Coral Bell Cove, Book Three

USA TODAY BESTSELLING AUTHOR
RENEE HARLESS

Coral Bell Cove, Book Three

USA TODAY BESTSELLING AUTHOR

RENEE HARLESS

Bailey Hart has mastered the art of staying small.
A lighthouse-bookstore, a quiet life in Coral Bell Cove,
and enough romance novels to drown out the
heartbreak she swore she'd never repeat. She's sworn off
big leaps, big risks, and especially the boy who once left
her love note—and her heart—on full display.

Crew Wright was supposed to have it all.
The charming quarterback with a Southern smile and a
future paved in stadium lights… until an injury sent
everything crashing down. Now he's back home to heal
his shoulder, his pride, and the parts of himself he
buried beneath fame. He's not expecting Bailey—the
girl who saw him before the world ever did.

What starts as borrowed tools, paint-splattered
afternoons, and late-night confessions quickly turns into
something neither of them can outrun.

Bailey wants to protect her heart.
Crew wants a second chance to prove he won't break it.
But when old wounds reopen and the world comes
calling for him again, they'll have to decide if love is
something you chase… or something you stay for.

**At First Play is a slow-burn, banter-filled, small-town
romance about forgiveness, falling again, and finding
the one person who feels like home—
no matter how far you've run.**

For the ones who were told they didn't belong.
This story is for the readers who found their place anyway—and
learned that love doesn't ask you to shrink to earn it.

Chapter One

BAILEY

The first rule of small-town living? Never underestimate a retiree with Wi-Fi.

By seven a.m., half of Coral Bell Cove already knows who ordered the gluten-free donuts, whose cat is pregnant again, and that Crew Wright—yes, *that* Crew Wright—is allegedly back in town.

Which is precisely why I'm hiding behind the counter of my lighthouse-turned-bookstore, pretending the espresso machine requires urgent emotional support.

Outside, gulls bicker over a dropped pastry on the boardwalk, and the wind coming off the bay smells like salt, cinnamon, and incoming drama. Inside, the air is all roasted coffee and old paper—the perfume of safety.

I give the copper espresso lever an affectionate pat. "Hang in there, girl. If we survive the gossip cycle, we get a muffin."

The machine hisses in agreement.

The bell over the door jingles, and Daisy Merritt blows in with the breeze, carrying a basket big enough to feed a football team and energy that could power the lighthouse lantern if it still worked.

"Morning, lighthouse lady!" she chirps. "I brought peace offerings—blueberry, chocolate chip, and one maple pecan you're going to lie about eating."

"I don't *lie*," I say, taking the basket before she can drop it. "I practice discretion."

"Sure." She pulls off her knit cap, cheeks pink from the chill. "You're going to need carbs. Everyone's buzzing about the Wright boy being home. Otter Creek's basically a reality show right now."

I freeze halfway to the pastry plate. "Define everyone."

"Mrs. Winthrop started the rumor, and the hardware-store guys confirmed it. Apparently, Crew's rehabbing his shoulder out there." Daisy plucks a chocolate-chip muffin and takes a huge bite. "Poor guy. Still looks disgustingly good, though."

Of course, he does.

I pour another shot of espresso to hide the way my pulse jumps. "Good for him."

"That's it? *Good for him?* Bailey, you once wrote that man poetry on notebook paper."

"Correction," I say. "I wrote a private letter that got stolen, read aloud in gym class, and is now archived in the town's collective memory like a national tragedy."

Daisy snorts. "Details."

"I was sixteen."

"And still blushing like you're sixteen," she sings.

"Out." I point at the door.

She grins, snags a napkin, and heads out into the crisp air. "Don't say I didn't warn you. Word is he's staying a while."

The door closes, leaving me with the whisper of waves and the low creak of the old lighthouse settling. I exhale through my nose, long and slow.

Crew Wright. Back in Coral Bell Cove.

Nope. Not today.

I can't keep letting myself get worked up. He comes and goes all the time in the summer when it's a break in his season. I'm just much better at keeping my distance from him during those warm months.

I distract myself by straightening the "Staff Picks" table —*Beach Reads for When You Hate the Beach*—and the stack of vintage novels near the round window. Early light slides across the shelves, catching on the brass fixtures I polished last night. The sea beyond the glass glitters like one of my best friend Ivy's sequins.

The bell jingles again.

"Morning, Mrs. Winthrop," I say automatically.

"Morning, dear." She totters in wearing her usual floral scarf and enough perfume to stun a man out at sea. "Anything new for a woman of refined taste and questionable morals?"

I smile. "Plenty. How steamy are we talking today?"

"Moderate," she says primly. "Enough to feel alive but not enough to alarm my cardiologist."

I hand her a paperback. "Widowed heroine, brooding neighbor, lots of lingering glances."

She beams. "Perfect. Oh, did you hear? Crew Wright's back for an undisclosed amount of time! Isn't that *wonderful?*"

My jaw tightens behind a professional smile. "That's the word on the street."

"He's such a nice boy."

"Sure."

She squints at me. "You used to tutor him, didn't you?"

"Briefly. Until he discovered that doodling football plays in the margins doesn't count as active reading."

Mrs. Winthrop chuckles. "Some people take longer to learn their lessons. Don't let yours slip by twice, dear."

Before I can reply, she wobbles out again, leaving a cloud of flowery perfume and unsolicited wisdom behind her.

I lean against the counter and let the quiet settle back over me.

My phone buzzes.

Lila: Rumor mill says my brother's back in town. Have you seen him yet?

Me: Not unless he's disguised as a seagull.

Lila: Give it time. Mom's already planning a "welcome home" dinner.

Ivy: Tell her to livestream it. I need content.

Me: I need bleach for my brain.

Lila: Come on, B. It's been years. Maybe closure time?

Me: I have closure. It's alphabetized under "never again."

Ivy: I'm not privy to the entire story there, but what if "never again" has abs?

Me: …Blocking you.

Ivy: You love me.

Me: Unfortunately, yes.

I LOCK MY PHONE, BUT THE GRIN WON'T QUITE FADE. That's the thing about Lila and Ivy—one is my ride-or-die and the other is literal pop royalty married into the Wright circus. Between them, privacy is extinct.

Still, their teasing hums in my chest like background music as I start shelving the new arrivals.

The wind outside shifts, rattling the glass panes. Leaves skitter across the boardwalk. Somewhere down by the marina, someone tunes a guitar, and the faint notes drift up the hill.

The lighthouse hums with it all—the rhythm of home.

I brush dust from the highest shelf, balancing on the

step stool, and whisper to the books, "We're not thinking about him."

The books, traitorous as ever, don't answer.

The coffee pot lets out a low, sputtering growl that sounds almost judgmental. I glance over at it from the ladder and sigh. "Don't you start, too."

It bubbles back at me like a gossiping aunt. Typical. Everyone in Coral Bell Cove has an opinion—even my appliances.

I climb down, pour what's left into a chipped lighthouse mug, and take a cautious sip. Bitter. Strong. Exactly how I like it. The mug's chipped handle fits perfectly against my thumb, and the taste grounds me better than any meditation app ever could.

The day hums along like it has every morning since I opened *A Page in Time*. There's comfort in the routine—the creak of the old floorboards, the way the salt air sneaks through the cracks in the windows, and the faint cry of seagulls diving near the pier.

Normal. Predictable. Safe.

Until the universe inevitably laughs and reminds me that safe doesn't exist in Coral Bell Cove.

A thud against the door nearly makes me spill my coffee.

"Delivery!" someone shouts, followed by something heavy scraping against the entry.

I hurry over to yank the door open and find Grayson from the post office wrestling a box half his size up the steps.

"You're gonna give yourself a hernia," I warn.

He flashes a grin. "Probably. But then you'd have to read to me while I'm recovering."

"Not unless it's your eulogy."

He laughs and drops the box with a groan. "It's from Nashville. Must be one of those book bundles Ivy ordered for you."

I crouch to check the label. Sure enough—*From: Ivy Quinn-Wright.* She's made it her personal mission to keep the kids' corner of my store stocked with her favorite titles.

"Thanks, Grayson. How's your mom's knee?"

"Better. She'll be back to stalking Mrs. Winthrop's Facebook posts any day now."

"Glad to hear it. Send her my love—and tell her to stop commenting heart-eye emojis on every photo of my dog."

He tips his hat and wanders off, whistling.

I drag the box inside, slice the tape open, and start unpacking. Children's books, bright and colorful, tumble out like confetti—*Goodnight Lighthouse, The Little Seagull That Could,* and a stack of Ivy's latest picture book about following your dreams. She always includes a note written in gold ink.

For Bailey's littles, who already know stories make the world brighter.

My throat tightens. Ivy might be a pop star, but her heart is pure.

I tuck the books under my arm and head to the reading nook. The space is small—two beanbags, a round rug, and a shelf shaped like a sailboat—but it's my favorite corner of the shop. Kids come here to escape. So do I.

I start arranging the books, lost in thought, when the bell jingles again.

"Tell me there's coffee," says a familiar voice.

Daisy's back, holding a steaming cup of her own and looking far too pleased with herself.

"I thought you were baking," I say.

"I was, until the fryer exploded. Minor incident. The fire department from the town over says it builds character."

"Should I even ask?"

She waves her hand. "Don't. But while we're talking character, do you want to know who I just saw down at the docks?"

"No."

"The rumors are true. Crew. Wright."

I glare. "Why do you insist on ruining my digestive system before lunch?"

"Because I care," she says sweetly. "And because if I have to suffer through my mother asking if I've 'found Jesus or a boyfriend yet,' you have to suffer too."

"Trade you."

"Tempting, but no."

She leans against the counter, eyes gleaming. "You remember that sweatshirt you used to wear? The Stallions one?"

"Vaguely. It probably died of embarrassment years ago."

"He's wearing the same one."

My stomach flips. I busy myself with loading a spool of receipt tape into the printer. "Coincidence."

"Sure, honey."

She finishes her coffee, clearly enjoying herself. "Anyway, he's back. Word is he's trying to 'reset.'"

I snort. "He can reset all he wants. I'm staying powered down."

"Fine. But if you're gonna hide from him, at least wear something cute. Makes avoidance look classy."

When she finally leaves, the shop feels too still again.

I blow out a breath and glance around. The midday light slides across the worn wood floors, turning them the color of honey. A couple of tourists wander past the windows, their laughter carried by the wind.

I wish I could freeze this—just the quiet, the scent of salt, the murmur of pages turning.

Instead, my mind drifts back to the first time I ever saw Crew Wright.

He'd been leaning against his locker, all crooked smile and reckless confidence, like the world existed to amuse him. I was carrying a stack of library books almost taller than me, and he'd taken one look and said, "You know they invented e-readers, right?"

I'd told him I preferred paper because at least it didn't talk back. He'd grinned like I'd just confessed a secret meant only for him.

And that was it. The moment I fell for a boy who'd never belong to me.

The memory stings like saltwater on a cut.

The bell jingles again, saving me from myself.

This time, it's two tourists—an older couple, matching windbreakers, holding hands like they've been doing it forever. They wander the aisles, murmuring to each other about Hemingway, until the man picks up a collection of poetry and reads a line out loud.

She laughs softly. "You still remember that one?"

"It's hard to forget the first poem I ever read to you."

They leave smiling, and I'm suddenly very aware that my own love story never made it past the prologue.

The wind outside picks up, rattling the sign against the glass. A storm brewing, maybe. Or fate getting impatient.

Because when I look up again, a shadow is moving on the boardwalk. Broad shoulders. Familiar stride.

No.

Absolutely not.

I duck behind the counter, heart thudding. My reflection in the glass case stares back at me like I've lost my mind. Maybe I have.

I peek over the register. He's closer now, head bent as he scrolls through his phone, hoodie tugged up against the wind. The same uneven gait from his old knee injury. The same careless posture that says *I own every room I walk into.*

Crew Wright, in the flesh.

I whisper to the espresso machine, "Play dead."

The bell above the door jingles.

I swear under my breath.

He steps inside, bringing the smell of ocean and October with him, and the room shrinks.

For a second, neither of us says anything. It's like time

folds—ten years collapsing into this one impossible moment. Of course, it's not like I have been actively avoiding any moment that would put us within the same space for years.

Then he grins. That same crooked, devastating grin that ruined my GPA.

"Hey, Book Girl."

My pulse jumps, my sarcasm scrambles for armor, and my heart whispers, *oh no.*

Of the fourteen snappy replies loaded in the chamber of my mouth, somehow the one that tumbles out is, "You can't just waltz in here and call me that."

He leans on the endcap like it's a casual choice and not a strategic decision to be within breathing distance of me. "I didn't waltz. This is more of a"—he glances down at his boots—"shove-in-from-the-wind and try not to slip on your antique floors."

"They're original hardwood," I say, because when flustered, my brain chooses *Home & Garden Magazine.*

"Still charming." His eyes flick over the ladder, the register lamp, the basket of maple pecan muffins, then back to me. He holds my gaze long enough to make my rib cage feel like it's trying to remember choreography. "You look the same."

"I do not."

"Okay," he concedes, mouth tipping. "You look like the upgraded edition. Hardback with a better cover."

I hate that my laugh escapes. "Flattery will get you nothing but store credit, Wright."

"Store credit's more than I've had in years." He says it lightly, but there's a hairline crack through the humor, and for a heartbeat, I see him without the grin—tired at the edges and that careful way he's holding his right shoulder like it's a secret.

I fold my arms. "What do you want?"

"A book."

"Try the giant shelves of them." I make a sweeping gesture with my arm.

He glances around. "You gonna curate for me, or do I wander until I fall in love with a spine the way people meet-cute on those shows my mother watches?"

"You can start in nonfiction," I say sweetly, "under *Consequences of Being a Teenage Coward*."

He winces, but his grin hangs on. "Ah. Going right for the scar tissue."

"Just keeping us honest."

He straightens, stepping away from the endcap, and the room somehow gets smaller. "Honest is good." He tilts his head. "You gonna come help me, or are you going to stand behind the counter like a force field of ISBNs protects you?"

"I don't need a force field," I lie, moving around the counter because apparently, I do, in fact, intend to help him.

As I pass, he smells like ocean and laundry soap and the kind of cologne that lingers in the best way possible. The awareness snaps across my skin like static. I pretend to nudge past him, but my shoulder brushes his chest, and six hundred tiny, ridiculous fireworks go off in my nervous system.

"Watch the merchandise," I mumble, when really I mean watch me not combust.

He falls into step beside me, a step too close. "What are you reading these days, Book Girl?"

"Everything you don't."

"Savage." He taps a spine with his knuckle. "Do you ever put your own stuff on the shelf?"

"My—what?"

"Your writing." He says it like it's obvious, like the town didn't weaponize my first attempt.

"We sell published books here," I say lightly. "Turns out *emotional distress* doesn't have an ISBN."

He goes quiet then, and I feel him seeing it—the place in me that still glows like an old burn. He doesn't reach for it. He doesn't look away, either.

"What about something funny?" he says after a beat. "I have a lot of rehab time. I could use a book that doesn't try to teach me how to be a better person."

"Low bar," I murmur, but head for the humor shelf anyway. "Here." I pull down an essay collection. "Smart, irreverent, heart under the snark."

"Is that your book's bio?" he asks.

I hand it to him without touching his fingers. He manages to graze mine anyway, and I am serenely, absolutely fine about it except for the part where my pulse sprints.

"Got anything about second chances?" he asks, like a man tossing a line into water to see what bites.

"Depends," I say. "Are we talking about second chances or recycled mistakes in a new outfit?"

He blows out a laugh. "You always hated easy answers."

"Easy answers are usually lies spouted to sound sensible."

He takes the essays but wanders, trailing me, reading titles out loud. "'The Art of Letting Go.' 'Small-Town Secrets.' 'Begin Again.' You alphabetize your trauma now?"

"It's called cross-merchandising," I say. "We keep the tissues near the sad section."

"Strategic," he murmurs. "So people cry, buy another book, and then wipe their eyes on the receipt."

"Now you're getting it."

When I stop by the round window to adjust the display, he stops beside me. The glass is cold enough to fog when he breathes on it. Outside, the bay is slate blue and choppy, the gulls wheeling like badly behaved kites. His reflection sits next to mine in the glass, too close, too familiar. We stand like that long enough for the moments to stack.

"Why are you really here?" I ask, still watching our blurring shapes.

He doesn't joke it away. "Coach wants me quiet. Home's quiet. You—" He breaks off, then shifts. "This place always made me settle."

Dangerous. That word is dangerous. I keep my voice breezy. "Well, we do sell books that teach breathing exercises in the self-help aisle."

He huffs a laugh and angles toward me. "You didn't ask how the shoulder is."

"I assume it's attached? I'm a small-town bookstore owner, not an orthopedist."

"True," he says. "But you used to be Bailey-who-knew-when-I-was-lying."

"Congratulations." I turn, meeting his eyes. "Now I won't have to hear it."

We let the silence sit, and it's not empty. It's full of every version of us that almost was.

The bell jingles. I step back so fast my hip knocks the table. A stack of paperbacks avalanches. He reaches out on instinct, one big hand circling my waist to steady me while the other catches three falling romances midair.

Time does that elastic thing where it stretches so wide a whole conversation fits in a breath without saying a word.

His palm is warm through my sweater. My body recognizes him faster than my brain allows permission. He smells like October and the kind of boy I promised myself I don't love anymore. He looks down at me like I'm a page he dog-eared and never returned.

"Got you," he murmurs.

I move first because self-preservation is muscle memory. I step out of his hold and crouch to right the books, pretending I'm not shaking.

"Careful," I tell the paperbacks, because it's easier than telling him.

He squats too—too close again—and passes me a novel. His knee bumps mine. We both pretend not to notice, which is unconvincing at best.

"Still got quick hands," he says.

"Congratulations." I stack the last book and stand. He does too. We're almost nose to nose, which would be annoying if it weren't doing criminal things to my heart rate.

The couple who just walked in clears their throat. "Is this the romance section?" the woman asks, barely hiding a smile.

"Apparently," I mutter.

"Back wall, left," Crew says smoothly, not taking his eyes off me as he points them toward it. The woman beams with delight and drags her partner away.

We share a helpless, stupid little grin that feels like a secret and a problem at once.

The register drawer chooses that moment to ding open of its own accord like it's auditioning for the role of *chaperone*. I mutter a curse and move behind the counter to fix it. He follows, of course, because he only understands the concept of boundaries in football.

"Want me to look at it?" he asks.

"Are you a cash register whisperer now?"

"I'm a man with two brothers and a farmer for a dad," he says. "I can at least pretend to fix things convincingly."

"You can convincingly *look* like you're fixing things," I correct. "Different skill set."

He rounds the counter anyway, which is apparently open season on my personal space. We both reach for the drawer. He gets there first. His forearm brushes mine, and I learn more about the tensile strength of self-control in three seconds than any self-help book could teach.

"Your coil's sticking," he says, peering into the mechanism.

"My coil?"

"Technical term," he deadpans. "Very advanced."

"Fascinating."

"Hand me a butter knife?" When I blink at him, he adds, "Gently."

I pass him the shop's sacrificial letter opener, which is at least knife-adjacent, and he uses it to wiggle the coil—fine, maybe that *is* what it's called—until the drawer slides true.

He looks up, triumphant, and the tiny flush of pride on his cheek warms something in me I didn't authorize.

"There," he says. "Fixed."

"You poked it and got lucky."

"Story of my life," he says without thinking, then winces. "That sounded—"

"In character," I supply.

He laughs, low and helpless, and I do not smile (I absolutely smile.).

We stare at each other, and the current between us hums like the transformer outside during storms. His eyes drop to my mouth. Mine drop to his. We both catch ourselves and pretend we are looking at anything else.

My phone buzzes against the register like it's trying to hop off the counter. I glance at the screen.

Lila: He's there, isn't he? He won't answer my texts.

Me: No comment.

Ivy: Omg live photo or I riot.

Me: It's a bookstore, not a zoo exhibit.

Lila: Did he apologize yet?

Me: For existing? No.

Ivy: For breathing the same air as you with that face. No apology accepted without an offering (flowers, pastries, firstborn, etc.).

Me: You're unhelpful.

Ivy: I'm honest. Also, fix your hair. He's looking.

I SHOVE THE PHONE UNDER A STACK OF SPIRAL NOTEBOOKS because apparently I'm a teenager again.

"Your security detail checking in?" Crew asks, amused.

"My friends don't trust me around fire hazards," I say. "You qualify."

"Fair." He sighs, and there it is again—his grin dimming at the edges, honesty stalking the perimeter. "Bailey—"

"Don't." I automatically hold up my hand because if he says *I'm sorry* in that careful voice, I might let the words stitch up places I've learned to live with being open.

He nods once and doesn't push. "Recommendation taken." He taps the book he's still holding. "I'll take this one. And... another. Surprise me."

I blink. "You're asking me to pick a second book without knowing what it is?"

"I'm asking you to pick a second book because you know me better than I'd like." And then, like he can feel me bolting, he adds with a crooked smile, "And because I trust your taste in fiction more than my own."

I hate that it lands, that sloppy compliment, right where I'm weakest—right where I'm proudest.

"Fine." I slide a copy of a coastal romcom from the shelf under the counter—sharp banter, slow ache, a lighthouse on the cover because I am a menace. "This. It's clever and a little devastating."

"Like you," he says, almost reflexively, then rubs the back of his neck like he wishes he'd had the good sense to keep that thought inside.

I ring them up, and he slides his card across the credit card scanner. Seeing his name on the plastic—*Crew Wright*—hits harder than it should.

The receipt prints in a stuttering line. I tear it off and reach out to hand it to him, but he doesn't move to take it at first. We're close again, the counter suddenly a narrow strip of land between two countries with very complicated treaties. He looks at me like he's memorizing the Cliffs-Notes before an exam he actually cares about passing this time.

The door opens; a gust of cold air threads between us. We step back as an older man wanders in, asking for nautical maps. I point him to the back corner. Crew tucks his books under his arm like contraband.

"I'll bring the romcom back," he says softly. "I owe you notes."

"Dog-ears are a crime punishable by banishment," I say.

"I'll underline with a ruler."

"Acceptable."

He hesitates, then nods toward the ceiling. "Your west eave's crying. I can hear it from the steps."

I roll my eyes. "She's dramatic in the wind."

"She's leaking," he says, and his voice, for once, is not cocky or teasing. It's practical and sure. "Flashing's loose. You'll get rot."

"I have a roofer," I lie.

"You have YouTube," he counters. "Let me help."

"I don't need—"

"Help rarely arrives because you *need* it," he says, that quiet seriousness back. "It arrives because it wants to make something better."

I stare at him because that's not fair, that line. It sinks into me like a nail pulled by a magnet.

He lifts a hand, not touching me, just hovering, palm up like an offer. "I'll come by tomorrow. Noon. If you don't want me to, lock the gate and I'll get the hint."

Something traitorous in me imagines tomorrow—him on the ladder, tools on the sill, the two of us squinting into the wind like we could muscle fate into behaving. The picture is so vivid I can smell the salt on his sweatshirt.

"Bring your own hammer," I say, because I am not agreeing to anything except the most mundane thing in the scene.

His grin is relief disguised as trouble. "Yes, ma'am."

He backs toward the door, like leaving is the hard part. "See you, Book Girl."

I hold my breath until the bell jingles and he's gone.

The old man in nautical maps mutters something about "kids these days," and I realize I'm gripping the counter like it's the last piece of a shipwreck.

My phone vibrates again.

Lila: B??

Me: He bought two books and offered to fix my roof. I told him to bring his own hammer.

Ivy: I just fainted. Are you okay? Do you need electrolytes? A hype playlist?

Me: I need witness protection.

Lila: Proud of you for not impaling him with a bookmark.

Me: Growth.

Ivy: Send me a pic of the eave. I'll send you a roofer and a publicist.

Me: No. You know how I feel about that.

I SET THE PHONE DOWN AND PULL IN A BREATH. THE register hums softly. The lighthouse settles. Outside, clouds gather like the festival committee.

"High-voltage slow burn is not a sustainable business model," I inform the espresso machine.

It burps in agreement.

I spend the next hour reorganizing shelves that don't need it and learning exactly how long ninety minutes can feel. Every sound yanks my attention to the door. Every shadow skimming the window sends my pulse sprinting. It's ridiculous. I hate it. My bones love it. Somewhere in the middle, I choose to act like I have sense.

Daisy pops back in at closing with a Tupperware of "accidental" brownies. "If you tell anyone I burned the first batch and salvaged them with frosting, I'll deny it to the grave."

"Your secrets are safe with me," I say, then ruin any mystique by slumping dramatically against the counter.

She narrows her eyes. "He came in, didn't he?"

"Define 'came in.'"

"Bailey."

"Fine. He breathed my air and said things."

"And?"

"And nothing. I sold him books. He fixed the cash drawer and... offered to help with the roof."

She squeals like I just announced a royal engagement. "Bailey."

"It's a roof, not a proposal."

"Yet."

"Out," I say again, but I'm smiling. I can feel it, traitorous and warm.

When the sun finally starts its slow drop and the tourists thin, I flip the sign to CLOSED. The shop breathes with me. I lock the register, turn the lamps low, and climb the spiral stairs to the little apartment that sits like a secret on the second floor.

From the landing window, the bay is all pewter and scattered light. The farm is a dark smudge across the water. I press my palm to the cold glass and pretend the chill is the reason my chest aches.

A truck idles down by the dock, taillights glowing red in the gray. The driver's door opens. A familiar silhouette leans against the frame, looking out at the same horizon I've stared at every day since I learned how to want things like they were allowed.

Crew tips his head back like the sky just gave him an answer. He turns toward the lighthouse, and even from this distance, I feel it when his eyes find the window.

We hold that line of sight across the evening like we're balancing on it. Neither of us waves. Neither of us looks away first.

The wind lifts. Leaves scrape the boardwalk. Somewhere, the diner's neon sign buzzes to life.

I drop my hand from the glass and whisper to the empty room, "Breathe. It's just a hammer."

Because tomorrow exists now, apparently. Because my life—the quiet, alphabetized, laminated version—just invited trouble back in and called it repairs.

Downstairs, the shop creaks like approval.

I make tea. Not because I want tea, but because doing something small feels like control. I curl on the old velvet chair with a blanket and the romcom I handed him—my copy, dog-eared and soft. I read the first page three times without absorbing a single word. My brain keeps replaying stupid details instead—the scrape of his stubble when he smiled, the way he guarded his shoulder, and the controlled softness when he said *let me help* like help was a verb he finally learned how to conjugate.

The kettle clicks cool. The lamp hums. The sea keeps breathing, relentless and sure.

I close the book and tilt my head back until my eyes sting.

"I can do this," I tell the ceiling. "I can be a functioning adult around a man I once wrote to like a fool and who let my heart get turned into gym-class entertainment."

The ceiling, a longtime realist, neither disagrees nor encourages.

My phone buzzes again, and even before I flip it, I know who it is.

Unknown: Noon tomorrow. Promise I'll bring a hammer. And muffins. -C

I STARE AT THE SCREEN. THE LETTER. THE NERVE.

I type three replies and erase them all, then land on the most responsible one.

Me: Don't be late. The eave is dramatic.

THREE DOTS APPEAR. PAUSE. DISAPPEAR. REAPPEAR.

C: Me too. See you, Book Girl.

I LET THE PHONE SLIP TO THE CUSHION BESIDE ME AND press my knuckles to my mouth until the ridiculous smile behaves.

Outside, the wind knocks once against the glass like a friend who doesn't need to come in to feel welcome.

I stand, switch off the lamp, and climb the rest of the way up to the lantern room. It's retired now, but the lens is still there—old glass and curved brass that throws back the last of the light like memory does.

I lean my forehead to the cold pane and say the quiet truth out loud because some truths don't count unless they get air.

"I'm not sixteen," I whisper. "And I'm not running."

The dark takes it, tucks it away. The lighthouse accepts the vow like a secret it was built to hold.

Downstairs, the espresso machine settles with a final sigh. Tomorrow, it will hiss like Coral Bell Cove's current gossip. Tomorrow, a man with a grin and a vulnerability he tries to hide will show up with a hammer and a peace offering. Tomorrow, I will let him climb my ladder and stand under my eave and pretend the current between us isn't loud enough to be measured in megawatts.

Tonight, I will sleep with the window cracked and the sound of the bay threading through the room. I will dream, if I'm unlucky, of hands catching my waist and of a note tucked into a book I swore I'd never open again.

I slide under the quilt and trace the familiar patchwork with my fingers until my breath slows. The last thing I see before sleep takes me is the pale reflection of the lens, a circle of ghost-light over the bed, like a promise that the dark is only ever half the story.

Chapter Two

CREW

The sunrise cracks open, and the horizon spills light across Otter Creek Farm. The barns catch it first—rust-red and gold—then the pastures, then the porch where I'm standing with a cup of coffee that tastes like regret and a shoulder that feels like it belongs to somebody older.

The Wright family doesn't sleep in. Never has. Even after I left for the pros, even after I told myself I was done with all this—dawn still finds me.

The air smells like hay, salt, and diesel from the tractor idling somewhere out of sight. Birds start their music. The farm is alive again, same as always.

"Let's get moving," Marcus, the team-approved physical rehabilitator, calls from inside the barn gym, his voice cutting through the quiet like a whistle.

Right. No point standing around pretending I'm part of the scenery.

I drain what's left of my coffee and step inside. This barn's been converted into half gym, half storage. One side has hay bales stacked to the rafters. The other is filled with equipment that looks like it was ordered off a "Rehab or Die" subscription box.

Marcus is already setting up resistance bands, his clipboard tucked under one arm. He's built like a linebacker and patient like a monk—which makes him the only person on earth qualified to deal with me right now.

"You're late," he says.

"I'm three minutes early."

"Late for a guy with nothing else to do."

I grunt, grab the nearest band, and start the warm-up. The stretch burns all the way down my arm. The muscle still trembles, still protests like it doesn't believe me when I say we're getting better.

"How's it feel today?" he asks.

"Like betrayal." Every time I think about the blindside hit that took me out, resulting in a torn labrum, my stomach drops, and I have to work to keep my mood above water.

He smirks. "That's progress. Yesterday, it was murder."

"Don't worry, I'll get nostalgic in a second."

Without rising to the bait, he just checks my form, adjusts the band tension, and makes a note. The quiet between us is easy—the kind that only happens when a man has seen you at your lowest and doesn't hold it against you.

I keep moving through the drills. The farm hums

outside—tractor engines and distant laughter from the chicken coop where my dad's probably wrangling Mom's newest batch of "emotional support hens."

By the time we finish, sweat runs down my neck, and my shoulder is on fire. Marcus tosses me a towel.

"Good work," he says. "Don't push past the threshold."

"Define 'threshold'."

"The part right before you do something stupid."

"So Tuesday."

He chuckles. "Exactly."

We clean up, and he heads out, probably to terrorize another client in town. I'm left with the echo of my own breathing and the faint creak of the barn settling around me.

The silence used to feel like home. Now it just feels like an echo I can't shake off.

I wander to the open doors, towel slung over my neck, and watch the morning unfold. My brother Rowan's truck pulls into the drive, and my sister Hadley's voice drifts in from the porch. The smell of bacon sneaks through the breeze, and my stomach growls loud enough to make a cow in the pasture look over.

"Come eat before Mom declares you malnourished," Hadley calls, hands cupped around her mouth. She's standing on the porch steps, messy bun, leggings, coffee mug that says *Good Moms Say Bad Words*.

"Already did rehab," I say.

"Rehab doesn't count as food."

"Tell that to my protein shake."

She rolls her eyes and disappears inside.

I grab my hoodie from the bench and follow, flexing my hand to keep the joint loose. Every motion's a reminder of the hit that ended everything—the way my arm twisted wrong, the pop, the crowd's gasp that swallowed the world.

Some days, I hear it in my sleep.

Inside, the kitchen smells like cinnamon and butter. Mom stands at the stove, flipping pancakes like she's feeding an army. She looks up when I walk in, smile bright and knowing.

"There he is," she says.

"Morning, Ma."

"Sit. Eat. Don't argue."

I sit. I eat. I don't argue. It's the Wright family way.

Hadley drops into the chair across from me, already scrolling through her phone. "So Bailey's roof is leaking."

I freeze halfway through a bite.

"Lila says Bailey's been patching it herself."

"She shouldn't be on a roof. That woman is so stubborn. She should hire someone to do it."

Her eyebrow arches. "Why do you sound personally offended?"

"I'm not. I just—roofs are dangerous."

"Uh-huh." She sips her coffee. "Maybe you should go help her. You know. Be useful while you're pretending to be retired."

Mom sets a plate in front of me, pancakes stacked high.

"She's a good girl, that Bailey," she says, as if that's relevant. "I don't know why you two don't talk."

"Because we're adults with separate lives," I say, stabbing at the pancakes.

"Separate zip codes don't mean separate lives," Hadley singsongs.

I give her my best big-brother glare, which works on everyone but her.

"I saw her yesterday," Mom continues, undeterred. "Still running that sweet little bookstore. Lighthouse looks beautiful."

Of course she did. My mother collects small-town updates like souvenirs. I don't add that I saw her, too. I wouldn't be surprised if she hasn't already sought out that information.

"Good for her," I mutter.

I finish breakfast, grab a thermos of coffee, and escape before they can orchestrate my social calendar. Outside, the air's warmer now, sun climbing higher. The fields glow gold and green. Somewhere, a tractor backfires; somewhere else, a horse snorts in protest.

I head toward my truck, keys spinning around my finger. The shoulder aches, the dull kind of pain that says *not yet but almost*.

The problem is, *almost* doesn't pay the bills.

My phone buzzes, and my agent David's name flashes across the screen.

I sigh and answer. "Yeah."

"Crew, buddy! How's the golden arm?"

"Rusty."

"Don't say that. Reporters hear you talk like that, they'll run it as gospel."

"Maybe they should. At least it'd be accurate."

He sighs dramatically. "Look, rehab videos perform better than silence. You've got sponsors waiting to see proof of progress. Post something. Smile. Pretend you're optimistic."

"Pass."

"You want a career or not?"

"I want to lift my damn arm without it shaking."

There's a sigh. "You'll get there. Just don't disappear. The public forgets fast."

I hang up before he can start another pep talk.

Silence again, broken only by the hum of cicadas and the faint echo of the bay. I look toward the road that leads down to town, where the lighthouse stands tall against the horizon.

Bailey's world.

Mine, once.

The image flashes again—her standing behind the counter, arms crossed, eyes like a storm she's holding back on purpose. The way her laugh still sounds like summer. The way guilt tastes sour every time I think of that stupid, stolen note.

I open the truck door, set the hammer on the passenger seat, and grab the thermos of coffee from the holder.

I could drive anywhere. Back to Nashville. Richmond.

Hell, the next county. But my hands don't turn the wheel that way.

The road bends toward Coral Bell Cove, and I follow it like I'm in a daze.

The closer I get to town, the more everything starts to look the same and completely different all at once.

The bait shop still leans like it's had one too many, but the windows are new. Mrs. Hollister's bakery smells like cinnamon and salt. Even the "Welcome to Coral Bell Cove" sign has been repainted—same pelican, brighter blue.

People wave when they recognize the truck. I wave back out of habit, pretending not to notice the quick double takes.

The fallen quarterback is back on his old turf. Cue the headlines.

If they hadn't been convinced yesterday that I was back for longer than a weekend, they are now.

I make a quick trip into the bakery to grab the muffins I know are one of Bailey's favorites. I may stalk her social media page in my downtime, and she's always posting her favorite books with these particular treats.

By the time I pull into the gravel lot by the lighthouse, the wind off the bay has picked up, bringing the taste of brine and rain. Yesterday, I was too eager to see Bailey and didn't pay attention to the building. The place still looks like something out of a postcard: white stone, black iron rail around the lantern room, and the little attached house that's now *A Page in Time*. The porch light is on even though it's midmorning, the kind of faint, cozy glow that hits somewhere beneath my ribs.

I sit there longer than I should, engine idling, coffee cooling in the thermos.

Just go knock, Wright. It's a roof, not a wedding proposal.

The wind slaps the tarp overhead, snapping like it's impatient. I grab the hammer, step out, and instantly remember how slippery these boards get with sea mist. Perfect conditions for public humiliation.

The door opens before I reach it.

Bailey steps out, sweater sleeves pushed up, hair twisted into a messy knot that's losing the fight against the breeze. She has a smudge of ink on her cheekbone and a cautious set to her shoulders—like she's been bracing for me all morning.

"Morning," I say, aiming for casual. It comes out like gravel.

She blinks, once. "You have impeccable timing. The roof's about to fly to Norfolk."

"Guess I picked the right day to remember my handyman phase."

"I didn't realize you had one."

"Briefly. Between Pop Warner football and my first concussion."

Her mouth twitches. Almost a smile. Progress. Better than yesterday at least.

I hold up the hammer and the paper bag from the bakery. "Peace offering. Muffins and minimal power-tool use."

She eyes the bag like it might explode. "Maple pecan?"

"Obviously."

That earns me a tiny, reluctant laugh. She takes the bag, fingers brushing mine, and every nerve ending I own sits up and pays attention.

"I was going to call a roofer," she says.

"Hadley told me you've been doing it yourself."

"Of course she did."

We stand there a beat too long, the kind of silence that hums. Then she steps aside. "Fine. But if you fall, I'm not doing the paperwork."

"Deal."

The stairs groan as I climb up to the roofline. The view from the top punches the breath out of me: the curve of the cove, the glitter of the water, the bookstore sign swinging gently below. The tarp's barely hanging on. One corner flaps like it's signaling distress.

I start securing it, the rhythm coming back like muscle memory—hammer, nail, pull, breathe. Below, I can hear her moving inside, the faint chime of the bell as someone comes in, and her voice, low and warm, as she greets them.

It's ridiculous how grounding that sound is.

When the last nail goes in, I sit back on my heels, flex my sore shoulder, and let the wind cool the sweat on my neck. For the first time in months, the ache feels earned instead of empty.

"Still alive up there?" she calls.

"Define 'alive'."

She laughs, and it rolls up through the salt air, settling right where the guilt used to live.

I climb down, boots hitting the porch, and she's waiting with two mugs of coffee that smell infinitely better than mine.

"Truce?" she asks, offering one.

"Depends on the terms."

"Terms are: you drink this, I stop pretending I don't appreciate the help."

"Fair trade."

We stand shoulder to shoulder against the rail, watching the tide roll in. The coffee's hot, the silence easy —almost.

She glances sideways. "So what's the catch? You fixing roofs for every woman in town now?"

"Just the ones with literary merit."

Her lips curve. "Smooth."

"Occupational hazard."

"Football or flirting?"

"Both require good aim."

That earns another laugh, and for a second, it feels like the years between us shrink down to nothing. The wind catches a loose strand of her hair, and without thinking, I reach out and tuck it behind her ear. My fingers brush her skin—soft, warm, real.

She goes still, eyes lifting to mine, and the air thickens.

One wrong move and we're both going to regret it.

I drop my hand and step back just enough to breathe. "You should probably have someone look at the flashing before the next storm. A dozen people in town with deep pockets would help you."

She exhales slowly, the sound half laugh, half something else. "You volunteering?"

"Maybe."

Her gaze lingers a heartbeat longer than it should. "You always did like playing hero."

"Yeah," I say quietly. "Didn't work out so well last time."

She doesn't answer, and she doesn't have to. We both hear the echo of that gym full of laughter, the paper note crumpled in my fist, and the way I didn't defend her.

A gull cries overhead, sharp and lonely.

I clear my throat. "Thanks for the coffee."

She nods. "Thanks for the temporary roof."

I start toward the truck, every step heavier than it should be. When I glance back, she's still on the porch, watching the horizon like it might tell her what to do with me.

The sky over Otter Creek turns that strange gold-lavender color it only gets in early fall. I drive the long way home, windows down, salt air rolling through the cab, trying to shake off the sound of her laughter. It clings to me like sawdust. The day passes in a blur.

By the time I hit the gravel road to the farmhouse, my coffee's cold and my pulse still hasn't slowed.

Moths orbit the illuminated porch light bulb like it's the moon. Mom's already inside. I can hear music—Fleetwood Mac, her "cooking therapy" playlist. The screen door groans when I push it open.

"You're late," she calls from the kitchen.

"I didn't know there was a curfew."

"There is when you miss dinner."

"I was fixing something."

She pokes her head around the corner, spatula in hand. "Fixing or avoiding?"

I smirk. "Can't it be both?"

She narrows her eyes, but her mouth twitches. "There's a plate in the oven. Eat before the dog does."

"Lila still around?" I ask about my older sister, wanting to talk to her about Bailey.

"She went home an hour ago. Told me you'd be brooding."

"Not brooding." I drop my keys on the counter. "Processing."

"Uh-huh."

I grab the plate—meatloaf, mashed potatoes, green beans—and sit at the table. The farmhouse is too quiet at night. Only the creaks in the walls offer any break.

Mom hums as she wipes the counter. "I hear you kept your promise and helped Bailey today."

I chew, swallow, and stare at the fork. "Temporarily fixed her roof."

"Of course you did."

"Lila tell you?"

"Lila tells me everything. It's her love language."

"She needs a new hobby."

Mom sits across from me, hands folded. "You know,

coming home doesn't have to mean repeating the same mistakes."

"Wasn't planning on it."

"Good." She stands and presses a kiss to the top of my head like I'm ten again. "Then start by being kind to her and to yourself."

When she leaves, the kitchen feels bigger. I finish eating, rinse the plate, and wander outside after grabbing a beer from the fridge.

The night hums with crickets and the low whisper of wind through the pecan trees. Stars scatter across the dark like spilled salt. I lean against the porch rail, stretching my shoulder until it protests.

The rehab pain is simple. Predictable. It gives me something to measure. Bailey, on the other hand—there's no scale for that.

I pull out my phone. Lila's name is already glowing on the screen.

Lila: Mom says you're thinking. That's dangerous.

Me: Temporarily fixed the roof. She's fine.

Lila: "Fine" the word or "fine" the woman?

Me: Go to bed.

Lila: So it's the woman. Got it.

· · ·

I shake my head, but the smile sneaks up anyway.

Me: You're insufferable.

Lila: You love me.

Me: I tolerate you.

Lila: She's different now, you know.

Me: So am I.

Lila: Then maybe try again, minus the public humiliation.

I stare at the last message until the screen goes dark. Try again.

The idea sits heavy in my chest.

I think about the way Bailey's eyes softened when she laughed, how the wind played with her hair, how every muscle in me wanted to reach for her and didn't.

There's a rustle at the end of the porch. Shadow, the old barn cat, hops up beside me. He head-butts my arm, demanding attention.

"Hey, buddy." I scratch behind his ears. "You ever screw up so bad you start measuring time by it?"

He blinks at me, unbothered. Typical.

"Didn't think so."

The cat curls up, purring, and I stare out toward the faint glow of town. Somewhere beyond those trees, the lighthouse stands—steady, stubborn, shining through the dark.

Kind of like her.

I drain the last of the beer from the bottle beside me and set it on the railing. My shoulder throbs, and my chest feels heavier than it should be.

Tomorrow, I'll tell myself it was just a roof. Just a favor.

But tonight, under the wide Virginia sky, I know better.

Chapter Three

BAILEY

The pigeon is back.

He plants himself on the sill like a judgmental gargoyle and stares at me through the round lighthouse window while I try to drink coffee without reviewing last night like it's game film. The espresso machine hisses. The ocean sighs. The pigeon blinks slowly—as if to say, *So. You let him on your roof, and now you're surprised there are feelings.*

"Don't," I warn, pointing my mug at him. "Not before caffeine."

He doesn't care. Coral Bell Cove birds are fearless. They know things.

I set the mug down and do the thing I do when life feels like it's trying to test me: I move. Lamps on. Front door cracked just enough for salt air and small-town rumors to slip inside. Rugs straightened. Display tables fluffed like throw pillows. I take out the day's cash envelope, stack the fives, and—because the register has a personality—tap the front panel twice like a bribe.

The lighthouse creaks the way it does when the temperature drops. Early fall has its own soundtrack here: wood settling, gulls arguing, water slapping the jetty in a rhythm that says storms are rehearsing offstage. Somewhere down the hill, a delivery truck backfires.

Normal. Familiar. The routine slides over me like a favorite sweater and almost—*almost*—mutes the memory of a warm palm on my waist.

The bell rings and Daisy herself barrel-rolls in, cheeks flushed, braid half unraveled, carrying a bakery box like an offering to a vengeful goddess. "Okay," she announces without preamble, kicking the door shut with her heel. "The group chat is unhinged, Mrs. Winthrop is high on espresso, and I have at least three customers who asked whether your *romance section* has a resident consultant who *knows her stuff* while wiggling their eyebrows like caterpillars. Tell me everything."

I adopt my most professional tone. "Good morning. How lovely to—"

She flips the pastry box open. Steam rises—maple pecan, glossy and indecent. "A bribe for the truth."

"Daisy."

"You're glowing," she says, like a detective revealing the murder weapon. "Which is actually rude before nine."

"It's my lamp."

"It's your feelings."

I reach into the box, break a muffin in half, and talk around a mouthful of forgiveness. "He fixed a tarp."

"And your register."

"And—fine—my pulse."

She shrieks—quietly, because she respects my shelves—and claps a hand over her mouth. "I knew it. You have the roof-ache."

"Is that like heartache, but with roofing metaphors?"

"It's when a man shows up with a hammer, and suddenly, your eaves aren't the only thing feeling tender."

"Out."

"Can't. I brought carbs." She perches on the stool by the counter, eyes dancing. "So what did we learn? The man still has a face that could cause a power outage. And?"

"And nothing," I say primly. "He bought two books and demonstrated unsafe levels of confidence around my personal space. End of report."

"Did he apologize?"

"Not... exactly."

She narrows her eyes. "Exactly how 'not exactly' are we talking?"

"He didn't say the words. But there was a tone."

"A tone."

"A tone," I repeat, because my brain has chosen vague nouns over vulnerable honesty.

She slides me a takeout cup with my name scrawled across it in loopy frosting-piped handwriting.

BAILEY, STOP PANICKING.

"Sweetheart," she says more gently, "you are six foot two of bravado away from revisiting your origin story. Of course, you're rattled. But men like him don't usually come back different."

"He's...quieter," I admit. "And he looked at my roof before he really looked at me."

"Progress," Daisy declares. "In this economy."

The bell jingles. Mrs. Winthrop enters like a weather system in a floral scarf. "Darlings," she coos, "I have excellent news. I saw Crew Wright at the pier in sweatpants that could have paid my mortgage."

Daisy elbows me. I choke on coffee air.

Mrs. Winthrop leans across my counter, her perfume doing violence to the concept of subtlety. "He purchased a black coffee like a man with sins and a conscience. Also a blueberry scone, which tells me he's still redeemable. Men who choose blueberry want a second chance."

Daisy nods gravely, playing along. "What do men who choose chocolate chip want?"

"Chaos," Mrs. Winthrop says without hesitation. "Anyway, Bailey, may I please have something tasteful yet invigorating? Preferably with a lighthouse and a man who knows how to wield a rope."

I hand her a coastal mystery. "Minimal rope play, maximum yearning."

"Excellent." She taps the lid then pats my hand. "And you, my dear, deserve both."

The door swings again and again. The morning becomes a parade: a contractor in need of maps, a toddler who "reads" upside down, a tourist couple who saw my shop on Ivy's Instagram and gasp at the spiral staircase like it's a ride at a theme park. I field questions, make jokes, sell books, and refuse—point-blank, with a smile—to discuss the quarterback in the town like he's a rare bird sighting.

Underneath it all, the memory of his voice keeps tapping on a closed door in my chest. *Help rarely arrives because you need it. It arrives because it wants to stay.*

My phone buzzes against the register. It's Lila, predictably.

Lila: Mom says you're "looking rosy."
Should I be excited or call an ambulance?

Me: It's cold. I'm a person with blood.

Lila: Blood that's been stirred by poor
choices and broad shoulders?

Me: Ban. Block. Delete.

Ivy: I volunteer to mediate. But by
"mediate," I mean "stir." 😇

Me: Don't you have a stage to dominate?

Ivy: Not until tonight. In the meantime,
send a pic of your roof so I can text a
contractor, a lawyer, and possibly a priest.

Me: It's fine. He nailed things. It held. (That
sounded...)

Lila: I'M SCREAMING.

Me: Out. Both of you. I have customers.

Ivy: We are customers. Support your local chaos.

I KILL THE SCREEN BEFORE MY SMILE GIVES ME AWAY AND ring up a stack of romances for a shy college kid who whispers, "Do these end happily?" like she's begging for proof the universe keeps promises.

"They do here," I tell her, bagging the books like keepsakes. "That's the shelf rule."

When the bell rings again, I brace for another wave, but it's only Grayson from the post office, hat tipped back, carrying a bundle of mail that looks like it lost a fight with a small boat. He thumps it onto the counter and leans his elbows there like he's about to deliver bad news with a grin.

"Morning, Bailey," he says. "We've got catalogs, a flyer for the *Back Bay Harvest Bash*, and one fancy envelope that smells expensive."

"Smelling mail is a federal offense."

"Only if you get caught." He winks at Daisy, pockets a muffin when he thinks I'm not looking, and disappears back into the weather.

I sort the stack. Catalog. Catalog. A postcard from a grateful customer traveling through Maine. A flyer asking for volunteers for the pumpkin regatta (no). A cream envelope with an embossed edge and no return address.

My palms go cold the second I touch the paper. Not in dread. Not quite in hope. In recognition.

I slide a nail under the flap and ease it open.

For the children's corner,

the note says in neat, stubborn loops.

To keep the light on. — A friend

My throat goes tight. The check is generous without being showy, almost like the person who wrote it knows the exact line between help and insult. I turn the paper over, looking for a signature I already know won't be there.

I fold the note back in and tuck the envelope under the counter with the care you give fragile things nobody else sees.

Daisy watches me watching myself. "Good thing?" she asks quietly.

I nod. "Good person."

She doesn't push. She passes me a napkin and a look that says *I'm here if you need to fall apart like wet cardboard.*

A gust rattles the windows. The lighthouse answers with a low groan, like an acknowledgment between old friends. I glance up toward the lantern room, praying she holds together this season.

"Okay," Daisy says briskly, switching gears the way

people who love you do when they sense the cliff edge. "Inventory. New arrivals. Which of these would you recommend to a woman who wants a book boyfriend who apologizes promptly and has excellent carpentry skills?"

"Does he also read labels before washing sweaters?" I ask, defaulting to banter because it's the rope I know the knots on best.

"Hot."

I laugh, and we fall into the easy rhythm of our morning: me tagging new stock and her taste-testing frosting "for quality assurance." The bell rings; we serve. The bell rests; we breathe.

By late morning, the drizzle starts—the soft kind that makes the world smell clean and the town move slower. A class of third graders squeezes in, damp and excited, as their teacher distributes scavenger-hunt lists with items like *Find a book with a dog*, *Find three different fonts*, *Find the word lighthouse*. They fan out like bees. I answer questions, point to spines, and ignore the kid trying to barter me his plastic dragon for a sticker.

When the last small body bounces out and the door closes, *A Page in Time* huffs like it's just finished running a race. I lean both hands on the counter and let the silence fill my bones.

The bell dings once, softly.

"Don't," I say without turning around. "If you're here to tell me he looked *positively edible* in sweatpants again, I'm going to start an anti-gossip jar and fund the teen reading program for a decade."

"Rude," says a voice that is not Mrs. Winthrop. "And weirdly accurate."

I spin. Lila stands in the doorway, raincoat half zipped, cheeks flushed. There's a streak of applesauce on her cuff, which means motherhood is still winning on points.

She holds out a paper cup. "You look like you haven't hydrated since you graduated from high school."

"I've had coffee."

"Not hydration." She sets the cup down, peels off the raincoat, and folds herself into the stool Daisy vacated. "So. How's your morning not-thinking-about-my-brother going?"

I take a long drink of actual hydrating water and try for mild. "Fine."

"Define 'fine'."

"Functional. No sobbing into Classic Literature. No narratively convenient power outage."

"Yet," she says, and bumps my knee with hers.

I could lie. I could dodge. I could make a joke about restraining orders for family members who ask invasive questions in my place of business. Instead, I blow out a breath and lean back against the shelves.

"He was kind," I say, surprising myself with the word.

"Yeah," Lila says softly, like that was her favorite answer, and she didn't want to sway the judge. "He has been lately. Past couple of years, actually. It's unnerving."

"It's disorienting," I admit. "Like somebody tilted the town ten degrees and forgot to warn us."

She tips her head. "You know you don't owe anybody a

performance. Not me. Not him. Not Mrs. Winthrop's thirst."

"What I owe them is hazardous to my hazard plan."

"That's because your hazard plan involves hiding in a lighthouse like a particularly literate sea witch."

"Sea witches have boundaries."

"Sea witches also steal voices." She grins. "Don't make me dangle your karaoke performance of 'Jolene' over you as blackmail."

"That was one time."

"It was *something*." She reaches across the counter and squeezes my hand. "Dinner Saturday. You. Me. Ivy. No boys. We're going to eat pasta, drink wine, and discuss your feelings like civilized women."

"My feelings are feral."

"Perfect." Lila stands, shrugs back into her coat, then hesitates. "He asked about you, by the way. Not...bluntly. But he wanted to know if you were okay. He always...asks."

I busily straighten an already-rectangular stack of notecards. "He could ask *me*."

"He would, except for the past five years, when he comes anywhere near you, you scatter away like you've left your flat iron plugged in and turned on," she says simply. She flashes me a smile that lives somewhere between mischief and loyalty. "Try not to redecorate the place to spell out 'go away' in book spines before then."

I watch her go, the door swings shut behind her, hissing in a goodbye of its own.

The rain thickens, fogging the windows. The bay

becomes a watercolor with the edges licked away. I make a lazy loop of the shop, checking for leaks—a reflex I've developed the way some people develop a sixth sense for when their toddlers go quiet. The west eave holds. The old glass in the lantern room sulks but stays intact.

At noon, I turn the sign on the main door to BACK IN FIVE and take my lunch to the covered porch. I carry Daisy's quiche disguised as respectability, a book I've read twelve times, and a blanket I pretend I don't keep out here to feel like I'm starring in the slowest indie film ever made.

The porch boards are slick, the air that tender, icy kind that smells like clean metal and far-off fireplaces. I tuck my feet under me and open the book, trying—failing—to make the words behave when my brain is still up on a roof with a boy who became a man without asking anyone's permission.

The sound of tires on gravel pricks my skin a second before the truck appears around the curve. Not his. I feel ridiculous for knowing that, for how immediately my heart rations disappointment into manageable bites.

It's the UPS guy. He jogs up the steps, leaves a box, tips an imaginary hat, and jogs back. The town's choreography is muscle memory: arrive, tease, deliver, leave with gossip.

I take the box inside and flip the sign back to OPEN. The afternoon flows: a lull, a rush, a lull. A teen who asks for "something like *The Hating Game* but with more dogs." A retired Navy man who tells me about a lighthouse in another country with a light so steady it kept him alive in a storm forty years ago. A mother who collapses on the rug while her toddler builds a castle of board books and calls it "Quiet Time" like a benediction.

After school, the teenagers come—hoodies, backpacks, the whole noisy perfume of kids trying to find their way in life. They edge around romance like the covers might bite. They whisper-laugh and point at titles and are so broadly earnest it makes something in my chest ache in a fond, brittle way.

One of them lingers at the counter, a girl with ink-stained fingers and a nervous mouth. "Do you...have anything about leaving," she blurts, "but also staying? Because I have a scholarship for spring, and my grandma needs a ride to dialysis, and the guidance counselor keeps saying 'there's always Uber,' like Uber is a person we all trust with our grandmas, and—"

I reach under the counter where I keep items for grief and pull out two essay collections and one novel that grabbed my throat when I was twenty and didn't let go. "Yes," I say. "I have exactly that."

She breathes out like she's been holding air for days. "Thank you."

"Keep the novel," I add, when she goes to count out crumpled dollar bills. "Bring it back when you're finished. Or don't. Let it have time to sink in. Either way."

Her smile is a whole weather system. "Okay."

The door closes behind her, and the shop and I collectively sigh. I slide my palms over the counter and let the warm, exhausted hum of usefulness flood me. This is the part that never leaves: the way a book can step in for you when your mouth can't make sense.

The bell dings. A gust of cold air rides in with a man I don't recognize—mid-thirties, storm jacket, and a clipped way of speech that says business. He browses like he's timing himself. Buys two biographies and a postcard for his mother. Leaves with a nod that feels like appreciation's introverted cousin.

When the door shuts, I notice the envelope he knocked loose from the flier display. The cream one with the embossed edge.

I pick it up on reflex—and freeze when I see the scrawl on the back I missed before. Not —*A friend.* Just a postscript, ink pressed a little harder into the paper like the writer argued with themselves before letting it exist.

P.S. The lantern glass can be set in place with rope and patience. Ask Sawyer. Or ask me, if you can stand it. — C

I don't realize I'm smiling until it hurts my cheeks.

"I cannot stand it," I inform the espresso machine, and the espresso machine—traitor, conspirator—sighs like a woman who knows better and does it anyway.

The rest of the afternoon becomes an exercise in avoiding my own hands. Do not text. Do not call. Do not climb to the lantern room and tie a rope to your sanity. I alphabetize like a penance. I vacuum. I wipe down the children's corner and find a glitter sticker on my elbow because fate respects no boundaries.

At four, the door flies open, and the weather invades with purpose. Crew's younger brother, Holt, staggers in wearing a poncho he clearly stole from a roadside stand. He's carrying a box of T-shirts with a logo that makes my soul leave my body.

BACKBONE & BUTTER BARS, the shirts announce in big block letters, with a cartoon lighthouse that looks feral and a pan of Daisy's famous bars drawn like an Olympic torch.

"No," I say, before he speaks.

"Yes," he says, already unpacking. "For the Harvest Bash. Fundraiser. I have fifty of 'em. We'll be millionaires by Thanksgiving."

"I refuse to sell merch that implies Daisy's baked goods are structural."

Daisy pops through the side door like Beetlejuice at the mention of dessert. "Excuse *you,* those are *my* butter bars. Bailey's department is paper cuts and passive-aggressive bookmarks."

"Team effort," Holt says. "We're a brand now."

"You're a menace," I tell him, then ruin my own moral stance by laughing until I'm folded against the counter while Daisy tries to wrangle him and fails because Holt, like the weather, cannot be wrangled. He can only be endured.

They leave me three shirts "for display." I hide them behind the checkout plant. Even the plant looks offended.

By the time the drizzle thins out, I've almost—almost— won my battle with impulse. Which is when the bell rings and the universe decides compromise is simply adorable.

Sawyer—tall, easy-boned, hat shoved back like the sky

isn't enormous—leans in and taps the brim. "Heard your lantern glass is sulking."

"Crew's just being dramatic," I say, and catch myself—God help me—checking the sidewalk beyond him for a taller, broader shadow.

"Wright came by asking about glass replacement," Sawyer continues. "Said I should stop here first with a glove lecture."

"A glove lecture?"

"You'll want 'em. You do it wrong, you bleed."

"Good to know," I say faintly, taking the gloves. He glances around the store, eyes snagging on the window where the pigeon has returned to do his little judgment dance.

"Nice bird," Sawyer deadpans.

"He's part of the board," I say. "Votes on acquisitions."

"Smart." Sawyer tugs his cap. "Call if you need a hand. Or two. Because, Bailey, it's okay to ask for help, you know?"

When he's gone, the gloves sit on my counter like a dare.

I stare at them until the angle of the light shifts and turns the fibers gold.

"Fine," I tell the empty shop and the meddling sky and the part of me that's been teaching herself to do things without permission since she was ten. "Tonight."

I lock the door when the sign says I should. I count the drawer. I turn the lamps low. And then I climb.

The spiral stairs are a hymn I know by heart. Step,

breath, hand to rail. The lantern room waits at the top with the same patience it has for a hundred years of weather and more than enough secrets. The glass is cold and clouded, the crack a white seam like an old scar.

I set down some duct tape and rope, strip off my sweater, roll my sleeves to my elbows like a battlefield nurse, and test each pane with careful fingers. Gloves and patience.

"Ask Sawyer," the note had said. "Or ask me, if you can stand it."

I tie the first anchor knot by memory—the one my grandfather taught me on the dock until my fingers bled and I cursed. The rope settles heavy against my palm, and the old glass looks at me like, *That's not going to hold very long.*

Halfway through the second tie, my phone buzzes on the floorboards, screen lighting the room with a square of blue.

Crew: Don't start without me.

A BEAT. THEN ANOTHER.

Crew: Fine. Start without me. But leave me something to fix. It's a man's fragile ego at stake.

. . .

I STARE AT THE SCREEN, EVERY MUSCLE IN ME TRYING NOT to move fast enough to be called a decision.

Me: Bring your own gloves.

A DOT. THEN TWO. THEN NOTHING.

I tie the last knot on the rope to secure the glass from moving anymore, with my mouth curved into something I don't name. The lighthouse breathes like a steady chest. The rope hums against my hands like a word I'm about to learn fully.

Down below, on the boardwalk, a truck door shuts. I don't go down to meet him. I keep my hands on the old glass, shoulders squared, breath even. I let the footsteps come up to me—spiral, spiral, nearer—and when his shadow finally spills into the lantern room, I'm ready enough to pretend I have always been.

"Gloves," he says, holding them up in triumph, then takes in the knotwork and whistles low. "Not bad, Book Girl."

"Don't sound so shocked," I say, but softer than I mean to. "I can tie more than metaphors."

He steps closer, the room shrinking to fit us both, salt air threading between our words. "Show me what you did," he says, and it's not an order. It's an invitation. "I'll follow your lead."

I do. He does. Our fingers learn the same language.

We do not kiss. We do not fall. We do not do anything that will ruin this, yet I walk down the stairs later feeling ruined in the best, oldest sense of the word. Changed by weather I invited on purpose.

At the bottom, in the shop, under the lamp that always turns everything gold, he finds the cream envelope I didn't tuck far enough and slides it back to me without comment, his mouth tipping like a secret he won't use against me.

"Harvest Bash this weekend," he says lightly, as if his pulse isn't banging in his throat in sync with mine. "They roped me into a pie auction. I'm terrible at pie."

"Don't bid on anything that your brother baked," I advise, pocketing the envelope like a talisman. "It's mostly hubris and possibly fireworks."

"I'll save my wallet, then," he says, then takes a deep breath. "You going?"

"I live in a lighthouse," I say. "They can't hold an event without me approving the lighting."

He laughs. The laugh lodges under my breastbone. "See you there, Bailey."

"See you," I say, and it is not a vow, but it might be a map.

He goes. The bell hushes shut, the room inhales, and the pigeon, for once, looks satisfied.

I flip the porch light on and stand in it a second too long, like a moth who's tired of pretending she isn't drawn to heat. The bay slicks itself with stars. Somewhere far out on the water, a buoy clangs, and the sound threads the silence like a needle through cotton.

I touch the knot-burn on my palm—small, stinging, real —and decide I can live with a little heat.

I lock up, climb to bed, and fall asleep to the sense that the lighthouse doesn't creak anymore. It settles. Houses remember the hands that tend them. Today, the house has ours.

And that's either the best or the most dangerous thing I have done in years.

Chapter Four

CREW

The farm wakes up mean and pretty, same as always.

Dawn smears orange streaks across the pastures, and the barn smells like hay and rust and a childhood I keep trying to pick up without breaking. I'm in the gym corner of the old barn before the sun clears the pecans, band looped around the fence post, shoulder whining like it filed a complaint overnight.

"Easy," Marcus says, stepping in to adjust my elbow. "Mobility first, heroics never."

"You say that like you've met me," I grunt.

"I keep hoping repetition will work where common sense has failed."

I snort and keep moving. The band pulls, and I breathe. The joint remembers we're doing this for the long haul, not the highlight reel. Sweat stings my eyes. Somewhere outside, Mom hums to her hens.

When we finish, Marcus jots notes and gives me the look he gives right before he says something I don't want to hear.

"What?"

"Rest this afternoon," he says. "And by rest, I mean *rest*. No acrobatics. No lifting hay bales to prove a point."

I lift my good shoulder. "What about lifting my mouth into a smile at a town function against my will?"

"That's cardio."

"Great. Consider me compliant."

He cracks a rare smile. "Harvest Bash?"

"Apparently, I'm pie-adjacent." I grab a towel. "The committee thinks 'community engagement' will remind folks I'm a person and not a cautionary tale."

"Are you bringing the person you keep not talking about?"

I stare him down. He lifts both hands like a cop in a sitcom and walks away whistling.

By the time I hit the kitchen, passing my brother, Rowan, and my brother-in-law, Dean, along the way, Lila's at the table with three to-do lists, and Mom's filling Tupperware dishes like the county might run out of food.

"There he is," Lila says. "The reluctant celebrity."

"Don't say celebrity," I say, opening the fridge.

"Bailey texted me a photo of your rope work from last night. You didn't embarrass us."

"Us?"

"The family." She sips her coffee. "And civilization."

I ignore the way my pulse perks at Bailey's name. "She did most of it. I just followed instructions."

"Growth," Mom says without looking up, which is both encouraging and rude.

Lila leans her chin on her hand. "So. Are you going to ask her to go to the Bash with you, or are you planning on pining like a handsome barn ghost in flannel?"

"I don't pine."

"That's adorable," she says. "Tell it to your face."

"Leave him alone," Mom says mildly, sliding a plate of scrambled eggs in front of me. "But also, if you *are* going to pine, at least take dessert to share."

I fork eggs into my mouth to avoid words. Neither woman is fooled.

My phone buzzes on the table. David again. I ignore the first call. The second. On the third, I give in.

"Wright," he says, voice caffeinated and already disappointed. "I'm sending media to the Bash. Local team with small-town fluff. Smile, hold a pie, pretend you love humanity."

"I do love humanity," I say. "I just prefer the parts that aren't holding microphones."

"Too late. They're coming. Be charming."

"Define 'charming'."

"Not the version where you brood and glare like a Regency duke at war with feelings."

I hang up to preserve the friendship.

"Agent?" Lila asks.

"Saboteur," I correct.

I escape before they can interrogate me more.

The hours drag until dusk, because that's what time does when you're waiting to put your body somewhere your brain already is. I take a long shower that does not fix my personality, stare at my reflection until the man in the mirror looks back, as if he might be the kind who can say what needs saying, then pull on a navy Henley. Jeans. Boots. Jacket. Keys.

At the cove, the park by the marina is dressed up like a memory. String lights zigzag from oak to oak. Booths line the path with homemade jam, carved birds, and Holt's questionable T-shirts that should require a permit. Kids run feral in tidy shoes. The band on the gazebo plays something that sounds like three different songs at once and, somehow, still works.

People notice me. There's an initial pop of attention—eyebrows, whispers, a few brave "Hey, man, good to have you back"—and then it settles. Coral Bell Cove gets bored with its own gossip faster than outsiders think. The town wants you to belong more than it wants to punish you for leaving. It's not a trap; it's a door you can walk through if you quit being dramatic.

Daisy materializes at my elbow with a pie I'd fight God for. "No touching," she warns. "That's for the auction."

"What if it falls and I heroically catch it with my face?"

"Then I sell you napkins," she says, shoving a fork into my hand anyway. "Emergency taste test. I need to know if the new crust ratio is illegal."

I take a bite and see colors. "This is a crime."

"Excellent," she says and vanishes in a flourish of apron.

A familiar laugh skates over the noise, and my spine recognizes it before my head finishes turning.

Bailey stands by the cider tent talking to Lila and Ivy, and for a second, I forget the concepts of feet, earth, or weather.

She's not overdressed, not showy—just...her. Soft sweater the color of late peaches, skirt that looks like it was cut from a cloud, and boots that could fight a hurricane. Her hair's half up, the other half conspiring with the wind, and there's a streak of flour on her wrist like she lost a fight with Daisy's kitchen. She tips her head back to laugh again at something Lila says, and I have to fight the urge to walk into traffic just to reset my brain.

I'm moving before I tell myself to. The crowd parts on muscle memory. People say my name like we share a secret that's not mine to keep. Ivy spots me first and grins like she's emceeing fate.

"Wright," she singsongs. "We were debating whether you'd last longer than the five minutes of hellos."

"Lucky me, I made it ten," I say, eyes on Bailey because lying is rude.

"Hi," Bailey says, and the word settles like a landing I've been missing for years.

"Hi," I say back, very sophisticated.

Ivy pops a caramel in her mouth. "God, I love being right in the middle of this."

"Go sing to people," Bailey tells her, even though we all know Ivy just finished up a worldwide tour.

"In thirty," Ivy says. "In the meantime, we have a pie auction to rig."

"Rig?" I echo.

"Strategically influence," Lila corrects. "Don't you want to raise money for the library roof?"

"Yes," I say. "I also want to survive the evening without becoming a meme."

"Impossible," Ivy chirps. "Okay, lover boys and girls, to the gazebo. The auction's starting."

We shuffle toward the stage. I end up beside Bailey on the bottom step, our shoulders almost touching. The air is bright and cold and tastes like cinnamon and nerves. A kid runs past and smacks my thigh by accident. I catch him by the back of his hoodie and set him upright. His mom mouths, "*Thank you,*" like I did something heroic.

Onstage, the mayor taps a mic until it shrieks. I flinch. Bailey grins without looking at me.

"Nerves?" she murmurs.

"Just don't like being told when to be loud," I say.

Her mouth curves. "Same."

The first pies go fast. People bid like it's a sport, which here it is. Daisy's triple-berry sparks a fight between two retired Coast Guard chiefs that ends with the mayor threatening to call their old CO. Holt auctions a Butter Bars monstrosity that shouldn't exist and still goes for $110 because Coral Bell Cove has lost its mind.

"Next up," the mayor crows, "a Wright family classic: Mom Wright's pecan pie—baked under the supervision of her semi-competent sons!"

The crowd roars. Mom blushes. Lila screams her bid of twenty. The number rockets to seventy, then ninety, then a hundred and thirty because nostalgia is a drug.

I clap and do not think about microphones or expectations or the way people still want us to be fine in public, even when, in private, we are all lopsided. Then the mayor says my name, and I remember the thing about microphones.

"And now—" he booms, winking like a magician about to saw a volunteer in half. "A special lot. Donated by *A Page in Time* and our very own lighthouse lady: a *Literary Lovers' Basket*—rare romance hardcovers, handpicked by Bailey, and one private after-hours story hour for two at the lighthouse —tea and cookies included."

The crowd oohs like it has rehearsed.

My ears ring. Beside me, Bailey goes very still and then very composed, like a cat deciding whether to panic in public.

She leans toward the mayor. "That's not what I called it."

"Artistic license," he stage-whispers. "Roll with it."

A man near the front yells, "Fifty!" and a woman from the boardwalk counterbids with "Seventy!" and suddenly, there's a whole buffet of strangers trying to buy time in a room I've only just remembered how to breathe inside of.

Something territorial and irrational rises in me like a tide that didn't check the schedule.

I do not like that feeling. I also do not ignore it.

"Two hundred," I say, hand up because apparently I like escalation.

The crowd pivots. Bailey's head whips toward me, eyes wide with startled amusement that she tries to throttle into exasperation and fails.

"Two ten," calls a fisherman I've known since I was ten.

"Two fifty," I say, because reason is on lunch break.

"Crew," Bailey murmurs, voice low. "You don't have to—"

"I want to." It's not smooth, and it's not a line. It's simply the truest sentence I have spoken in public in years.

Her throat works. The corners of her mouth soften. She looks away like the lights are too bright and then back at me like maybe they aren't the point.

"Two seventy," someone shouts.

"Three hundred," I counter, because at this point I'm bidding on air and the right not to watch a stranger sit where I plan to apologize properly.

"Three fifty!"

"Four," I say, and the murmurs go up an octave.

The mayor milks it. "Four hundred going once... going twice..."

"Sold," I say under my breath at the same time he does out loud.

Applause like rain on a tin roof. Ivy wolf-whistles. Lila

covers her mouth, eyes laughing. Mom dabs at her eyes like I just rode a bike without training wheels.

Bailey stands very straight, hands folded, cheeks pink. "Congratulations," she says softly when the noise dips. "You just paid four hundred dollars for cookies."

"Bargain," I tell her. And then, because I cannot help myself, I ask, "Does the basket come with a translator for your sarcasm?"

"Unfortunately, no."

The auction rolls on, and I don't hear most of it. The band tunes behind the gazebo. People drift off toward cider and gossip and the dance lawn where couples start swaying out of habit. The sky goes that deep cobalt that makes the string lights look like constellations that sat down to rest.

"Walk?" I ask, when the crowd thins enough that we can slip away without three aunties drafting a marriage license.

She considers, then nods once. "One lap."

We skirt the edge of the pier, boots thudding soft on planks gone damp with the evening. The bay lifts and lowers itself like it's breathing. Far out, a buoy clangs, the sound as steady as the beat I can't slow down.

"You didn't have to bid," she says finally, eyes on the water.

"I wanted to keep the lighthouse on our schedule," I say. "Not the internet's."

She huffs something that's almost a laugh. "You and Lila with your schedules."

"I'm a middle child in a loud family," I say. "Schedules are the only way to be heard."

She glances over, amused. "You were very heard tonight."

"Yeah," I say, and rueful doesn't even begin to cover it. "About that."

We stop at the end of the pier. The town noise turns to a wash. The wind is a careful hand on the back of my neck.

"I'm sorry," I say, the words landing quieter than I planned, truer than I let myself hope. "For the hallway. For the way I didn't stop him. For how I let *silence* do my talking and pretended that wasn't the same as choosing a side."

She closes her eyes, then opens them again. "You were a kid."

"So were you," I say. "And you deserved a man even then."

Her breath fogs. "Heroics don't fix it."

"I know," I say. "But I can tell the truth about it. And I can do better now if you let me. If you don't, I'll still do better. You just won't have to see it."

We look at each other long enough for the cold to find the open edges of our clothes. The lights back onshore swing in their own breeze. Somewhere behind us, Ivy's voice climbs a scale and rides it like a bird that finally remembered the air is hers.

Bailey breaks first, but it's not retreat. It's mercy. "You paid four hundred dollars for cookies," she says, mouth curving. "You get at least one."

"Just one?"

"Don't be greedy."

"Can I be specific? Chocolate chip?"

"Chaos," she says automatically, and then blinks because she already knows the whole stupid lexicon of my life.

We start back toward the park. On the last plank before dirt, my boot slips. Reflex has me grabbing for the rail with my left hand. Her hand hits my chest at the same time—steadying me, steadying us—and stays there a beat longer than gravity requires.

The air goes loud as blood.

"Careful," she says, not moving her hand.

"I'm trying," I answer, not moving mine when it finds her wrist.

We stand like idiots with our bodies inventing a language we're barely qualified to speak. Then she slides her hand away. I let her, yet she doesn't step far.

At the gazebo, the band counts off. Ivy leans into the mic, eyes on the crowd like she's about to make trouble and call it harmony. I stand beside Bailey in the soft spill of light and pretend the beating thing in my chest is a drum the band can hear.

"Tomorrow," I say, surprising myself because the word sounds like a plan.

She arches a brow. "What's tomorrow?"

"Lantern inspection," I say. "And cookies."

She pretends to deliberate. "Bring your own thermos."

"Always."

We don't touch again. We don't kiss. We don't make promises with our mouths that our bodies can't hold. We just stand there while Ivy sings something that sounds like the start of a life, and for once, I don't mind being seen.

When the song ends, and the crowd roars, and the night leans in close, I know two things with the clean certainty rehab never gives me: I am not running. And I am not playing to the cameras that secretly film my every move.

I'm playing to the light.

Which is to say, I'm playing to her.

Chapter Five

BAILEY

The day after the Harvest Bash tastes like cinnamon and consequences.

I unlock the door to *A Page in Time* with one hand and balance a paper bag of Daisy's "I Won't Bake Again Until Noon (Lie)" pastries on my hip with the other. The porch boards are still damp from last night's fog; the string lights I forgot to take down from the windows glow faintly in the gray. I'm not saying I left them up for ambience. I'm saying I left them up because they make the lighthouse look like it took a deep breath and remembered it was allowed to be pretty.

Inside, I flick on the lamps, and the shop wakes in warm layers—brass, wood, paper, and sea-salt air sneaking through the old casements. The espresso machine hisses as if it's rolling its shoulders, which is rude because I'm the one who tied rope knots until my palms stung and then stood in a park pretending I didn't notice a six-foot-something problem bidding on cookies like a man with intent.

Not a date, I remind the ceiling. A fundraiser. A basket. A rash decision made by a quarterback with generous pockets.

The ceiling, as usual, refuses to referee.

I move—rugs straightened, windows cracked, cash counted, muffins plated. Normal is a choreography I can do by muscle memory. It helps. It always has.

The bell over the door jingles, and Mrs. Winthrop drifts in wearing a cape and an expression like she's already shocked by whatever I'm about to say. "Darling, I have terrible news. I woke up this morning and discovered I'm still not twenty-five."

"Tragic." I slide a maple pecan in her direction. "Carbohydrate condolences."

She accepts, bites, then sighs dramatically. "I suppose we must go on. Tell me everything."

"About?"

"Don't play coy," she scolds gently. "It ages you. The *basket*, Bailey. The *literary lovers* nonsense invented by the mayor. You allowed a public man to buy a private hour. I require details so I can live vicariously and give excellent advice."

"It's not—" I stop, realizing I'm about to say *a date* out loud to a woman who once told me plants thrive when you talk to them about scandal. "It's an appointment. After hours. For tea and cookies. The end."

She hums like a woman who has never once accepted *the end* as a reasonable conclusion to a story. "Hmm. Well, when you inevitably wear that soft blue sweater your eyes like, tell him to sit on the rug. Men open up closer to the ground."

"Is that...science?"

"It's experience." She pats my hand, purchases a mystery, and sails out again, leaving perfume and prophecy in her wake.

I set the bell to ring a little louder because I refuse to be ambushed by any more wisdom before nine.

The morning rush trickles—tourists finishing out long weekends, teachers hunting for class read-alouds, a fisherman who buys a book of poems and claims they help his casting rhythm. I let the town talk itself out around me, answering to *Bailey*, *lighthouse lady*, and, once, *book witch* (which, honestly, is flattering).

At ten, the side door creaks, and Daisy backs in with a tray of scones balanced like a tightrope act. "I brought tributes for your not-date," she singsongs, nudging the door shut with her heel.

"It's not—"

"I know." She sets the tray down, peels off her jacket, and studies my face. "You slept?"

"Like a woman who tied rope knots for fun."

She grins. "Sawyer said your lines were clean. Also he said if you're going to keep using that old glass, you might want to rub in a little linseed oil. But that could've been about bread. He was eating toast at the time."

"I'll ask him."

"Or," Daisy says, "you could ask the person who clearly

wrote you a donation check like a man trying not to be noticed."

I do not look at the drawer where the envelope lives. "You anointed yourself as treasurer of my secrets, when?"

"The minute I learned how to make frosting. It's in the bylaws." She leans on her elbows. "Have you set a time?"

"For the...appointment?" I aim for bored and land somewhere near breathless.

"For the not-date in your lighthouse with baked goods and moonlight," she corrects.

"I was thinking tomorrow," I say, because apparently my mouth has decided to live dangerously before my brain has a chance to file a safety report. "After close."

"Perfect," she beams. "Do your hair. Wear the blue sweater."

"Mrs. Winthrop texted you, didn't she?"

"She added me to a sub-thread. It's me, her, and your pigeon."

The door opens, and the pigeon—my nemesis—stares in as if on cue before deciding the weather is beneath him and flapping away. Daisy waves. "See? He's invested."

"Fantastic. A bird and two women over seventy are managing my love life."

"Please. I'm not over seventy." She kisses my cheek, snags a scone, and disappears with a parting, "Call me if you need reinforcements or have a hairbrush emergency."

The shop settles. A father and daughter browse the nature section, arguing about whales with the kind of intensity that says they're going to be fine. I ring up a stack of cookbooks for a customer who confesses he's never baked a pie but is suddenly deeply competitive about it. I recommend a recipe. He vows to return with samples. I support his dreams because I, too, am not immune to sugar.

The bell rings again, and this time four things happen at once: a gust of cooler air tumbles in, two young reporters I don't recognize step over the threshold with mics clipped to their shirts, the taller one says "We're with Channel Seven doing Harvest Bash follow-ups," and the fourth thing—the one that knocks my balance—is that Crew, of course, is right behind them holding a takeaway tray of coffees like they're a peace treaty.

I remind my face that it has edges and a position. "Hi."

"Hi," he says, and the room shifts because his *hi* says more than it should.

The reporters spin, light snapping on. "Mr. Wright! Do you have a second for a quick feel-good piece?"

He flinches a millimeter. Just enough to make me want to form a protective circle with my arms. He recovers, a smile sliding into place. "I have sixty seconds. After that, I'm a hazard to your equipment."

They laugh. "Perfect. We're doing post-Bash human interest. Local hero returns, supports library, bids on literary basket—"

"It was for cookies," he says, shooting me a side glance that asks permission to keep telling our joke in public.

"Cookies," I echo, playing my part because if the town expects anything of me, it's that I can commit to a bit.

"Right." The shorter reporter checks her notes. "And

the basket includes—let me get this right—an after-hours 'story hour for two' hosted by…" She squints at her card. "Bailey Hart."

"So," the reporter barrels on, "tell us—what moved you to bid?"

He could feed them lines: community, literacy, sister's influence, nostalgia. He could turn the charm up two clicks, and they'd eat out of his hand. And for a second, I think he will.

Then he glances at me, breathes once, and chooses a different stage.

"I like lighthouses," he says simply. "And books seem to bring out the truth in people."

The taller reporter blinks. The shorter one recovers. "That's…poetic."

"It's accurate." His smile tilts. "Also, I hear there are cookies."

"There are," I say, because someone has to steady the scene, and it turns out it might as well be the girl who wore flour on her wrist the night before. "But only to approved bidders following rigorous cookie protocols."

"Fortunately," he says, eyes warming, "I come pre-approved."

"Debatable."

The interview lasts exactly sixty seconds and feels like walking across a frozen pond that decides mercy is fashionable today. They get their footage. He gives them a quote that will play well. I do not flip a microphone into the bay. Everyone's a winner.

When they leave, he sets one of the coffees on the counter in front of me without fanfare. "Oat milk, minimal sugar. You're chaotic but disciplined."

"Stop reading my diary," I say, fingers curling around warmth I will not name.

He lifts the other cup. "Truce?"

"Terms?"

"You don't ban me from the premises for being a public nuisance. I don't let anyone else bid on your time."

My pulse, unhelpful traitor, leaps like it was waiting to be told to. "You can't stop—"

"I can try."

"Intimidation isn't a personality."

"Tell my agent," he mutters.

I fight a smile and fail, because in the light morning, he looks exactly like a man who would pay four hundred dollars to keep a promise to himself.

"So," he says, casual like the world isn't slanting, "about my winnings."

"Your cookies," I say, for the cameras that no longer exist. "And the...hour."

He nods once, all the joking sluicing off his face for something steadier. "Tonight? After close? If you're not—"

"I was hoping for tomorrow, but tonight works," I say, as if my mouth has separated from my central nervous system and run off with my best impulses. "Seven thirty."

"Perfect." He reaches into his jacket and pulls out a small paper bag. "Peace offering."

"I thought the coffees were—" I open it and pause.

Inside are two brand-new pairs of work gloves. One small, one large. Both soft, broken-in, like someone took the time to oil the leather last night while thinking about my hands.

"I like my book witch with skin," he says with a shrug, laughing at his own chivalry before it can embarrass him. "Also, Sawyer said to tell you he'll come up on Wednesday to look at the lantern frame."

I swallow past the feeling gathering in my throat. "Thank you."

"Don't thank me for gloves."

"For not making a joke when the mics were on," I say. "For choosing the boring, honest answer."

His mouth does something that isn't a smile, yet is heading that way. "Trying out this whole 'man' thing."

"How's it going?"

He glances down at my wrist. The flour streak is still there despite my early morning shower (don't ask me, Daisy's work is witchcraft). Without thinking, he reaches out and rubs at it with his thumb. The touch is light. The charge is not. And the damn thing disappears. Not even super flour is immune to his charm.

"Better," he says, thumb withdrawing like he can feel the scaling heat he left in his wake.

We stand in the quiet hum of the shop, two coffees between us like a treaty, two pairs of gloves like a dare, and the after-hours hour hovering overhead like a promise I wrote myself and then forgot to deny.

A kid barrels in with a dollar and a mission to buy a bookmark with a dragon on it. We both jump, ridiculous and guilty, and the moment slides toward sensible again with a small, shamed laugh from my rib cage.

"Seven thirty," he says, backing toward the door before we both make choices we can't fold back up. "I'll bring... something."

"Bring your inside voice," I say. "It's a library-adjacent event."

"Yes, ma'am."

The bell sings, and he's gone.

I look down at the gloves in my hands and only realize I've been smiling like a fool when Daisy appears at my shoulder and whispers, "Oh, this is catastrophic."

"It's not—"

"Bailey," she says, head tipped, eyes kind, voice relentless. "Honey, you're already in the lighthouse. You might as well turn on the light."

I make a face at her. She makes one back. We're both twelve and thirty and ancient in the way women are when they stand behind counters and decide where their lives will go and who will be allowed to walk in.

At six, I flip the sign to CLOSED.

One minute later, the group chat lights up like a bonfire.

Lila: Need me to deliver a bodyguard/babysitter/baked goods?

Ivy: I wrote you a playlist titled "Tea & Tension." Do not waste it.

Me: If I don't respond, I was kidnapped.

Daisy: You're welcome.

Mrs. Winthrop: Blue sweater. Rug seating. Also a dab of vanilla behind the knees. It's science.

Me: ABSOLUTELY NOT.

Mrs. Winthrop: Your loss.

I laugh alone in the middle of my shop and don't feel alone at all.

At seven, I boil water and set out cups and cookies and the hardcover stack he paid for like a ridiculous, perfect man. At seven fifteen, I check the lantern ropes even though they're fine. At seven twenty-eight, I stand with my hand on the light switch and breathe like I am not about to invite history up a narrow staircase.

At seven thirty on the dot, the bell rings.

I open the door. He stands there, wind-tousled, jacket unzipped, hair damp at the edges. He lifts a thermos like an offering.

"I know this night comes with tea. But I brought a peace offering," he says. "Again."

"What's in it?"

"Cinnamon tea," he says, and smiles like a man about to tell the truth.

I step back, let him in, and close the door behind him.

The lighthouse settles around us, patient and old and extremely nosy.

"Books first," I say, because control is a warm blanket, and I like being warm. "Tea second. Then cookies. Then—"

"Questions," he says, and I blink.

"Science," I mutter.

He grins. "Lead the way, Book Girl."

I pick up the gloves and the thermos. He takes the books. We climb—step, breath, hand to rail—and at the top, in the lantern room, the glass holds steady, the rope hums, and the air goes sweet with cinnamon and the hope of something like repair.

Not a date, I tell myself one last time, purely for tradition.

Then I sit on the rug beside him, set the cups between us, and admit, quietly, when the room is listening and nobody else is, "I'm nervous."

"Me, too," he says, and says it like an invitation instead of a warning.

We don't kiss. We don't touch. Not yet. We drink tea, we eat cookies, and we read a page aloud from a book about second chances because I am who I am and he is who he has decided to be.

We ask each other questions we should have asked a decade ago.

And when the hour we auctioned finally runs out, neither of us moves to stand. Until, with the strength of one thousand men, I walk Crew to the door and bid him good night. Even though I want to do anything but.

Chapter Six

CREW

The morning after tastes like dry cinnamon and a decision I didn't let myself make.

Sun slams through the east windows as if it owns the place while the kettle screams like it's filing a complaint with management. The old farmhouse floors carry every sound the way Coral Bell Cove carries a rumor—straight through the bones.

I stand at the sink in yesterday's T-shirt, pour coffee that could file a restraining order against water, and try not to run last night on a loop. It runs anyway. Her laugh tripping over steam. The soft *click* of porcelain on old wood. The way our knees touched and pretended not to. The lantern room catching our breath and keeping it.

I take a swallow too big, burn my tongue, and mutter at the mug like it started this. The air smells like butter, salt, and the faint iron of rain that might or might not happen. Every wire inside me hums like the lighthouse lamp before it flares. This is ridiculous. I'm a grown man. I've broken ribs, separated shoulders, stood in front of eighty thousand people, and told a defense to come and get me. Yet one woman in a blue sweater says *honest questions*, and I'm a live wire with legs.

Move. That's the rule. When thinking gets loud, you move.

I grab a sweatshirt, and head out to the porch where the morning is trying like hell to be charming. Early fall at Otter Creek tastes like apples and diesel. Pecan trees stand black and confident against a sky that's already forgetting summer. Cows move in the lower pasture. Somewhere, a tractor coughs awake like an old man with opinions. I breathe it in and pretend there isn't a lighthouse-shaped outline stamped against the inside of my eyelids.

Marcus shows up at eight with resistance bands and that smug monk patience that makes me want to be better and punch him, in that order. "Morning, prodigal shoulder," he says, stepping into the barn gym like a man entering church with snacks. The barn's cool and smells like hay and lemon disinfectant. Dust floats in the light slats, polite as parishioners.

"Mobility, not machismo," he adds, which is rude because I haven't even made a poor decision yet.

"You flirting with me?" I ask, hooking the band around the post, rolling my shoulder like I've been taught.

"You're not my type," he says. "Too tragic."

"I'm a delight," I groan through the first rep. A burn kisses across the front of the joint—clean, mean, honest.

"You smell like shame and drugstore coffee," he says, setting a timer on his watch.

"It's called cologne—*Eau de Quarterback at a Crossroads*."

He smirks without looking up from the clipboard. "Notes from yesterday: external rotation improved; internal still tight; scapular winging decreased. Notes for today: stop trying to win rehab. And for the love of your grandma, take it easy, Crew. You're overdoing it."

"Winning is a lifestyle."

"Not when your rotator cuff is one sarcastic comment away from spitting you out like a sunflower seed."

We work. The barn breathes with us. Band pulls, spine stacks, breath drops lower when the burn gets sharp. I close my eyes and look for the click—when the motion stops being a fight and starts being a conversation. It arrives, late and worth it, like most good things.

"How's the lighthouse?" he asks, casual as a loaded question.

"Tall."

"Girl?"

"Woman," I say, automatically. "Bossy. Dangerous. Good with rope."

"Sounds like a country song." He tips my elbow half an inch. "You two talk?"

"Yeah."

"Kiss?"

"No."

He whistles low. "Voluntary?"

"There were rules," I say. "And tea."

"Wow. Tea. You two are wild." He stares, not blinking. "And you didn't die."

"Define 'die'."

He raises his hands and steps back. "My bad. I'll update your chart to *Alive, reluctantly*."

We move into YTWs, and my shoulder vibrates like an overcaffeinated phone. "You ever screw up so bad you still taste it?" I ask, eyes on the rafters because I won't hold his.

"I coach men who think pain is a proof of masculinity," he says. "So yes. Daily. Tell her."

"She's not a garbage can," I mutter.

"Right," he says, softer. "She's the reason your face looks ten percent less haunted."

The next rep falters. Just barely—a tremor most people wouldn't catch. Marcus does. He always does. He adjusts the angle of my wrist, not the man, guiding me back into the line of motion.

Something in the quiet of it pulls at a loose thread inside me.

The barn fades for a breath—not in a cinematic way, just that split-second slide into memory I never asked for.

Friday before playoffs.

Tile floors slick with Gatorade and ego. Tanner kicking the locker room door like he owns the place.

He had a note in his hand—folded twice, blue-lined paper, the crease worn from someone worrying it. *Her* handwriting, even then, was soft around the edges.

He read it out loud with a grin he didn't earn.

Good luck in the big game. I'll be in the stands cheering for you. Stay gold, C. -B.

The laughter came fast. Too fast. A pack of boys who didn't know what to do with sincerity except kill it. Tanner tacked the note dead center on the board like it was a joke. And I...

God help me, I laughed too. Not because it was funny. Because I was seventeen and stupid and thought approval was oxygen.

She didn't come to the game.

Or the next.

And I learned the cost of choosing an audience over a girl who meant every quiet thing she wrote.

"Wright," Marcus says softly.

I blink hard, the barn rushing back around me—hay dust, oil, the steady drag of breath.

"You here?"

I clear my throat. "Yeah."

Too fast to be believable.

We finish in silence that isn't empty. He claps my back at the door. "Rest this afternoon," he says. "And by rest, I mean do nothing spectacular."

"No heroics," I say.

"Not with your shoulder," he says, then grins like a man who knows a loophole when he writes one.

The house is empty when I go in. Mom's left a note on the counter—

Market run. Lila says hydrate. Don't glower too much.

I pour more coffee against my better judgment, and last night unfurls again like rope from a neat coil. Her hands. Her voice on the words we read out loud. The way she said *"not yet"* didn't feel like a denial. It felt like scaffolding. It felt like an adult thing—built, checked, trusted.

Sitting still is a crime, so I take my show on the road. The coffee shop bell jingles, and the place fills with espresso and milk and the kind of jazz that cleans the corners of rooms. Kelly looks over the espresso machine like a cat at a terrarium. "He lives," she says. "You want your usual or something seasonal and humiliating?"

"Just coffee. Strong enough to make my regrets apologize."

"Got a new roast called *Poor Choices at Dusk*."

"Perfect."

She sets the order in motion, a shoulder/hip rhythm people get when they do a thing they understand. I breathe through my nose and practice not checking the door every four seconds. I make it to seven. The bell rings. The universe has a sense of humor.

Bailey walks in like she paid the light bill and the day's grateful. High bun, sweater sliding off one shoulder. There's an ink smudge on her thumb. I want to kiss it off. Jesus. Get a grip.

She sees me. There's the microsecond of flinching—the muscle memory we both have—then the half smile that means *I'm choosing this* and *don't make me regret it*. "Morning," she says, stepping into my entire nervous system.

"Morning," I manage. "You forgot to bring the marshmallow man. I was going to fight him."

"He's in HR training," she says. "Workplace boundaries and such."

"You ruin everything."

"Only mascots and men who deserve it." Her mouth curves like a threat softened by fondness. "What are you doing today besides pretending your shoulder is fine?"

Pretending I don't want to kiss you in a coffee shop, I say in my head. Out loud, I reply, "Chores. Rehab homework. Avoiding my agent."

"Busy." She steps up when Kelly calls her name and receives a cup labeled BOOK WITCH in bubble letters that will haunt me. We stand shoulder to shoulder while a retired couple behind us argues about oat milk.

"Tonight?" The word is out before I agree. She arches a brow at my lack of finesse. "Lighthouse," I clarify. "After close."

"Tea," she says.

"Honest questions."

"Science," she returns, eyes bright, and we are such children we walk out before we kiss in front of Kelly and traumatize the oat milk couple.

"Don't get hit by a gull," she tosses over her shoulder.

"Don't fall off your roof," I fire back.

"Bring better lines," she says, not turning. "You're rusty."

Mom ambushes me at home with cornbread and

prophecy. "Your face is at a thirty percent less sulk factor," she says, sliding a pan on the counter. "Who do we thank? The Lord? The lighthouse? The girl you've been in love with since she corrected your grammar in tenth grade?"

"I'm leaving," I say, already eating with my hands like a man who never owned a fork.

"She was mean about it," Mom continues dreamily. "*It's whom, Crew.* Half the kitchen giggled. You looked at her like she'd invented air."

"I'm moving," I say. "New name. New life." I'm smiling. I can feel it. It feels like breaking a rule and getting away with it.

"Second chances aren't miracles," Mom says, softer now. "They're work. Do the work."

"I am."

"Do it with your whole chest," she adds, tapping the center of me with two fingers. "Not with your helmet on."

"Please stop speaking in metaphors."

"Never." She kisses my cheek. "Tell Bailey I said hi."

"I'm not—"

"Bye," she sings, already at the sink, smirking.

I do chores like I'm getting paid by the thought, not the hour. Fence line. Feed. A loose hinge. A tarp that needs a better tie-down. My brother is enjoying having me home and making good use of me.

My shoulder cooperates, mostly. Sweat is good. It makes the body honest. I check the time every ten minutes and pretend I'm not. I shower, do the thing where I stare at the mirror and give speeches I'll never admit to, pull on the navy Henley Lila calls "the bay during a murder plot" (rude), and the boots that make me taller when I don't need to be.

The lighthouse appears exactly where it always is and somehow closer. The bay looks like a sheet of slate on which someone wrote secrets. Her porch light is on. The shop glows behind the glass. I park, breathe, do a shoulder roll to keep the tremor away, and walk like this isn't the most consequential small distance of my adult life.

"Hi," she says at the door, and it hits me in the spine.

"Hi," I say, because apparently that's our entire vocabulary when it matters.

"You brought tea?" She eyes the thermos.

"Damn, I forgot."

"On brand," she teases, flipping the sign to CLOSED. "Come on."

We climb—spiral, breath, hand on rail. My palm hovers behind her back and never touches because restraint is religion tonight. The lantern room greets us the way an old dog greets a child—tail thumping, polite, hopeful. Her rug is a dare. She sits cross-legged, and I swear my pulse calibrates to the length of her exhale. We pour. We drink. The air smells like fall and storms that haven't decided yet.

"Honest questions," she says, and it isn't the news. It's the law.

"God," I say. "Okay." I set my cup carefully because my hands aren't the steadiest.

"Why didn't you stop it?"

I thought she'd ease me in. She doesn't. It's very Bailey to rip the bandage when I've brought extra gauze.

"Because I was a coward," I say, and it's almost a relief—the word finding air. "Because the room was louder than I was brave. Because I thought if a crowd loved me, the one person I wanted to love me would feel obligated to catch up."

Her eyes don't flinch. She takes it like she takes rope—measured, strong. "You hurt me."

"I know."

"Do you still have it?" she asks, and the question lands gently and surgically.

"Yes," I say, because there's freedom in not lying to yourself or to the woman who might still own you. "It goes with me everywhere."

Something in her breath stutters and then smooths. "I hated you."

"I earned it."

"Good," she says, and there's the ghost of a smile that doesn't make it past her mouth. "Now we can stop pretending to be polite."

We talk. About then. About now. About how silence is also an answer, and how we both gave too much of it. She tells me about winter break and how leaving for two weeks felt like two years because the town kept asking her questions like quizzes, and she failed all of them. I tell her about the hit that ripped my shoulder and a part of my certainty, and how the silence after the crowd gasped felt like the first time the world told me *maybe not you*.

"Are you afraid?" she asks.

"Every minute," I say. "Of doing it wrong again. Of

loving the *idea* of you more than the person in front of me." I run a hand over my jaw because it feels like the only true gesture left. "I don't want to put you on a shelf. I want to stand next to you and be useful."

She watches me like she's grading a paper, and I might pass if I show my work. "What are you afraid I'll do?" she asks.

"Fold," I say, and she blinks. "That you'll fold yourself small to make me fit. That you'll give me the lighthouse and leave yourself in the dark corners."

"Crew." She says my name like it's heavy and she's strong. "Rule one: I don't fold. I reorganize with extreme measures."

"Hot," I say, because the alternative is crawling across the rug and learning the taste of her shoulder, and we're not doing that yet.

She rolls her eyes, fondness smudging the edge. "Rule two: if you want to touch me, you ask. Out loud."

My spine goes electric. "Out loud."

"So I can say yes," she says, more serious now, "and you'll know it's yes."

"Rule three?"

"No assumptions," she says. "About the past or the future. I decide what forgiveness looks like. You decide what you can carry. We both decide if we're building something or playing house."

"Building," I say, instantly. She looks relieved and annoyed that I didn't agonize. I grin. "What? I'm decisive about two things: breakfast and you."

"That's unfortunate," she says, smiling despite herself. "I'm complicated."

"I like complicated," I say. "It keeps things interesting after the awkwardness."

She laughs and presses her palm to her mouth like she can keep it in. Her eyes are warm and dangerous. Somewhere out over the water, a buoy clangs. The windows hum in their frames like a satisfied cat. We drink more tea. We read a page each from a book about people who almost ruin it and don't—because they choose to be grown instead of dramatic. We don't kiss. Every cell in my body yearns for it, though.

When we finally stand, it's slow. Gravity changes when you leave a room that holds a version of you you like. Down the spiral, her sleeve brushes my arm, and restraint becomes an Olympic sport. At the counter, she slides two cookies into a paper bag and writes RULES on the front, underlining it with a flourish like an executioner with manners.

"Same time tomorrow?" I ask, light so she can say no without bruising anything.

"Maybe," she says, which is woman for *yes, if you don't screw up between now and then.* "If you're good."

"Define 'good'."

"Honest. On time." She tilts her head.

"Always."

At the door, I do the thing I've been practicing all night: I ask. "Can I touch you?" The words feel like they cost something and buy everything.

Her chin lifts. "Where?"

"Your waist," I say, voice dropping without my permission. "For two seconds."

She thinks about it like a jeweler, like a captain, like the woman she is when she's deciding whether to open a door and let a man inside her house and her life. "Two seconds," she says.

I step closer, set my palm lightly at the warm place between the sweater hem and the pants, and the universe changes shape. I don't pull. I don't push. I just learn the temperature of her bare skin. One. Two. I drop my hand and step back before I make a menace of myself.

"Good night, Crew," she says, soft and seismic.

"Good night, Bailey," I say, and it tastes like belief.

Outside, the air is cooler, the fog gathering itself into a low, thoughtful animal. I stand on the porch long enough to memorize the sound of her turning the lock and the way the lamp inside paints gold into the doorway like she's made of it. My truck engine coughs awake. I pull out and don't turn on the radio because I want to hear the world think.

Halfway home, at the overlook where the road shoulders out, I park and kill the lights. The newer lighthouse throws its beam across the bay, slow and steady, like a promise practiced into muscle memory, while Bailey's smaller lighthouse shines a beacon barely discernible to any passing boats. I take out my phone. Her name sits there, simple and dangerous. I type *I can still smell the book pages. And you.* The letters gleam back like they want to be history.

One tap would do it.

I don't tap. I watch the words breathe on the screen and then erase them, letter by letter, a small act of worship to a bigger thing—patience, maybe, or respect, or the way my mother told me to show up with my whole chest and not my highlight reel. The message box goes blank. The want doesn't. Good. Let it live. Let it make me better or make me wait or both.

The night air is cold enough to bite. I roll the window down and breathe until the ache settles into a bearable shape. The light sweeps the bay, again and again like a heartbeat. When I finally pull back onto the road, I say it to the dark, to the water, to the boy I was and the man I'm trying to be, a line that's been sitting inside me like a compass. "Stay gold, B."

I don't send anything. I don't need to. The light's already carrying it.

Chapter Seven

BAILEY

The smell of tea haunts me.

It's in the rug, the kettle, the memory of him sitting too close. I try to pretend it's just plain tea, but it's not. It's *him*—his laugh low in his throat, his knee brushing mine, his stupid, perfect smile when he realized I'd made rules.

I pull the blanket over my head like it might erase him. It doesn't. It just makes the air smell more like salt and him and last night.

The lighthouse creaks as the wind picks up, the same way it always does, but everything sounds different today. The tide feels higher. The light sweeps slower. Even the gulls sound smug.

I groan, roll over, and stare at the ceiling. "You're not sixteen," I tell myself. "You are a grown, emotionally stable woman with a mortgage and a business license."

The ceiling, traitorous, says nothing back.

By the time I drag myself downstairs, the shop smells like vanilla and ocean air. Sunlight slants through the front windows, hitting the shelves like a spotlight. *A Page in Time* looks beautiful this morning. Unforgivably romantic. Even the damn books look like they're conspiring.

The bell above the door jingles as I flip the sign to OPEN. "You," I mutter to the novels in the front display, "are not allowed to look smug."

Jane Austen doesn't respond, but she's definitely judging me.

I brew a fresh pot of coffee, open my ledger, and try to focus on anything other than Crew Wright's hands. It's hopeless. Everything reminds me of him. The way he carried those boxes as if they weighed nothing. The way his voice wrapped around my name like it had been waiting a decade to repeat it.

There's a knock on the side door before I can spiral too far. I don't have to check who it is—only one person knocks like they're trying to summon the dead.

Lila strides in holding a pastry box the size of a toddler. "I come bearing muffins and judgment."

"I'm not on trial," I say even though I absolutely am.

She plops the box on the counter, grinning. "You're glowing."

"It's called morning light."

"It's called *my brother kissed your emotional stability right in the face.*"

"He didn't kiss anything," I say, and she raises an eyebrow so high it could pierce clouds.

"Didn't have to," she says. "You look like a woman who's been thoroughly eye-fucked."

"Language," I hiss even though she's not wrong.

She laughs, pouring herself coffee like she owns the place. "You forget, I've been married to Dean for long enough to recognize the post-slow-burn look. It's adorable. You're doomed."

Before I can argue, her phone buzzes on the counter, and she flips it toward me. Ivy's name flashes across the screen, along with approximately seventeen heart emojis.

Lila grins. "Speak of the glamorous devil." She taps Accept. "Morning, superstar. You're on speaker with the emotionally constipated one."

Ivy's voice floods the shop like sunshine and chaos. "Hi, my favorite book witch! Why are you emotionally constipated? Did Crew finally remember how to use his words?"

"Goodbye," I say, reaching for the phone. Lila dances away like a mischievous toddler.

Ivy gasps theatrically. "Wait—he *was there last night*, wasn't he? Lila said she saw him leaving the lighthouse."

"I'm surrounded by spies," I mutter. Sometimes I have to remind myself that even though Ivy and Crew were a PR relationship a few years ago, she's happily married to Crew's brother.

Lila smirks. "Small towns are basically social media with better pie."

Ivy hums. "So... did he apologize?"

"Yes," I say carefully. "He apologized."

"And?"

"And *nothing*, Ivy. We talked. Like adults."

The silence lasts for approximately two seconds before they both burst into laughter.

"You two talking like adults is about as believable as me retiring to a farm," Ivy says. "You're both one shared glance away from spontaneous combustion."

"Not helping," I mutter.

Lila sips her coffee, her tone suddenly softer. "Bailey, he looks at you like he's been starving."

My chest tightens. "He looked at me like that in high school, too. Right before he didn't defend me and went on to laugh at me with his friends."

Lila winces. "People change."

"Sometimes they don't," I say, quieter this time.

Ivy's voice gentles through the speaker. "You know, Crew's not the same guy who laughed with the team. He's the guy who left fame to come home and rebuild something broken. Sounds like a man who's learning."

I pick at the edge of a muffin wrapper. "Maybe. Or maybe he just got good at pretending."

Lila leans across the counter, eyes sharp and kind. "Or maybe you're scared because the only thing more terrifying than him breaking your heart again is him *not* doing it this time."

I hate that she's right. I hate even more that she knows it.

Ivy claps once. "Okay! That's enough emotional honesty for one morning. Bailey, go sell some books. Lila, go kiss your billionaire husband. I'm hanging up before I start writing a song about it."

The call ends, and the shop goes quiet again.

"Traitors," I mutter, but my chest feels a little lighter anyway as Lila scurries out the same way she came.

I busy myself restocking a few shelves, humming under my breath, pretending everything's fine. That's when I hear the rumble of a truck outside.

Of course.

Crew Wright has the worst timing and the best jawline.

He steps through the door like the storm he is—dark jeans, worn boots, Henley sleeves rolled to the elbows. The sunlight hits his hair just right, because apparently God likes to torture me.

He's carrying a box of new releases. "Delivery guy left these by the fence," he says, voice low and smooth.

"Thank you, though I'm pretty sure you shouldn't be lifting that," I say, keeping my tone polite. Professional. Not murderous.

He sets the box down, his hand brushing mine for half a second—just long enough to short-circuit my entire nervous system.

"Your shoulder?" I ask, desperate for neutral ground.

"Better." He nods. "Still a little tight."

"You're supposed to rest."

"You're not supposed to lift boxes alone."

"I manage fine."

"I noticed." His eyes flick down to my hands before returning to my face.

The air between us shifts.

We're standing too close, the kind of close that remembers things bodies shouldn't. The books around us might as well be cheering for all the noise my pulse is making.

I reach for the box, and he reaches for the same corner. Our fingers brush. Electricity.

We freeze.

He doesn't move his hand. "Bailey."

I swallow hard. "Yeah?"

"This counts as breaking at least one rule."

"Which one?"

He smiles. "The one where I don't think about kissing you when you look at me like that."

I blink up at him, every muscle in my body vibrating. "Crew..."

He steps back first. Always the gentleman. Always the one who leaves me breathless and unfinished. "You have a smudge on your cheek," he says quietly.

"I—what?"

He reaches out, thumb brushing the spot, skin against skin, a flash of warmth that shouldn't feel like a promise.

"There," he murmurs. "Got it."

He leaves before I can say a word, the door closing behind him with a soft jingle that sounds like trouble.

I lean against the counter, heart pounding, face flushed. "Idiot," I whisper—to him, to me, to the universe.

Outside, the lighthouse shadow cuts across the ground like a line I already know I'll cross.

The door shuts, and the quiet that follows feels personal. The kind of quiet that remembers.

I stand there too long, pulse still thrumming where his thumb brushed my cheek. The smell of cedar and sea air lingers, like he left part of himself behind on purpose. My brain, the traitor, replays the moment on repeat: his eyes locking on mine, the heat there, the restraint. That deliberate *not yet*.

I press a hand to my chest. "Nope," I say out loud to the empty shop. "Absolutely not. We are not doing this again."

The books, naturally, disagree.

Even the display table looks smug—stacked high with slow-burn romances and second-chance tropes. There's one on top titled *When He Came Back*. Of course there is.

I grab it, flip it upside down, and mutter, "You hush."

It's ridiculous, this whole thing. I'm not fifteen. I have responsibilities, deadlines, invoices, and an aging lighthouse with a leaky roof. I don't have time for Crew Wright and his stupid kind eyes and his big, apologetic hands.

But as the hours crawl by, I can't shake it—the way his voice dropped when he said my name. The careful way he stepped back, like he knew exactly how close *too close* really was.

By late afternoon, the sun paints long gold streaks across the counter. The bell above the door rings occasionally— locals stopping in for used paperbacks and tourists snapping photos of the spiral staircase—but it all feels like static. Every time the door opens, I half expect him to walk back through it.

He doesn't.

By the time I close up, the shop smells like candle wax

and sea salt, and my head is a mess of thoughts I can't catalog. I sweep the floor twice because sweeping is easier than feeling. When that doesn't help, I do what I always do when my heart won't quiet down—I pull a book off the shelf and start reading.

It's one of the ones I inherited from my grandfather's attic. The spine is cracked, and the margins are full of notes in his sharp handwriting. He said books teach you what people can't say out loud.

Tonight, the words don't comfort me. They feel like accusations.

I set it aside, pour the last of the tea from this morning, and step outside. The wind carries the scent of the bay, sharp and briny. The light above the tower sweeps out over the water, steady as a heartbeat. I lean on the railing, mug warm between my hands, and try to breathe around the knot in my chest.

I should feel proud. The shop's doing better than ever. The roof's getting repaired next week. I've built something solid out of the wreckage of what used to be heartbreak.

But all I can think about is how solid doesn't feel the same as alive.

I used to tell myself that what happened with Crew was ancient history. A bad high school chapter I'd long since closed. But then he came back, looking like temptation and redemption in one very inconvenient package, and suddenly, the past doesn't feel that far away.

And the worst part? I don't even hate him for it anymore.

I tip my head back, look up at the stars peeking through the cloud cover, and whisper to no one, "You're going to ruin me again, aren't you?"

The wind doesn't answer, but the lighthouse hums softly—a low, steady sound like the sea remembering something it promised to forget.

I take a long sip of tea, the cinnamon faint now but still there, haunting the edges of every thought.

Later, upstairs, the house creaks the way old houses do. I try to distract myself with busywork: folding laundry, organizing receipts, alphabetizing romance novels by author. But my brain won't stop wandering back to the way his hand felt against my skin.

It wasn't even a kiss. It was nothing. A touch. A second. A heartbeat.

And somehow it's everything.

I sink onto the couch, wrap myself in the blanket, and stare at the window. From here, I can just barely see the glow of Otter Creek Farm across the bay. One warm light still burns in the distance.

It feels like he's looking back.

"Don't do this," I whisper. "You know better."

But my heart doesn't care about rules. It's already moving—stupid and soft and hopeful—toward the one man who's both my biggest mistake and my favorite memory.

I close my eyes, let the sound of the waves pull me under, and pretend I don't want what I want.

But I do. God help me, I do.

. . .

Saturday mornings in Coral Bell Cove smell like peaches and audacity. The farmers' market unspools along the marina in tidy rows—pop-up tents like little circus hats, strings of pennants doing their best against the wind, and everyone pretending they didn't read the town thread speculating about *the quarterback and me* over breakfast.

I tell myself I'm here for apples and honey. I tell myself I'm not scanning the crowd for six foot two in a navy Henley that did dangerous things to my judgment last night. I tell myself a lot of lies before 9 a.m.

Lila appears at my elbow with a smirk. "Hydration, sarcasm, and the knowledge that Holt is selling T-shirts that say LIGHTHOUSE LOVE with your face on them." She hands me an iced coffee like a peace offering.

I choke. "Tell me you're kidding."

She points. Holt waves from three stalls down, wearing his own merch. It's...a caricature. My hair looks like a shampoo ad, and Crew's jawline could cut rope. Daisy is in his space, swatting him with a tea towel. "He printed six," Lila says. "We'll burn them at noon."

"Make it eleven."

We weave through the booths. Everybody has opinions. The high school principal pretends not to stare and then asks if the library can host an author talk "with...ambience." Two teenagers in Wright jerseys take a selfie and whisper, "Do you think they've kissed?" One of them sees me looking and mouths, "Sorry," with the terrified sincerity of a child who's seen a ghost.

I laugh because the alternative is moving to a cave.

We stop at Sawyer's produce stand. He tips his cap. "Book witch. Heard you're keeping dangerous company."

"I keep *excellent* company," I say. "Gala apples, please."

He bags the apples like he's defusing a bomb. "Remember, the town can smell a story from three coves away."

"I hate you all."

"You don't," he says easily, passing me the bag. "You love us so big it makes you mean."

Lila plunks peaches into her basket. "Speaking of mean love, my brother is—oh." She breaks off, smile tilting. "Never mind. He's already here."

I don't turn. Don't need to. My skin tells me before my eyes do—the little electricity that wakes up under my ribs. I face the basil instead, because I am strong and mature and definitely not rattled by a man who can make a crowd vanish just by looking at me.

"Morning, Bailey," Crew says, voice warm enough to melt butter but somehow not my spine. I turn, and there he is: jeans, T-shirt, a baseball cap shading eyes that still find mine without asking permission. He's holding a paper bag and a bundle of sunflowers.

"Morning," I say, proud that my voice doesn't crack. "Running errands for your mother?"

"Two kinds," he says. "The ones she asked for and the ones she'll pretend she didn't." He holds out a small jar. "For your tea. Local honey. For medicinal purposes."

"Bribery," I say, taking it anyway. Our fingers brush. One second. Maybe less. My stupid heart files it under Evidence.

Sawyer, traitor to all privacy, clears his throat like a gong.

"Quarterback, you gonna help me load up the empty crates or are you just here to buy flowers and make my customers swoon?"

Crew sets his bag down and reaches for the crate. His shirt pulls just enough to be rude. Daisy, who sidles up beside me quietly, makes the face of a woman who still enjoys the art of flirtation. "Unhelpful," I hiss.

"What?" she says.

"Haul that to the truck." Sawyer nods at Crew. "And try not to flex about it."

"I'm not flexing," Crew says, flexing.

I should leave, but of course I don't. We migrate down the row together like the tide decided we were a matched set. Holt intercepts us and attempts to put a LIGHT-HOUSE LOVE shirt over my head. I duck. Crew takes it across the chest like a bodyguard and glares until Holt backs away, muttering, "Art isn't appreciated in my lifetime."

Daisy pops up between us, flour on her cheek, a tray I missed earlier balanced like a miracle. "Taste test," she declares. "New maple bars. Bailey first."

I bite, and my eyes roll back in my head. "I hate you."

"You love me," she says, then turns to Crew with a brand-new tone that makes me narrow my eyes. "And you—how's the shoulder? Do I need to fight Marcus for you?"

"I'm fine," he says, and Daisy flicks the edge of his cap.

"Men are never fine," she says. "Okay, children. Be adorable on your own time. Some of us have capitalism to perform."

She vanishes into the crowd, leaving the two of us with one maple bar and too much air. I break it in half and hand him the bigger piece. He looks at it, then at me. "Rule two says I should ask, but...can I lick the sugar off your lip?"

Heat detonates low in my stomach. He's teasing. He has to be. My mouth betrays me and curves. "Absolutely not."

"Worth a try," he says, his grin quick and private, and takes a bite like he didn't just weaponize food.

We're three steps from freedom when a local news camera materializes. The reporter—bangs, blazer, relentless—plants herself in our path. "Bailey! Crew! Quick question for the Harvest Minute—how does it feel to be Coral Bell Cove's favorite love story?"

I choke, swallowing air. Crew's jaw ticks. He schools it into a smile before I can say *run*.

I beat him to the mic. "Feels like a town with great pie and poor boundaries," I say, nice as a church lady holding a knife behind her back.

The reporter blinks. Crew bites back a laugh. "We're just here for fruit," he says. "And honey."

"And basil," I add, because why not. "And discretion."

The camera guy bites his lip like he wants to clap. The reporter pivots to a safer target (Mrs. Winthrop, who is *always* a quote machine), and we slip away toward the end of the pier where the wind is louder than people.

We stop by the railing. The sun glints off the bay in hard, pretty shards. For a second, the noise falls off the edge of the world.

"Thank you," I say.

"For what?"

"For not...selling us. For not feeding the rumor mill." I twist the honey jar in my hands. "It's not that I'm ashamed. I just—"

"Want what's yours to be yours," he finishes. "Me, too."

We stand in that soft agreement, the closest thing to quiet we've had all day. A gull screams profanity in the middle distance. A kid drops a strawberry and wails like it betrayed him personally. The market roars back to life. I look at Crew's hand on the rail—big, scarred, careful—and realize I'm the one who breaks our no-touch détente first.

"Crew," I say, voice steady. "Can I—"

He looks at me like he heard the rulebook rustle. "Where?"

I slide my fingers over his wrist—light, brief—and feel the jump of his pulse under my fingertips like a secret. "Here," I say, barely above a whisper. Two seconds, the way I allowed him last night. I let go before I change my mind. "Thank you. For the honey."

His eyes go softer than I'm ready for. "Anytime," he says, and it lands like a promise he didn't mean to make out loud.

We head back into the chaos because real life always wins. Ivy texts a photo of our joined shadows with the caption: *Tell me you're not in love without telling me you're not in love.* I text back a single pumpkin emoji because I refuse to be bullied by pop royalty before lunch.

By the time I lug my bags up the lighthouse steps, the day has worn me down to the necessary parts. I unload fruit, rinse basil, and set the honey by the kettle like a dare.

The shop bell rings twice with late stragglers. I recommend a thriller to a man who wants to be scared and a historical to a woman who wants to be seen. I hold a baby for a minute while a mom digs for her wallet and try not to cry when the baby sighs like the ocean.

When the door finally clicks shut, and the sign flips to CLOSED, the quiet comes back—the good kind this time. I take the honey down from the shelf, unscrew the lid, and let the scent float up—warm, floral, stubborn. I dip a fingertip and taste it, sweet and golden, and think about a boy who didn't defend me and the man who is learning how.

I make tea and take my mug to the porch. The light sweeps the water. Somewhere across the bay, in a farmhouse I know too well, another light turns on. I don't need to see him to know he's there. I feel it—the same way you know when a storm has chosen a direction, the same way you know a book is going to end happily, even when it's still making you work for it.

"Okay," I say to the horizon, to the rules, to myself. "Okay."

I don't text him.

I don't need to.

Tomorrow is soon enough, and for the first time in a long time, *soon* feels like something I can live with.

Chapter Eight

CREW

There's a headline in the *Coral Bell Gazette* that reads:

Lighthouse Love Story: Quarterback and Book Witch Brew Up Buzz

I wish I were kidding.

The photo underneath is of me handing Bailey a jar of honey at the farmers' market. The camera caught her mid-laugh, my head tilted toward her like I'm about to confess a state secret. Which, honestly, isn't far off.

I set the paper down on the kitchen table like it might explode.

"Good picture," Mom says, appearing out of nowhere with her mug of chamomile tea.

"Good morning, invasion of privacy."

She smiles. "You're welcome. I only bought six copies."

"Why?"

"For my scrapbook," she says, completely serious. "And your sister's kids. And possibly the church bulletin."

"Jesus Christ."

"Language," she chides, sipping her tea. "You look happy, Crew. Don't ruin it with sarcasm."

"I'm not happy," I lie.

She raises one eyebrow, that maternal *don't waste my time* look that's scarier than any linebacker. "Mmm. So the smiling, glowing, talking-in-complete-sentences thing is just a phase?"

"I'm going to town," I mutter, grabbing my cap.

"Tell Bailey I said hi!" she calls as I escape out the door.

The day stretches out slow and golden, the kind of early autumn day that looks like a movie.

The horses are restless, the air sharp and sweet with hay dust. I work until sweat darkens my shirt, until the ache in my shoulder feels like something earned.

Still, I can't stop thinking about her. The way she looked at me yesterday—half exasperation, half challenge, all heart. The way she touched my wrist at the pier. Two seconds, soft and sure, like she was returning the exact weight I'd given her the night before.

I've been touched by hundreds of hands—fans, teammates, trainers—but hers is the only one that ever felt like home.

Sawyer pulls up in his truck mid-afternoon, dust pluming behind him. He hops out with two crates of feed and a grin that means trouble.

"You're famous, and not for football this time," he says.

"Die."

He laughs, tossing me a bottle of water. "Seriously, man. My niece texted me the article. Said, and I quote, *Crew Wright is in his lover-boy era, and I'm here for it.*"

"I hate everything about that sentence."

"She's twelve," he says. "She knows things."

I flip him off.

He laughs harder. "So, the bookstore girl, huh? The one who wrote you that note in high school?"

"You know about the note?"

"Crew, everyone knows about the note. Half the town cried when they found out you kept it."

"That was supposed to be private."

"This is Coral Bell Cove," he says. "Privacy is a myth, like cold sweet tea or functional family boundaries."

I groan, rubbing the back of my neck. "I'm just...trying to be careful."

"Careful," he repeats. "That what we're calling falling in love now?"

"I'm not—"

He holds up a hand. "Don't say it unless you mean it. But maybe stop pretending it's not happening. We all see it. I mean, you could have stayed in Nashville for rehab, my man. Why else would you have chosen to rehab at home?"

I look away, out toward the pecan trees. The light filters through the branches, dappling gold over the pasture. "Yeah," I say quietly.

By sunset, I'm standing at the lighthouse again.

I tell myself it's because I forgot my thermos from the other night, which is true. Mostly.

Bailey's outside on the steps, barefoot, hair down, wearing an oversized sweater that looks like something you could live in. She's holding a mug, watching the horizon turn pink and copper. The sight punches a hole clean through my chest.

She looks over when I step up the path. "You're stalking me," she says.

"You make it sound weird."

"It *is* weird."

"I forgot my thermos."

"You mean this?" She holds it up with a smirk.

"That's evidence."

"Of what?"

"That you're a thief."

She laughs, low and warm, and I swear the sound changes the air.

I sit on the step beside her, leaving a respectful six inches of space. It feels like both too much and not nearly enough.

She glances sideways. "You know, if you keep showing up here, people are going to think you like me."

"I do like you."

Her mug pauses halfway to her mouth. "You're supposed to deny it."

"I'm bad at lying," I say. "Ask anyone."

Her lips twitch. "You're infuriating."

"You've mentioned."

We sit there, side by side, watching the tide roll in. The waves lap against the rocks, steady and patient. It smells like salt and cinnamon again, or maybe that's just my memory playing tricks.

After a while, she says, "You didn't have to come."

"I wanted to."

"That's not the same thing."

"I know," I say softly. "But it's honest."

She's quiet for a long moment. "You scare me, Crew."

I nod. "You scare me, too."

Her laugh is a breath. "At least we're consistent."

The wind picks up, tangling her hair. Without thinking, I reach out and tuck a strand behind her ear. My fingers graze her skin, light as a whisper.

She stills.

"Crew," she says, voice barely audible.

"Yeah?"

"Don't."

I drop my hand. "Okay."

But she doesn't move away. She just looks at me—eyes wide, pulse flickering at her throat—and every bit of her body language says *don't stop, but don't rush either.*

Her voice wavers. "You can't keep doing that."

"Doing what?"

"Making it impossible to breathe."

I swallow, throat tight. "Guess we're both out of practice."

She huffs out a laugh, shaky and soft. "You're impossible."

"You love impossible."

"I used to," she whispers. "I don't know if I can again."

"Then don't yet," I say. "Just...sit here with me. That's enough."

Her eyes meet mine. For a heartbeat—one single, suspended second—it feels like gravity tilts. Her hand brushes mine on the step, fingers grazing, hesitating.

Neither of us pulls away.

The contact is light. Barely there. But it's everything.

When she finally stands, she looks dazed. "You should go before the town writes another article."

"Let 'em," I say quietly. "They'll never get the good parts right anyway."

She shakes her head, but she's smiling as she goes inside.

I stay on the steps a while longer, staring out at the water, every nerve in my body humming with her.

When the light sweeps over the bay, I look up and whisper, "I'm trying, B. I really am."

THE FOLLOWING MORNING, THE FARM SMELLS LIKE coffee and the kind of trouble that comes dressed as peace.

I wake early, mostly because I didn't sleep. Every time I closed my eyes, I saw her face — the way her breath hitched when my fingers brushed her hair and the war playing out in her eyes.

When I finally gave up and came downstairs, Mom was already in the kitchen, flour dusting her hands like snow.

"Morning, handsome," she says, without looking up. "Someone dropped off books for me."

My brain short-circuits. "Books?"

"From Bailey," she says casually, shaping biscuit dough. "Said she thought I'd like the new collection for the community library drive. Sweet girl. Smart."

"She's—yeah. She is."

Mom glances at me. "You gonna stand there grinning, or are you gonna grab the butter?"

I move on autopilot, reaching for the butter dish while trying not to picture Bailey standing in this kitchen, sunlight on her hair, her laughter echoing off the walls.

Mom hums. "She didn't stay long. But she looked happy."

"Happy's good," I say, too quickly.

"Mm-hmm," she says, and I know that tone—the one that means she's storing information for later use. I escape outside before she can weaponize it.

The morning's sharp, the air smelling like dew and pecans and hay. Horses flick their tails lazily, and the world feels too still for the noise in my chest.

I'm elbow-deep in feed when I hear footsteps behind me.

"Morning, Wright."

I freeze. Then turn.

Bailey stands there, holding a paper bag and wearing that same oversized sweater, jeans cuffed at the ankles, hair tucked behind her ears. She looks like autumn showed up just to compete.

"Didn't know we offered delivery," I say, trying for easy.

"Your mom forgot her receipt," she says, holding it up. "And she bribed me with biscuits."

"Classic."

"She said to tell you to stop sulking and come eat."

"I'm not sulking."

She smirks. "You're literally hiding in a barn."

"Working, because it's the best kind of therapy," I correct. "It's different."

"Sure it is."

She sets the paper bag on a hay bale and glances around. "This place is beautiful. Always has been."

"Yeah," I say, watching her instead of the view. "It is."

She catches me looking, blushes, then crouches to pet the barn cat weaving around her ankles. "Hey there, handsome," she says softly.

The cat purrs, traitorous bastard.

"You're clearly his type," I say.

"He's clearly everyone's," she counters. "You could learn from him."

I laugh. "I'm not licking anyone to say hello."

"Your loss," she says, straight-faced. It hits me right in the ribs—that mix of humor and heat she wields without trying.

We end up walking toward the house together, and it feels domestic in a way I didn't realize I missed. So much better than her running in the opposite direction whenever she saw my face. The smell of biscuits pulls us into the kitchen, where Mom and Hadley are in the middle of some covert operation involving jam jars and chaos.

Mom beams when she sees Bailey. "Oh good! I was just telling Hadley that I need your advice about shelving the new donations."

Hadley looks up, grinning. "And I was telling her that what she *really* needs is more gossip."

"Please, don't," I mutter.

Hadley ignores me. "So, Bailey. Any exciting lighthouse news? New lights? New visitors? Possibly new *romantic developments?*"

Bailey blushes, pretending to examine the biscuit tray. "Just repairs. And tea."

"Tea," Hadley says, nodding sagely. "Right. Nothing says innocent like cinnamon tea at midnight."

Mom laughs so hard she has to put down the jam knife. "Hadley, you're awful."

"I'm efficient," she says, pouring herself more coffee.

Bailey looks at me, eyes sparkling with amusement and embarrassment all at once. "Your family's relentless."

"They're good at it," I admit. "It's a full-contact sport."

She smirks. "You should warn your opponents."

"I'm better on defense."

Her gaze flicks to my shoulder. "Still holding up?"

"Getting stronger."

"That's good," she says softly, and for a second, the whole room disappears—it's just her and me and the weight of what almost happened last night.

Mom clears her throat loudly. "Crew, the porch rail's

loose. Maybe Bailey could help you fix it while I finish these jars.”

“Subtle,” I mumble, knowing she could ask my brother, Rowan, who pretty much runs the farm with my dad now.

Bailey grins. “Sure, Mrs. Wright. I’m handy.”

Outside, the morning has softened into something golden. The porch smells like sawdust and sugar, sunlight slanting through the pecan trees. I hand her a screwdriver, and our fingers brush—light, familiar, too much.

She kneels beside me, holding the board steady while I tighten the bolts. Every movement pulls us closer. Her shoulder grazes mine; her hair brushes against my arm.

She glances up once, smiling. “You’re distracted.”

“Occupational hazard.”

“Being around me?”

“Trying not to kiss you.”

She freezes, then whispers, “Crew.”

“Yeah?”

“Rule two,” she says softly, but she doesn’t move away.

I lean in just enough that she can feel my breath when I speak. “Ask, right?”

Her throat works as she nods. “Ask.”

“Can I?”

Her eyes meet mine, dark and searching. “Not yet,” she says, voice trembling.

I nod, step back, and swallow the ache in my chest.

She smiles faintly, like she’s grateful and wrecked at once. “Good answer.”

We finish the porch in silence, but it’s not uncomfortable. It's charged and alive—the kind of quiet that hums with the promise of something that hasn't happened yet but will.

When she leaves, she touches my arm as she passes—a small, deliberate thing that undoes every ounce of composure I have left.

I watch her walk down the drive, her sweater catching the wind, her hair gleaming in the sunlight.

Mom leans out the kitchen window, waving like she's in a parade. "Nice work, honey!"

I look up. "We fixed your rail."

"I meant with Bailey," she says, smiling. "Pace yourselves."

I groan and drop my head back, but I can't stop the grin.

That night, when the farm has gone quiet and the air smells like woodsmoke and distant salt, I sit on the porch with a beer and stare out toward the lighthouse.

The light sweeps across the bay, steady and sure, just like her.

I whisper into the dark, "Not yet," and for the first time, waiting doesn't feel like punishment.

It feels like hope.

Chapter Nine

BAILEY

f joy had a sound, it would be Coral Bell Cove at festival season. They find a reason to put one on almost every weekend in the fall.

Children laughing. Music drifting. The low hum of gossip dressed as small talk.

It's the kind of noise that vibrates right through your bones—and the kind of day that feels like it could save you or ruin you, depending on which way the wind blows.

This morning, the wind's on my side. Probably.

I have three folding tables, two boxes of donated paperbacks, and zero patience for the ninth argument about whether the pumpkin tower should have a theme. (Mrs. Winthrop insists it needs an "emotional arc.")

The whole town's out. Booths line the marina. The Wright family's pie stand smells like heaven. Cider simmers somewhere, and Daisy's bakery has already sold out twice.

And then there's me—librarian, book witch, accidental lightning rod of small-town scandal.

I'm halfway through labeling the donation jars when Lila shows up with that look—the one that says she's about to be unhelpfully supportive.

"You're glowing," she announces.

"I'm sweating."

"You're glowing *and* sweating," she says. "Multitasking queen."

"I hate you."

"You love me."

"I tolerate you."

She laughs, but there's affection in it. "You've been smiling more."

"That's because I've been threatening fewer people."

"Sure," she says. "And not because someone has been walking you home every night like a romance montage?"

I open my mouth to deny it, but she's already sashaying away, calling over her shoulder, "You're welcome for the setup!"

Setup?

Before I can demand clarification, I hear a voice that turns my stomach to static.

"Morning, Book Witch."

I turn.

Crew Wright stands there, wearing a gray Henley that should be illegal, a backward cap, and a grin that could start wars. He's carrying lumber on one shoulder, helping Sawyer set up the stage for the evening concert.

The sight of him hits me like gravity. Every inch of him is solid, familiar, and infuriatingly attractive.

"You're early," I say.

"Mom said there'd be cinnamon rolls."

"She lied."

"Then I'm leaving."

I roll my eyes, but I'm smiling before I can stop it. "You're insufferable."

"You say that like it's a bad thing."

"It *is* a bad thing."

"Nah," he says, flashing that grin again. "You like it."

"Prove it."

His smile turns dangerous. "Challenge accepted."

By midmorning, the festival's in full swing. I've sold out of bookmarks, misplaced three rolls of tape, and been asked by two separate people whether Crew and I are "official."

We're not.

We're not *anything*.

Try telling that to the *Coral Bell Gazette*.

They've got a photographer roaming the square like a bloodhound. The poor guy's been chased off twice by Daisy and once by Ivy, who told him that "consent is sexy, Greg."

Ivy Quinn has adjusted to small-town life disturbingly well.

Speaking of which, she appears beside my booth in dark jeans and a loose white sweater that probably costs more than my car. She smells like vanilla and fame.

"You look gorgeous," she says.

"You look like a magazine cover."

She beams. "Rowan says I'm blending in."

"In what—Paris?"

"Be nice," she says, mock pouting. "Anyway, I came to warn you."

"About?"

"Crew."

My stomach tightens. "What about him?"

She lowers her sunglasses dramatically. "He's in a mood."

"What kind of mood?"

"The kind where he's smiling too much. He only smiles like that when he's trying to hide something."

I fold my arms. "And you're telling me because?"

"Because I like you," she says. "And because Lila says you're pretending not to be in love with him, which is adorable but tragic."

"I'm fine," I say.

"Sure," she says. "And I didn't write a breakup album about my mother."

"Valid."

She grins. "Anyway, if you two kiss tonight, I called it first."

Before I can respond, she's gone—all sunshine and chaos, leaving me standing there wondering how one person can be both a friend and a human pop-up ad for emotional vulnerability.

Afternoon drifts by in a haze of caramel, conversation, and exhaustion.

Crew shows up again with Sawyer and Rowan, both

sweaty and smug from building something tall and danger-ous-looking near the bandstand.

"Need help here?" he asks.

"I'm good."

He ignores that and crouches beside me, picking up a box of books.

I glare. "You can't help everything."

He smirks. "You're welcome to test that theory."

"Crew."

He glances up. "Yeah?"

"Don't."

He tilts his head. "Don't what?"

"Don't look at me like that."

"Like what?"

"Like I'm something you want."

He breathes, slow, careful. "That's because you are."

My chest tightens. "You shouldn't say things like that."

"Then stop looking at me like you want me to."

My jaw drops. "You're impossible."

"Consistent," he corrects.

"Annoying."

"Honest."

We stare at each other, and the air thickens until someone yells, "Pumpkin emergency!" and he laughs, standing.

"Saved by the gourd," he says, walking off, leaving me melted and muttering curses under my breath.

By sunset, the marina glows under a canopy of string

lights. Music spills from the stage, a blend of fiddles and heartache. The smell of cider drifts through the crowd, mingling with laughter and the occasional shriek of a child who lost their balloon.

I'm handing out raffle tickets when I feel him before I see him.

That pull, that awareness, is magnetic, like my body recognizes him before my brain can issue a warning.

"Dance with me." He appears beside me.

"I don't dance."

"You said that last time."

"I meant it."

He smiles. "And I meant it when I said I do."

The band strikes up a slow song, and before I can find an excuse, his hand finds mine. The contact steals my breath. His thumb slides over my knuckles, gentle but firm.

"Crew," I whisper.

"Bailey."

"This is a bad idea."

"Probably."

He pulls me close, and the rest of the world blurs.

His hand settles on my waist, warm through the fabric of my dress. My other hand lands on his chest—solid, steady, familiar. We move slowly, our steps matching like muscle memory.

He smells like cedar and wood smoke. My heart beats too loud.

"Still think it's a bad idea?" he murmurs.

"Yes."

"Liar."

I huff a laugh, but it dies when he leans in—so close that I can feel his breath against my temple.

"I've been trying not to want this," he whispers. "It's not working."

My throat tightens. "Then stop trying."

He pulls back just enough to look at me, eyes dark and searching. "You sure?"

"No," I admit. "But I want to be."

Something flickers in his gaze—hope, fear, hunger.

And then, because fate loves irony, Holt yells from somewhere behind us, "Yo, Crew! The cider tent's flooding again!"

Crew groans, forehead pressing lightly to mine as if he can will the interruption away. "I swear this town has bad timing."

"Maybe it's saving us," I whisper.

He smiles, small and bittersweet. "From what?"

"From doing something we can't take back."

He steps back, reluctant, like every inch costs him something. "Too late for that," he murmurs, before walking toward the chaos.

I stand there, heart racing, every nerve in my body alive with the weight of everything unsaid.

Later, when the festival winds down and the lanterns flicker low, I find him again. He's alone, sitting on the steps of the gazebo, elbows on his knees, head tipped back like he's listening to ghosts.

I hesitate, then sit beside him.

"You okay?"

He smiles without looking at me. "Define 'okay'."

"Tired. Emotional. Still mildly sticky from cider."

"Then yeah," he says softly. "I'm okay."

We sit in silence, the kind that doesn't need fixing. The bay reflects the string lights like a second sky.

After a while, he says, "You make it easy to forget how hard things used to be."

I glance at him. "That's because I'm amazing."

He laughs, low and rough, and it does something to me I can't name. "That you are."

He turns then, really looks at me, and my breath catches. His gaze drops to my mouth, then back to my eyes. "Bailey."

"Yeah?"

He leans in, slow and sure—like he's giving me time to stop him. I don't.

Our noses brush. His breath hits mine. The world narrows to that single moment suspended in time—almost, but not yet.

Then a burst of fireworks lights the sky, bright and loud, and he pulls back, laughing softly.

"Even the universe has terrible timing," he says.

"Or perfect," I whisper, heart aching.

He looks at me for a long second, like he wants to argue, then shakes his head, smiling. His oversized hand, perfect for his job, runs along my neck and collarbone as if he's measuring my pulse. "Good night, Bailey."

"Good night, Crew."

He leaves before I can say what I really mean.

That maybe I'm tired of waiting. That I'm already his.

That *not yet* is one heartbeat away from *finally*.

Chapter Ten

CREW

Sunlight slants across the kitchen table, catching the crumbs of yesterday's biscuits and the headline of the *Gazette*: **HARVEST FESTIVAL SUCCESS: WRIGHT BROTHERS SAVE THE DAY, BOOK WITCH STEALS HEARTS.**

Subtle.

Real subtle.

Mom hums at the stove, spatula in hand, like she isn't the unofficial PR director for Coral Bell Cove gossip. Hadley's sitting at the counter, legs crossed, sipping coffee with the kind of smug smile only siblings are genetically programmed to perfect.

"Sleep well?" she asks, knowing full damn well I didn't.

"Define 'well'."

"Define 'sleep'," she fires back. "Because I heard you pacing the porch like a ghost all night."

Mom hides a laugh behind her mug. "He's been restless since the dance."

I glare at both of them. "Do you people meet at dawn to coordinate attacks?"

Lila shrugs. "Only on Sundays."

"Good," I say. "It's Saturday."

She grins. "I'm proactive."

I try ignoring them, focusing on the paper instead, but the headline's too much. Bailey's picture—smiling mid-laugh, eyes crinkled, hair shining under lantern light—sits beside mine. The camera caught something raw, something that looks a hell of a lot like what we've both been denying.

And it does something to me I don't have words for.

"You could just go talk to her," Mom says, not even pretending she isn't listening in.

"I have talked to her."

"Without your usual sarcasm?"

I grunt.

"She's helping with cleanup," Hadley offers way too innocently. "At the lighthouse. Something about repairing the donation booth and drying out books that got caught in the cider-flood incident."

I narrow my eyes. "You're meddling."

"Call it divine intervention," she says, hopping off the stool. "Dean and Lila are coming over tonight for dinner. Bring her, or I'll invite her myself."

I hate how easily they see through me.

I hate it more that they're right.

By the time I reach the lighthouse, the sky's shifted

from blue to the gray that means trouble. The air feels heavy, charged—like even the weather's waiting for something to break.

Bailey's outside, kneeling beside a stack of damp boxes, hair in a messy bun, sweatshirt sleeves shoved to her elbows. She looks tired, focused, and utterly beautiful.

She doesn't hear me at first, humming softly under her breath—something old, maybe Fleetwood Mac.

"You know," I say, "that humming could summon sailors."

She jumps, dropping a stack of flyers. "Jesus, Crew. You can't just materialize like that."

"I knocked."

"You did not."

"Knocking's implied when you're this charming."

She groans. "You're impossible."

"Consistent," I say, crouching beside her. "Need help?"

She opens her mouth—probably to tell me no—but the wind cuts her off, sending a fresh spray of bay air across the dock. The edges of the boxes flap, threatening to scatter.

"Fine," she mutters. "But only because you have longer arms."

"Finally, my best feature gets recognized."

She gives me a look, somewhere between amusement and exasperation. "Pretty sure your best feature is ego."

"Close second," I say. "Right behind my self-awareness."

"Which is nonexistent."

"Exactly."

Her laugh slips out before she can stop it. That sound—

God, that sound—hits me square in the chest. I'll take it over applause, over cheers, over the roar of a stadium any day.

We haul the boxes into the shop just as the first drops of rain hit. The air smells like paper and storms, like nostalgia and maybe-love. She pushes a strand of hair from her face and looks around the room, sighing. "Half these books are soaked."

"Then we'll dry them," I say.

"You say that like it's simple."

"It is," I say, finding a towel. "Watch."

I pick up the top book and start gently patting the pages dry.

She folds her arms. "That's not how paper works."

"It's working fine."

"You're smearing the ink."

"It's abstract now."

She groans again, snatching the towel from my hand. "Give me that."

"Bossy."

"Competent," she corrects, kneeling to show me the right way—spreading the books slightly open, fanning the pages, spacing them apart. Her voice softens as she explains. "You treat it gently, or it falls apart. Paper remembers roughness."

I get the feeling she's not talking about paper anymore.

I nod slowly. "Yeah. I get that."

Her eyes flick to mine, then away, cheeks flushing. "I didn't mean—"

"I know," I say. "But you're right."

The rain gets heavier, drumming on the roof like a heartbeat gone wild. Thunder rolls low, steady. She glances toward the window. "We should close up."

"Storm won't last long."

"It's not the storm I'm worried about."

Her voice is quiet, but the meaning's loud enough to rattle the walls.

We work in silence for a while. She moves around the shop with this quiet grace, collecting candles, stacking towels, making something safe out of chaos. Watching her feels like watching someone build a home one motion at a time.

When lightning flashes, I see her flinch—not big, just a tiny tremor. I don't think she knows she does it. I move closer, not touching, just near enough that she can feel my presence.

"You okay?" I ask softly.

"I'm fine."

"Bailey."

She stops and turns toward me. Her breath catches. "Then what do you want?"

I could lie. I could joke. But the words come out raw, honest.

"You."

She blinks. "Crew…"

Lightning flickers again, the brightness slicing across her face. I see every line of her expression: defiance, desire, disbelief. Her fingers twitch at her sides like she wants to reach for me but doesn't trust herself.

And then thunder cracks, sharp and sudden, and instinct wins over caution. She stumbles a half-step forward. My hand finds her waist. Reflex. Reflex that feels like fate.

She looks up. The space between us disappears.

The kiss isn't careful.

It's every second we've spent denying this, every half smile, every almost. Her hands clutch my shirt, pulling me closer. My fingers slide into her hair, tangling in the strands, tasting the rain that's started to leak through the door. She makes a sound—quiet, broken—and I swear I'll never hear anything better.

When we finally break apart, both of us are breathing hard.

Her forehead rests against mine. "We shouldn't have done that."

"Probably not."

"Do it again."

I laugh, half disbelieving, half undone, and then her mouth is on mine again, slower this time, deeper. The world tilts. The storm howls outside, but inside is nothing but heat and heartbeats.

When she finally pulls back, she's trembling, eyes wild. "Crew..."

"Yeah?"

"This changes everything."

"Good," I whisper. "It was about damn time."

The storm rages for another hour. We stay inside, sitting close on the floor beside the counter, her head on my shoulder, my hand tracing circles on her wrist. We don't talk much. We don't need to. The silence feels like something sacred.

When the rain finally eases, she stands, smoothing her hair, trying for composure. "You should go."

"Probably," I say, but I don't move.

"Crew..."

"Yeah."

Her silence should sting, but it doesn't. Not this time. Because now her unspoken *not yet* doesn't sound like no. It sounds like a promise.

I nod. "Okay."

She smiles, small and unsteady. "Okay."

That night, back at the farm, I can still taste her.

The rain, the warmth, the way she said *do it again* like a prayer.

For the first time in a long time, the ache in my shoulder doesn't hurt.

But my heart? My heart's on fire.

Sleep doesn't come. I lie in bed staring at the ceiling fan, every slow turn syncing to the rhythm of her kiss. It's there on my tongue, in the ache of my jaw, in the pulse that won't settle. When lightning flashed behind her, she looked like the storm had chosen her as its favorite. And now my whole body hums with the memory.

Around three a.m., I give up, pull on a T-shirt, and step onto the porch. The air still smells like rain and salt and something faintly sweet—honey, maybe, or her. The fields glitter darkly.

I'm half tempted to text her, but I can already imagine her response: *go to sleep, quarterback.*

I don't know how long I stay outside on the back deck, but it's long enough to watch the sun rise over the tree line.

Inside, the kitchen's a battlefield of clinking dishes and judgment. Mom's making pancakes, Dean's at the counter eating them like he earned them, and Lila's pretending to help while mostly watching Oliver and Evelyn, Dean's niece and nephew, who he is now the guardian of, play a game of Guess Who?

Dean looks up. "You look like a man who got struck by lightning."

"Funny story," I say. "I did."

Lila freezes mid-scroll. "Oh my God. You kissed her."

I blink. "What?"

"You totally kissed her. Gah, why didn't she tell me?" Her blond hair immediately veils across her face as she types on her phone like a madwoman.

Mom raises a brow but doesn't stop flipping pancakes. "Finally," she mutters.

"Do I have no privacy?"

Dean grins. "This is Coral Bell Cove, brother. The gulls probably know."

Lila leans forward. "Was it romantic? Or, like, 'oops our faces collided in a hurricane'?"

"Can we *not*—"

"Was there tongue?"

"Lila!"

She cackles. "I'll take that as a yes."

Mom slides a plate toward me. "Eat before you pass out from embarrassment."

I drop into the chair, muttering, "Remind me to never have a personal life again."

"Too late," Dean says. "You're in a Hallmark movie now. Enjoy the montage."

By afternoon, the rain's cleared, but the clouds still hang low, soft, and heavy. I drive out to the lighthouse under the pretense of checking on the flooded books. Really, I just need to see her and make sure last night wasn't something I dreamed up between thunderclaps.

She's out front, sweeping the porch, wearing cut-off shorts and a sweatshirt that's two sizes too big. My sweatshirt. She looks up, startled, then wary. "You left this on purpose, didn't you?"

"Maybe," I say. "You wear it better."

"Don't start."

"Start what?"

"The thing," she says, gesturing vaguely. "The charming-your-way-past-boundaries thing."

"Right." I step closer, grin crooked.

She laughs despite herself, and that's all the permission I need to lean against the railing beside her. We stand there, side by side, watching gulls swoop low over the water.

After a while, she says quietly, "About last night..."

"Yeah?"

"I don't regret it." She sighs. "But I don't know what to do with it."

"Same," I admit. "Except for the part where I definitely want to do it again."

Her breath catches. "You really don't have a filter, do you?"

"Nope. Tried one once. It broke."

She laughs again, shaking her head, but there's color high on her cheeks. "You're impossible."

"You keep saying that like it's a bad thing."

She sets the broom aside, facing me fully now. The wind lifts a strand of her hair, and it brushes across her mouth. I have to fist my hands in my pockets to keep from reaching out. "You scare me," she says finally.

"I scare *you?*"

She nods. "Because you make me forget how hard I worked to be fine."

My chest tightens. "Then let me help you remember you can be *happy* instead."

She stares at me, eyes shining, and for a second, it feels like she might step closer. Instead, she whispers, "You say stuff like that, and I don't stand a chance."

"Good," I say, a half smile tugging. "Neither do I."

We end up spending the afternoon fixing a loose shutter and reorganizing books she swears are alphabetized but clearly aren't. She keeps pretending to be annoyed, and I keep pretending I believe her. The air hums between us like a held breath.

At one point, she's on a small step stool reaching for the top shelf. I move behind her—just to steady it, I tell myself—but my hands find her waist automatically. Warm. Solid. Real. She freezes, glances down over her shoulder, our faces only inches apart.

"Careful," I murmur. "Wouldn't want you falling."

Her voice is barely a whisper. "Too late."

It hits like a jolt, the truth in it. I could kiss her again right here, surrounded by books and dust and sunlight, but I don't. Instead, I ease back, hands sliding away slow enough to feel every heartbeat between us.

She exhales shakily, climbs down, and the look she gives me could burn through brick. "You're dangerous."

"Only if you run."

That night, after she locks up, I help her carry the last box of dry books to her car, ready to take them over to the school. The moon hangs low, swollen and yellow. She sets the box down, dusts her hands off, and turns to me.

"I'm still figuring this out. I spent so many years trying to ignore the fact that you even existed," she says.

"I'll wait," I tell her.

She studies me for a long moment, then steps close enough that her fingers graze my chest—just once, featherlight. "You're going to ruin my peace."

I grin. "You ruined mine first."

Her lips curve, soft and dangerous. "Then I guess we're even."

She walks away before I can respond, keys jingling, taillights glowing red against the dark road. I stand there until they disappear, the night wind curling around me, carrying her scent and the taste of rain.

The morning smells like warm paper and cinnamon again, like the lighthouse baked something overnight and left it on the windowsill just to mess with me. I show up early, pretending I'm there to help her set out chairs for story hour. I'm terrible at pretending. Bailey's already moving through the shop with that efficient grace, a stack of picture books balanced on one hip, hair twisted up with a pencil. The pencil is a hazard to my health. It makes me think about tugging it out and watching her hair fall.

"Left side needs three," she says, pointing with the book. "We've got five toddlers and a baby who thinks books deserve a personal attack."

"I can handle a baby," I say.

"You can't even handle me."

"Accurate," I admit, and she bites her lip like she wasn't planning to smile, and her mouth betrayed her.

Parents drift in with little kids who look sticky and hopeful, the way small humans do when there's a promise of crayons and sugar. I end up on the rug with a foam otter puppet someone thrust into my hands, the otter making eye contact with Bailey across the semicircle like he knows secrets. The cat decides I'm furniture and sits on my thigh, tail flicking, smug as a senator.

Bailey opens the first book, a lighthouse story naturally. Her voice changes when she reads—slower, warmer, like each sentence is a small boat she's easing across the bay. Kids lean forward. One leans into me. The puppet leans back into him. I do the otter's voice, and it's ridiculous, and the room laughs. Bailey shoots me a look that says *you're a menace* and *don't stop*. The pencil in her hair is going to be the end of me.

Halfway through, a little girl crawls into Bailey's lap and announces, "You're pretty like my mom when she's not mad," then sticks a sticker to Bailey's cheek. The entire row of adults tries not to cry, including myself. Bailey catches me swiping at my eye like a coward and tilts her head, a soft little question in the corner of her mouth. I shrug. The puppet nods solemnly on my knee, as if offering commentary.

When I read the second book—because someone asked and because I'd do anything if a small army of toddlers asked politely—my shoulder complains at the reach. Bailey notices. She drifts closer under the pretense of turning a page. Her hand lands lightly on my upper back, warm through cotton, just enough pressure to make the joint settle. It's a tiny correction, the kind Marcus would make. It hits like a benediction, and the shoulder behaves. The room keeps breathing, and for a brief, profound moment, I can see the whole of a different life stretch out: me on this rug once a week, her next to me, this small chorus learning what light is. It's all a new revelation I wasn't ready for.

After parents scoop up kids and scatter crumbs like confetti, Sawyer arrives with a box of supplies and an entire weather system of smug. "Delivery," he calls, stepping over a spilled cup with the grace of a man who's dodged stickier threats.

"What is it?" Bailey asks.

"Tarps, twine, a new nozzle for your outdoor spigot." He lifts the box onto the porch and winks at me.

We take the box around back to check the spigot, and I swear to God the nozzle is sentient. It waits until my hand is directly in front of it to cough a surprise jet of water straight into my face. Bailey claps a hand over her mouth, failing spectacularly to pretend she's not delighted.

"You did this," I accuse.

"I would never," she says, eyes sparkling. "Nature did this."

"Mother Nature's cruel," I say, flicking water off my chin.

Her smile turns into a dare. "Maybe she thinks you need cooling off."

"Is that so?" I say, reaching for the nozzle. It obeys me once, streams politely in an arc. Then it sputters and decides on chaos, spraying both of us. We yelp, then laugh, then it devolves within seconds, the way these things do, into a war that's mostly hands and shouting and the knowledge that if I look at her too long with water dripping from her jaw, I'll forget the rules, the town, my name. She darts left, and I catch her with one hand on the small of her back. The water hits us both in a clean sheet, like the sky joined in. Her sweatshirt darkens, clinging. Her hair slips free of the pencil. I go still.

She does too.

The hose falls, thudding onto the grass and slumping into a harmless snake. My palm stays on her back, fingertips memorizing the scallop of bone, the heat, the yes. She's looking up at me with rain-wide pupils, mouth parted, breath quick. We're alone except for Sawyer, which is a lie —town is around us, the bay, the light, the history—but for a moment, every witness goes mercifully blind.

"Crew," she says, warning and want and the last thread of a boundary.

"I know," I say, and I do. I move my hand first because restraint is something I can offer when the rest of me is a lit match.

We stand side by side under a sun that can't decide on full forgiveness. She flicks a drop from my ear with two fingers, carefully not. We call a truce without calling it. The nozzle surrenders as Sawyer fixes it, docile now that it has chaos to remember.

Inside, I hang her sweatshirt over the back of a chair while she changes upstairs. The fabric is heavy with water and hints of vanilla and something that is just her. I lay it flat, smoothing it without thinking, and have a brief, insane thought about sharing a drawer one day, about sweaters that hold the smell of two people's days.

She comes down in a dry T-shirt, damp hair tucked behind her ears, bare feet whispering over the floorboards. We fall into work again—mending a loose hinge, re-shelving drying books, bickering about alphabetization while secretly re-ordering our lives.

Afternoon drops a quiet over the cove. The shop grows that amber hush I like best, the kind that makes you lower your voice without knowing why. Bailey brews tea and pretends not to watch as I reach for the jar of honey without flinching when the shoulder pulls at the far edge of my reach. I catch her pretending and make a face. She rolls her eyes like she isn't fond enough to go soft around the edges.

"Dinner at my mom's," I say a little later, when the day has collected itself toward evening. I don't plan it. The words just...arrive. "Lila will be there. Dean. Maybe Ivy and Rowan if she's done threatening journalists. Come. Please."

Her shoulders go up, then down. Fear, then the calm right after a wave breaks, and you realize you're still here. "That's a lot of Wrights."

"It is," I agree. "We can take my truck. We can bail at any second. We can sit on the porch and make faces. It'll be —" I search for the right thing and land on honesty. "It'll be them loving whoever sits at the table and me being an idiot and you laughing."

Her mouth tugs. "And your mother trying to send me home with jam like she's recruiting me for her army."

"She is recruiting you," I say. "We're at war with anyone who alphabetizes historical romance by cover color."

She gasps in mock horror. "Someone did that?"

"Savage," I say grimly.

She thinks, the way she thinks about everything—with her whole face for a second and then with her eyes only. Then she nods. "Okay. I'll come."

"Yeah?" I try to say it like a normal person. It comes out like a sunrise.

"Yeah." Her gaze softens. "Stop smiling like that. People will think you won the lottery."

"I did," I say before I can remember to be cool.

She looks like she wants to argue with that and also like maybe she doesn't.

As promised, I help Bailey into my truck. My hand lingers a bit too long as I click her seat belt buckle, inhaling her sweet scent because I just can't get enough.

As predicted, dinner is chaos—in the precise way I promised and in a few I didn't. Mom insists Bailey sit next to her and keeps refilling her plate, as if to prove hospitality is a performance art. Lila interrogates me with eyebrows. Dean rescues me by asking Bailey about a book he pretends he finished. Ivy shows up late with cupcakes and a halo of perfume that smells like stage lights and sugar, kisses Bailey's cheek, and whispers, "Glow level: illegal." Bailey threatens to revoke her library privileges. Ivy vows to go underground with a fake mustache. Rowan follows shortly after doing a round about the farm. Everyone talks over everyone. It's a hymn I forgot I knew the words to.

Somewhere between salad and dessert, the room shifts around a smaller sound—Bailey's laughter at something my mom says about the first week she moved back after her parents decided being childless was easier. The laugh is bright enough to push back a shadow I didn't know she still kept. Mom reaches without thinking and touches the back of Bailey's hand for just a second. Bailey squeezes once, quick. It is the most intimate thing that happens all night, including the part where Ivy absolutely corners me at the sink and says, "Break her heart, and I will write a five-minute pop song with your whole legacy in the chorus." I assure her this is off the table. She narrows her glittered eyes as if to say *I know where you sleep.* I love her a little for it.

After dinner, Bailey and I drift to the porch while the house digests and the family continues to argue whether football is a metaphor or merely a convenient scheduling excuse for snacks. The night air is summer's last sigh. The pecan trees stitch dark lace against the sky. The part of the bay that touches the far end of the property shines on its own. We sit on the steps because chairs would formalize a thing that doesn't want suits. Steps let your knees knock by accident and make space for silence.

"I'm around families all the time, but I forget how loud they are," she says, not unhappy about it.

"Mine particularly," I admit.

"It feels like being inside a weather pattern," she says. "You just...lean."

"You can go whenever you need to," I offer, meaning the evening and not meaning only that. "Anywhere. Anytime. You say the word, and the truck starts. You say the word, and the lighthouse goes dark for a night. You say the word, and I shut up."

"You're doing good," she says, like I did something brave by speaking little.

We fall into one of those quiets that is all wideness and

no withdrawal. Crickets chirp like they're on salary. An owl tries a thesis from the pecans. Her bare toes land on the next step down, and I track the tiny movement like it announced a plot twist. Without thinking, I turn my palm up on the step between us. A space. A question. Not a pressure... a possibility.

She looks at it without looking at me.

It takes her a full minute. I count every second and put each one carefully on a shelf. Then she slides her fingers into mine, palm to palm, the way yeses sometimes prefer. Our hands fit as if they've been practiced. We don't look at each other. We look across the fields, at the tree line, at the night. The moment is full of the kind of heat that needs air to keep from burning wrong.

When I walk her to the truck later, my family shouts twelve things about leftovers and borrowing Tupperware. Bailey pretends not to hear, laughing into her shoulder. Lila texts a photo from the window—the two of us on the steps, hands under the rail—and adds *Ivy's album cover*. I send her a single ghost emoji, and she replies with seventeen knives and a heart.

The drive back to the lighthouse is a ribbon of dark road and low talk of tiny stories we haven't told yet, with no stakes and somehow mattering anyway. My shoulder is quiet in the way injuries get when you forget to be mad at them. I park, and I walk her up. We stop at the porch because rules and because I want the next time I cross her threshold to be a choice we make after we say the things that belong out loud. I know I need to take my time with Bailey. She's still too skittish around me despite every ounce of my body yearning for just another taste of her.

"Thank you," she says, arms crossed like she's cold, but I know it's a shield she hasn't bothered to lift all the way.

"For what?"

"For inviting me," she says. "For the porch. For the... hand." She flushes at her own vagueness and shakes her head. "You're bad for my sentences."

"I'll buy you more," I say. "Whole boxes. Fancy ones."

She huffs a laugh. The pencil is back in her hair. It's a better moon than the one over the bay. "You're not kissing me," she says, and it's not a complaint, it's an observation charged with 10,000 volts.

"I want to," I say. "Too much."

"Good," she says, so soft I almost miss it. She steps in the smallest amount closer, and that inch is a field of wildflowers in my chest.

She reaches up—slow, asking without words—and curls her fingers at the back of my neck. Just the warmth of her hand, and I'm a goner. I lean in, but only enough to share breath, to memorize the exact point where our mouths are not yet kissing, and our bodies think they are. Two seconds. Three. She lets go. I step back. We both look like we almost did something wrong and instead did something holy.

"Good night, Crew," she says.

"Good night, Bailey," I answer, and walk backward down the step like distance is a trick I have to do facing her so I don't forget how.

I don't start the truck right away. I stand by the rail and

look up at the lantern room where we invented patience and broke and remade it under rules we wrote with shaky hands. The light sweeps, the rope sings against the wind, and I realize I'm not afraid of the quiet between moments anymore.

Back home, when the house sleeps and the stars do their bright, stubborn thing, I go inside, pull open the dresser, and take out the note I have no business still owning.

Stay gold, C. —B.

I lay it on my palm, then press it flat on the table, and I write another line beneath it—not touching the letters, just sharing the page: *Trying like hell.* I don't know who I'm telling—her, myself, or God. Maybe all three.

When I finally fall asleep, it's with the sound of her laugh braided into the rain that isn't falling and the knowledge that we have moved, together, from *not yet* to the narrow bright shoreline of *almost now*. The difference is one decision and a breath. I hold both like they're a breakable treasure because they are.

In the morning, I'll bring her a breakfast sandwich I burned on purpose because I'm a menace, and she'll make fun of me and eat it anyway, and we'll argue about whether the mystery section should live near the stairs, and I'll watch her decide yeses like a captain. In the evening, I'll stand in the lantern room and not kiss her until she says *now*, and when she does—because she will—it will be because we built something steady enough to hold it. The light will turn. The town will gossip. The bay will keep our secrets and sell them at the market, marked up as legend.

For the first time since the hit that took my season and the laugh that took my boyhood, I'm not lost. I'm exactly where I'm supposed to be.

Chapter Eleven

BAILEY

The lighthouse wakes up before I do.

It creaks and settles and hums like it stretched in its sleep and decided to forgive me for everything I confessed to the ceiling last night. Downstairs, the shop smells like paper and lemon oil and the ghost of pie, which is rude, because I was trying not to think about his mouth.

I open early because my hands and mind need something to do. The kettle hisses. The bell chimed when I flipped the sign to OPEN, but now it's quiet enough that I can hear gulls heckling the tide. I tell myself I'm fine. I'm an adult woman with budget spreadsheets, a broom, and a very reasonable collection of boundary rules. I am not a teenager who got kissed in a storm and is now floating around her own house like a balloon.

I do inventory. I restock romance—alphabetical by author, not by "vibes," which is how Holt shelved an entire shelf last week when I let him help ("look, Bailey, these all *feel* like yellow"). I rearrange the display because the spine on *Stay Gold* is showing at a dangerous angle, and my heart is made of poor choices.

By nine, the front door *thunk-thunks* open with a bustle of sunshine and perfume. Lila sails in, one hand on a tray of muffins, the other dragging Ivy, who is in leggings, sunglasses, and a sweatshirt that says LOCAL MENACE across her chest in glitter.

"Intervention," Lila declares.

"Good morning," I say, suspicious, because nothing good ever follows that tone unless it's pie. "Is there pie?"

"Muffins," she says, sliding the tray onto the counter. "And judgment."

I glance at Ivy. "Do you bite?"

"Only paparazzi," she says, lifting her sunglasses and beaming. "Hi, lighthouse. You look like romance lived here last night and forgot its earrings."

"Get out," I say, but my mouth betrayed me with a smile before my brain could veto it.

Lila leans over the counter, chin on her hands. "How's the 'not yet' going?"

"It's... fine," I say, which is the kind of lie you tell to the TSA and your best friends. "We're—taking it slow."

"Slow like a glacier?" Ivy asks. "Or slow like thunder where you can count the seconds and feel it shaking the windows anyway?"

I aim a muffin at her. She catches it without looking. Popstars are unnecessary.

Lila unwraps a blueberry muffin and takes a bite, eyes all sisterly knives and soft edges. "Did you kiss him?"

I stare. The kettle clicks off. The cat appears on the counter because rules were invented to be ignored. "There was... weather."

Lila squeals into her muffin. Ivy claps like she's at an awards show. "Yes! I knew the hair looked post-storm."

"It's just wavy," I protest.

"It's *sinned*," Ivy says cheerfully, then sobers, pulling her sunglasses up onto her head. "Are you okay?"

The question lands exactly where it needs to, and suddenly, my throat is a tightrope. I fuss with the sugar bowl to buy a second. "I'm... more okay than I thought I'd be."

Lila's eyes soften. "Because it's him."

"Because it's him," I admit, and the truth feels like setting down a box I've carried too long.

Ivy reaches, squeezing my fingers once. "Then let yourself be happy. You can be careful and still say yes."

"I *am* careful," I say automatically.

"You're also stubborn," Lila adds. "Which is why we baked muffins and staged a gentle siege."

"I hate you both," I say, voice unsteady.

"You love us," they chorus, which is rude and true.

They stay for an hour under the pretense of helping, which means Ivy signs two old CD inserts for tourists who pretend they don't recognize her, and Lila reorganizes the children's corner by reading one book out loud and crying at the page with the sea otters.

When they finally leave—with three romance recs, two jars of jam Mom mysteriously delivered "for morale," and the promise to text when Holt inevitably sets something ablaze during festival cleanup (which is funny since he's training to be a firefighter)—my shoulders drop. I am full of muffins and friendship and a trembling that isn't fear anymore. It's anticipation wearing my sweater.

I try not to look at my phone. It sits on the counter like a glittering trap. I make it twenty-seven minutes. Personal best. Then it buzzes.

Crew: How's the menace level?

Crew: Do I need to come over and install a fire suppression system for Ivy?

I DON'T SMILE. I'M A PROFESSIONAL.

Me: Under control.

Me: Your sister-in-law only threatened two journalists and one candle.

THREE DOTS, THEN A PAUSE.

> Crew: Proud of you.

> Crew: Proud of us.

> Crew: Can I bring lunch? Promise to stay out of your way. Will do an impression of a quiet shelf.

IT'S RIDICULOUS HOW FAST MY HEART FLIPS LIKE A PAGE IN the wind. I stare at the message, and the rules appear in my head like kindly traffic cones. We're building something. It needs air and time, not my panic.

> Me: Later.

> Me: Story hour again at 3. Parents asked for you and the otter.

> Crew: The otter negotiated for better snacks. But I'll be there.

I PUT THE PHONE DOWN AND BREATHE. THE SHOP HUMS back to life: a couple browsing travel memoirs, a teen asking for dark academia, an older man with calloused palms looking for a book about small towns that isn't "too romantic" (Good luck, sir.).

Every time the door opens, my body thinks it's him. It isn't. And I go to war with my heart every time.

And then it is.

He arrives with the sun behind him, tall and easy, carrying a paper bag that absolutely contains something burned and heartfelt. His smile is softer than the day. He looks at me like we're the only two people inside this light.

"Hi," he says.

"Hi," I echo, because my brain does not, apparently, own a thesaurus.

He holds out the bag. "For you."

I open it and find a sandwich as advertised—edges too crisp, cheese melted into the deli meat—and a folded napkin that says *for the prettiest book witch*. I wheeze-laugh and then choke and then want to kiss him and then remember that wanting is a delicious, necessary torture right now.

"Terrible," I say, biting into the sandwich anyway. It tastes like butter and smoke and a man trying. "Perfect."

We fall into an orbit that makes sense to my bones. He fixes a squeaky hinge, and I ring up a stack of romances for a woman who whispers that she "hopes you two are a thing, but like, not in a creepy way." He reads to toddlers like the otter puppet has a degree in comedy. I shelve returns and pretend I'm not cataloging the precise timbre of his laugh when a three-year-old howls "again" from the rug. We move around each other like we're learning a dance without counting, a series of almosts and gentle passes, touches that are somehow *not* touches until they are.

After story hour, when the parents have reclaimed their tiny tornadoes and the rug looks like a sticker bomb went off, he finds me by the spiral stairs, palms braced on the rail above my shoulders in that not-caging, not-trapping way that steals breath only because it's him.

"Thank you," he says.

"For what?"

"For letting me be in this room," he says simply, and I swear my whole chest rearranges. "For the otter. For the… moment."

"We're doing okay," I manage.

He nods. "We are."

We stand too close and don't move away because moving away would require more bravery than I have when his mouth is right there. He leans the smallest amount nearer, and I swear I can feel the exact place air turns into decision.

"I have to close early," I blurt. "Town hall meeting. I volunteered."

"Of course you did," he says, amusement fond and quiet.

"Are you—" I swallow. The rulebook shuffles pages. "Coming?"

"If you want me there."

"I do," I say before I can be clever. The truth is quicker than my defense. "I want—" I stop, because the thing I want is too big for between the stairs. "I want you at the meeting," I say instead, which is not the whole sentence and also is.

He smiles like he heard the rest of it anyway. "Then I'll be there."

He is. And it's a circus the way only civic responsibility

can be. Holt has a bullhorn, which should be illegal. Mrs. Winthrop presents a color-coded spreadsheet of "emotional arcs" for garbage pickup after the next festival. Daisy bribes compliance with snickerdoodles. Crew carries folding chairs like they're paper and endures a round of applause from a table of teenage girls who whisper feral analysis into their sleeves when he walks past. He exists inside it like someone who knows he can't fix everything but can be the one who carries what he can. It is, infuriatingly, the sexiest thing I've ever seen.

After, we walk back to the lighthouse in a stretch of evening that the sky forgot to tighten. The wind is almost gone. The bay is a mirror trying to remember what it wanted to reflect.

He stops at the bottom step and looks up at the lantern room, then at me. There's a question in it. There's also a promise.

"Come up," I say, the two words a door I didn't know I had the key to.

We climb without speaking because there's too much to say and also nothing that would improve what the air already knows. In the lantern room, the world spreads flat and endless. The rug is a map I pretended would always be safe. I put the kettle on because ritual makes brave things feel like tasks.

He waits by the window, hands in his pockets, shoulders relaxed in a way they weren't when he walked in the first time. The light makes his jaw look like someone invented structure just to justify this view. He's not trying to be beautiful. He just is.

We sit. The rope hums in the wind. The room makes a quiet that belongs to no one else.

"I want to try something," I say, voice steady because if it shakes, I'll laugh, and if I laugh, I'll never survive it.

He straightens, attentive. "Okay."

"We can keep our rules," I say. "We can protect the parts of this that need time to grow tight. But—" I inhale. Exhale. I am not afraid of naming the thing I want. "When I say *now*, I want you to kiss me like you mean it."

His eyes go soft and dark all at once. His throat moves. He answers without words. He waits with his whole chest. He waits like a man who has learned patience the hard way and decided it is a worthy altar.

The light sweeps. The bay answers with a glitter that could be a coincidence or a blessing. I set my mug down to hear my own pulse. I move my knees closer to his because I need the physical sensation of a decision. I look at his mouth. I look at his eyes. I look at the place my hand will go when the rules allow it.

Licking my lips, I let out a breathy whisper, "Okay. Now."

I barely finish the word before his mouth is on mine, and the world rearranges to make room for this exact heat. He kisses me like he promised he would in a language made of both restraint and hunger. There's a sound from me I have never made before. It startles me and doesn't. His hand is at my jaw—careful, asking—and at my waist—

claiming without taking. I open for him because my body has wanted this longer than my pride, and because my yes is a house I built, and I am finally home inside it.

When we break, it's only far enough to breathe the same air. Foreheads together. His thumb rests just under my ear like a keepsake. He laughs a breath, stunned and grateful and a little wrecked. "Hi," he whispers, ridiculous.

"Hi," I whisper back, equally ruined.

Hauling me onto his lap, I straddle his thighs, pressing my center against the growing ridge in his pants. We kiss again, slower, and the room stretches to hold us. Outside, the town minds its own business for once or pretends beautifully that it does.

We don't rush to the edge. We don't spill over. We stack this on top of last night's kiss, on top of the porch hand-hold, on top of a note kept in a drawer and one kept in a dresser, and we make it a foundation instead of a fire. My hands learn his shoulders, the healed places and the tender ones; his mouth learns my laugh and my silence; my body learns the weight of his not hurrying me; his body learns the way *now* sounds when I mean it and when I mean *enough for tonight,* too.

When the wind picks up, slamming a loose shutter against the outside wall, we finally sit again, flushed and very alive. He takes my hand without asking. My fingers slot into his like we've had more practice than we do.

"I don't know how to do this without wanting everything all at once," he admits into the quiet.

"You don't have to know," I say. "You just have to learn. With me."

He nods. "That I can do."

We say very little after that because our mouths are busy with smiling and occasionally checking that the kiss wasn't a dream. When he finally stands to go, he doesn't ask if I want him to stay. The wanting is a bright, loud thing between us. The choosing is louder.

At the landing, he touches my cheek with the backs of his fingers like a superstition. "Tomorrow?"

"Tomorrow," I say, confident in a way that would have terrified me last month. "The otter and I will be waiting for you."

He grins. "Always."

I watch him descend the spiral, that long body sliding out of the room. The light sweeps once, twice. The night carries him toward the farm. The lighthouse—my stubborn, creaky, unwavering house—holds me steady while my heart does a dangerous, beautiful thing.

I lock the door and turn off the lamp. I press my palm to my mouth and laugh because my whole face won't stop smiling and because Lila and Ivy are going to be unbearable and because I am not scared anymore. Not of being happy. Not of wanting. Not of being seen.

Downstairs, I flip the chalkboard to tomorrow and write, *open for miracles at ten*. It's obnoxious. It's true. I leave it there for the gulls to read.

Then I go to bed and dream of a storm that didn't ruin

anything and a boy who came home as a man and learned how to wait at the threshold until I was ready.

Chapter Twelve

CREW

The light that spills through my window isn't blinding—it's forgiving. The kind that touches everything before it wakes it up, testing if it's safe to shine there. I lie still long enough to feel it move across my chest, over the scars and the places I still call ruins.

For years, my mornings started with noise. Alarms. Coaches. Reporters. The thick smell of antiseptic and liniment and adrenaline, all of it pretending to mean purpose. Now it's quiet. There's no stadium. No shoulder brace hanging on the bedpost. Just me, my breath, and the echo of her voice saying *now*.

My chest tightens around it.

I get up slowly, stretch until the scar tissue protests, then push through the ache. Pain used to mean weakness. Now it's just proof that I'm still here.

Outside, the world's already awake. Cows low in the field. Chickens gossip by the feed bins. The air's heavy with dew and the faint sweetness of cut hay. I take it in like a prayer, one slow breath at a time, until it steadies the pulse tripping inside me.

Rowan finds me in the barn with coffee in one hand and sarcasm in the other.

"Morning, lover boy."

I roll my eyes.

"You're pacing. Again. Thought the barn was haunted."

"Maybe it is."

He smirks, leaning against a stall. "You look like a man who hasn't slept since he finally got what he wanted and doesn't know how to keep it."

I don't utter a word because of course my older brother knows exactly how I'm feeling.

He takes a sip, eyes flicking to my shoulder. "How's the arm?"

"Better."

"Because of therapy?"

"Because of her."

He whistles low, shaking his head. "Knew it. Bailey's got you soft."

"Or sane," I counter.

"Same thing," he mutters, but there's no bite to it. Only understanding.

We work in silence after that. Grain, stalls, repairs. Every motion muscle-deep, automatic. But my thoughts keep drifting to her laughter, her eyes in the lantern light, and the taste of rain between us. I catch myself smiling once and immediately scowl, which only makes Rowan laugh from across the barn.

"You should tell her," he calls.

"Tell her what?"

"That you've got that look."

"What look?"

"The look of a man who finally came home."

I don't answer. Because he's right, and saying it aloud would make it too real.

By midday, the late heat sets in. The kind that sticks to your skin and makes the horizon shimmer like it's holding secrets. I park the tractor, wipe the sweat from my neck, and sit for a minute in the cab, engine idling low. The ache in my shoulder flares, dull but persistent. I press my thumb against it until it quiets.

That hit—*the* hit—still lives in my bones. The moment the stadium went silent and the world tilted under me while the medics ran. I'd known pain before. Sprains, bruises, the usual currency of the game. But that day felt different. Like the universe cracked something open that wasn't supposed to break.

The doctor called it a "partial rotator cuff tear." The team called it a timeline. The press called it career-defining. No one called it what it was: grief.

I stare out at the fields stretching wide, green, and unbothered. The same land that raised me and waited for me to come back when I swore I wouldn't. Bailey once said the lighthouse was built for sailors who lost their way. Maybe the farm has been doing the same thing all along.

I shut off the tractor and head inside.

Mom waits on the porch with lemonade and that look that always means she's about to say something important and gently ruin me.

"Long day?" she asks.

"Not really."

"You're thinking about something."

I huff out a laugh. "Do all mothers come with GPS for their sons' emotional lives?"

"Only the good ones."

She hands me a glass. The condensation slides cold down my fingers. "You've always run toward things, Crew. The next play, the next win, the next fix. Maybe this time you let something run toward you."

Her words stick. "What if I mess it up?"

"Then you learn," she says simply. "That's what love's for."

Love. The word lands heavy and soft, like the first drop before rain.

By dusk, I'm already driving toward the lighthouse.

The road curls around the bay, the sky melting into golds and bruised purples. The water mirrors it all, endless and calm. My pulse isn't calm. It's a storm that's been waiting for somewhere to land.

When I park, the light from her apartment window already sweeps across the horizon—steady, rhythmic, patient. Just like when the beam from the lighthouse guided sailors. The first time I saw that beam as a kid, I thought it was magic. Now I know better. It's work. It's care. It's someone remembering to keep the light on for people who can't yet see the shore.

The door's open. I knock anyway.

"Crew?" Her voice floats from the back room.

"Yeah."

She appears in the doorway, hair loose, cheeks flushed from whatever she's been doing. She's barefoot, wearing an oversized gray sweater that hangs just off one shoulder. My heartbeat does something reckless.

"You hungry?" she asks.

"I'm always hungry."

She tilts her head, nodding toward the small kitchen. "Good, because I cooked enough pasta for a small village."

"Guess it's your turn to feed the strays."

Her smile curves slowly. "Dock?"

"Always."

The dock hums beneath our feet, wood still warm from the day. The tide is low, gentle. The world smells like salt and garlic bread and the faint hint of rain carried in from somewhere far off. There is a small covered section off to the side, and she spreads a blanket, pours wine into mismatched mugs, and sits cross-legged, the sunset painting her in firelight.

I sit across from her, knees brushing hers. "You do this often?"

"Eat on docks with men who drive me crazy? Only on Thursdays."

"Good. It's Friday."

Her laugh slips out before she can stop it. "You're impossible."

"Consistent."

"Persistent," she corrects.

"Accurate."

She shakes her head, but her smile lingers. "You always do that."

"What?"

"Make me laugh right when I'm trying to stay guarded."

"Maybe that's my defense mechanism."

"Or your superpower."

"Depends on the villain," I say, and she laughs again, softer this time, like it's just for me.

The food's simple—pasta, vegetables, bread that crunches too loud—but it tastes better than any five-star meal I've ever had. Maybe it's the company. Perhaps it's the sound of her humming under her breath while she eats, or the way the wind catches the end of her hair and brushes it against my hand.

When we're done, she leans back on her palms, head tilted toward the sky. "You ever miss it?" she asks quietly.

"Home?" I ask at first, but she shakes her head.

"The game?"

She nods.

"Every day," I admit. "Not the pressure, not the travel. Just... the rhythm. The way your body knows what to do before your mind catches up."

Her eyes find mine. "That sounds like love."

"It was," I say. "Until it wasn't."

She doesn't press. She just waits, the way she always does—patient, present.

"It's weird," I continue, voice low. "Everyone talks about the comeback. The recovery. But no one talks about what happens when you're finally healed and realize you don't know who you are without the injury."

She studies me for a long moment. "Maybe that's what you're doing now. Redefining what healed means."

"Maybe."

Her gaze softens. "You don't have to prove you're whole by running again."

The words hit so hard I forget how to breathe for a second. "You always know what to say?"

"Only when it's the truth."

I laugh under my breath, shaking my head. "You're dangerous."

"I've heard," she murmurs.

We fall into silence then—the good kind, full and heavy with all the things we're not ready to name. The new lighthouse beam down the street sweeps over us every few seconds, a slow pulse of light like a heartbeat.

When she looks at me again, her eyes catch that light, and something inside me snaps quiet. I reach out, tracing my thumb along the edge of her wrist. She doesn't pull away. Her pulse flutters beneath my skin, steady and quick, matching mine.

"This feels right," I say.

She tilts her head. "What does?"

"This." I gesture back and forth between us, the air electric. "You. Me. The quiet. The mess. All of it."

She swallows, voice barely a whisper. "You're saying dangerous things again."

"Then stop me."

I lean in, slow enough to give her every chance to pull away. Her breath catches, her fingers tightening in the blanket. When my forehead meets hers, the world breathes.

Her lips part just enough for the smallest sound—a sigh, a prayer, maybe both. I kiss her softly, the way a man kisses a truth he's waited too long to speak aloud.

The taste of her, of salt and warmth and courage, is enough to undo every wall I've ever built.

When we break, her eyes stay closed. "You shouldn't do that," she whispers.

"Do what?"

"Make it feel like this."

"Like what?"

"Like home."

I touch her cheek, thumb tracing the faintest line of rain that's begun to fall. "Maybe it is."

Her eyes open slowly, and for a moment, the world is just that gaze—steady, searching, and impossibly kind.

"Crew..." Whatever she meant to say disappears when thunder rolls over the water. We both laugh, quiet and breathless, as if the storm's in on the joke.

"You and your timing," she says.

"It's a gift."

She shakes her head, smiling, and the motion brings her

close enough that her hair brushes my jaw. The wind carries her scent—vanilla, paper, and something wild underneath. I want to memorize it. I probably already have.

We stay like that, close but not crossing that invisible line again, letting the rain fall around us in silver streaks. The water ripples below, small waves lapping against the wood. Every sense sharpens—the wet air, the taste of wine on her breath, the sound of her heart beating where our arms almost touch.

She leans her head on my shoulder. "You make it hard to remember all my reasons."

"Then let me remind you of better ones."

Her laugh hums low against my arm. "You think you're the good reason?"

"I'm trying to be."

"You're succeeding," she admits softly. "That's what scares me. I'm not used to being the first choice. Not even to my parents."

I turn just enough to see her face, the raindrops clinging to her lashes. "Don't be scared of what's meant for you."

She smiles, small and trembling. "You sound sure."

"I am."

When the rain finally eases, she stands, holding out a hand. I take it, rising beside her. Our fingers stay tangled as we walk back toward the lighthouse, the air cool and clean around us. The world feels scrubbed new.

At the door, she turns to me. "Thank you."

"For what?"

"For not rushing. For making this feel like it's more than temporary."

I brush my thumb along the back of her hand. "That's the point, Bailey. I don't want a comeback. I want a home."

Her breath catches. She looks at me like she's seeing the rest of our story just over my shoulder. Then she nods, slow and certain. "You already found one."

And just like that, she leans forward and presses her lips to my cheek. A whisper of a kiss. A promise in lowercase. Then she's gone, disappearing inside with the soft click of the door.

I stand there for a long time, rain dripping from my hair, the scent of her still clinging to my shirt, the dock behind us humming with what we didn't say.

When I finally head home, the road glows slick and silver. The lighthouse beam sweeps over the bay, steady as breath, and I realize it isn't guiding anyone tonight. It's just shining because it can.

Chapter Thirteen

BAILEY

The morning after a storm always feels like the world pressed a reset button.

The air tastes new, and the daylight forgives everything.

I wake before the alarm, tangled in sheets that smell faintly of salt and smoke. The lighthouse hums around me —old wood stretching, pipes murmuring, the bay whispering against the rocks below. Somewhere out there, a gull laughs like it knows secrets. Somewhere out there, he's probably already awake.

I roll onto my back and stare at the ceiling beams, the ones Grandpa carved initials into back when this house was still half storage, half home. The grain runs straight and sure, just like his handwriting. For a second, I imagine adding mine next to his—B.H.—then realize I'm already thinking like someone who plans to stay. That's the dangerous part: how quickly *hope* starts unpacking its boxes once you open the door.

The kettle clicks in the kitchen. I didn't remember setting the timer. The ghost of routine, I guess.

I move through the motions: mug, sugar, coffee strong enough to count as an apology to my nerves. The steam swirls as I step onto the porch. The world is wet and quiet. The dock across the way gleams darkly in the light.

I sip my coffee and watch the gulls argue over breakfast. For once, I let the quiet stay. I don't fill it with what-ifs or why-nots. I just breathe until the caffeine catches up to my courage.

By ten, the lighthouse smells like fresh scones from Daisy's bakery next door and new paperbacks. The shop door creaks open every few minutes—locals grabbing beach reads, tourists hunting postcards, and the occasional teenager looking for the romance section and pretending not to blush when I point it out. Normal. Familiar. It helps.

Lila texts around eleven.

> Lila: You alive or did the storm sweep you into a Hallmark movie?

> Me: Define alive.

> Lila: Staring at the horizon like it owes you money?

> Me: Maybe.

> Lila: Good. Tell crew I said hi. And by hi, I mean if he hurts you, I'm hiding frogs in his truck.

. . .

I SNORT INTO MY LATTE. THE STORE CAT GLARES, unimpressed. *He already lives dangerously,* I think, and type nothing back because she'll hear my smile through the screen anyway.

Ivy calls next because, of course, she does.

"Are you glowing in puppy love bliss?" she demands, no greeting, all drama.

"I'm working."

"You didn't answer the question."

"I'm *glowing* from caffeine and stress."

"Lies. Spill."

"Ivy—"

"I'm your sister now by unofficial decree, which means I get updates. Did he kiss you again?"

I groan. "You're impossible."

"So he did," she sings. "Good for you, lighthouse Barbie."

"I will block you."

"You won't," she says, smug. "Because you love me and because I'm right."

I lean against the counter, smiling despite myself. "He's... different this time."

"Good different?"

"Scary different," I admit. "Like he's not just visiting anymore. Like he's thinking of staying."

There's a pause. Then her voice softens. "Maybe you should open up and let him."

I don't answer. Because maybe I should. And maybe that's what terrifies me most.

By afternoon, the sky starts to shift again—one of those gray-blue moods that rolls in from nowhere. I light a candle that smells like cedar and sea salt, put on the playlist Crew made last month for the kids' story hour (mostly old country songs and one Taylor Swift track he swore was an accident). The melody curls through the shop, low and sweet. Every lyric feels like a secret note addressed to us.

I busy myself with restocking—fiction first, then travel guides. Anything to keep my hands moving. The bell over the door chimes every now and then. Familiar faces, easy smiles. Coral Bell Cove at its finest: small, nosy, loyal.

When the last customer leaves, the clock reads six thirty. Dusk is already licking at the edges of the water. I close the register, straighten a stack of bookmarks, and tell myself not to check my phone.

He hasn't texted today. Not once. It shouldn't sting, but it does.

Maybe he's busy. Maybe Rowan dragged him into another farm emergency. Maybe—

No. I promised myself no maybes today.

I pull on a sweater and head down to the dock with a book and the leftover scone from Daisy's that no one bought. The boards creak under my weight, familiar music. I sit at the edge, legs swinging above the water, the pages fluttering in the breeze. The smell of rain lingers—sweet, clean, almost electric. I read three paragraphs without understanding a word.

Behind me, the lighthouse hums. The beam flickers once, twice. The bay answers in silver ripples.

I tell myself I'm fine and that I don't need him to show up. That the calm in my chest isn't just waiting for the sound of his truck.

I even believe it—for maybe thirty seconds.

Because that's when I hear it.

Gravel crunching. A low engine idle. Then silence. My heart trips. I don't turn right away. I tell myself it's anyone —a tourist lost, a delivery, a ghost. But then his voice drifts down the path, low and certain.

"Couldn't stay away."

The words ripple through me like warm water meeting cold skin. I close the book, pulse pounding, and turn.

Crew stands at the top of the dock, half silhouetted against the dying light. His hair's damp, shirt clinging in a way that should be illegal, jaw shadowed, eyes locked on me like he's memorizing the way I breathe. He's carrying a takeout bag and that small, infuriating smile that says *I thought about this all day*.

He steps closer, boots thudding against wood, every one of them a heartbeat I can feel in my ribs.

"I was going to wait till tomorrow," he says, voice rough. "But waiting's never been my thing."

I try to speak. The words tangle. "You—You didn't have to come."

"I did."

He sets the bag on the railing, hands sliding into his

pockets like he's trying not to touch me too soon. The air between us hums. The bay hushes, listening.

"I missed this," he says quietly. "Missed *you*."

My throat goes dry. "It's been one day."

He smiles, slow, dangerous. "Longest damn day of my life."

The wind lifts my hair. He reaches out before he can stop himself, tucking a strand behind my ear, fingertips trailing against my skin. I forget how to breathe.

He steps closer. Close enough that the space between us feels like it's about to catch fire.

"Crew—" I start, warning, pleading, everything at once.

His eyes drop to my mouth. The world holds still.

"Tell me to go," he whispers.

I don't. Can't.

Lightning flickers far out over the bay, quiet and harmless. It's the time of year when storms linger. The lighthouse beam cuts across his face, then mine, painting us in alternating light and shadow.

He exhales, slow and steady. "Guess that's a no."

I try to look away. I fail spectacularly. "You're trouble."

"Yeah," he says, voice low enough to shake something loose inside me. "But you're mine to get in trouble with."

And before I can think of a single good reason to stop him, he closes the distance—just one breath, one heartbeat—and his hand finds my waist, warm and sure.

The dock creaks. The wind stills.

He doesn't kiss me. He just looks at me like everything

is about to break open between us, and the world goes silent around it.

Chapter Fourteen

BAILEY

The first thing I notice is the smell—salt, coffee, and something sweet baking downstairs. The second is that I slept through my alarm for the first time in... maybe ever.

Sunlight slants through the window, slicing the room into ribbons of gold and dust. I roll over, stare at the ceiling beams, and try to remember how to breathe like a person who didn't spend last night standing on a dock with her almost-something pressed against her.

Crew Wright kissed the air between us. I let him. And now the entire world smells like the aftermath.

The kettle shrieks downstairs. I throw on the first sweater I find, tug my hair into a knot, and head down the narrow staircase that groans under every step. The lighthouse walls always sound like they're gossiping—old, wooden, and unashamed.

The kitchen is chaos in its purest form: flour dust on the counter, the oven timer blinking, the cat sitting like an unimpressed supervisor beside a tray of scones left over from yesterday. "You could help," I tell him. He yawns. Typical.

By the time I pour my coffee, the calm has almost convinced me. Then my phone buzzes.

MOMENT OF THE YEAR: LOCAL BOOKSELLER CAUGHT IN LIGHTHOUSE LOVE STORY?

The headline belongs to the *Coral Bell Gazette*. The picture—blurry but criminally accurate—shows Crew and me on the dock, the lighthouse beam washing over us like we'd rented a movie crew for the occasion.

"Oh no."

The cat looks equally horrified.

I scroll past the caption—something about "the hometown hero's return sparking more than nostalgia." My pulse is already sprinting. Coral Bell Cove doesn't do privacy; it does popcorn. By noon, the entire town will have opinions, and by dinner, they'll have slogans. It was bad enough when everyone assumed, but now there is hardcore evidence. The kind that would be impossible to deny.

The shop bell clangs downstairs. Because, of course, someone would show up early on *today* of all days.

The bell over the shop door clangs again, louder this time—three sharp notes that mean whoever is on the other side isn't here for browsing.

I wipe my hands on a towel, force a smile, and call out, "We're open, but only marginally civilized."

"Good," a familiar drawl answers. "Civilized sounds overrated."

Crew's standing in the doorway with that easy, unbothered posture that says *nothing touches me* even though last night proved plenty does. Ball cap, gray T-shirt that clings in ways gravity approves of, a paper bag dangling from one hand. He smells like early morning and trouble.

"You can't just appear out of nowhere," I say.

"Technically, I used the stairs." He sets the bag on the counter. "Brought muffins. Thought I'd earn points."

"You brought muffins on the morning the town decided we're headline news?"

He raises an eyebrow. "You saw it?"

"Front page. They called me a 'book-loving siren.' I'm not sure if I should sue or send them cookies."

"Depends on the cookies," he says, unwrapping a muffin. "Blueberry. Best bribe I had."

"Crew." My voice comes out softer than I mean it to. "This is bad."

He leans against the counter, all easy shoulders and apology hidden under the grin. "Bailey, it's gossip. Nobody dies from gossip."

"Tell that to my blood pressure."

"Already did. It says it's fine."

I glare. He takes a slow bite of the muffin and chews like a man with no conscience.

"Do you even care?" I ask.

He swallows, wipes his thumb across his lip. "About what they say? Not really. About how it makes you feel? Yeah, I care a lot."

The room shrinks. The sound of the ocean outside fades to a pulse that syncs with mine.

By midmorning, half of Coral Bell Cove has stopped by *A Page in Time* pretending to buy greeting cards while casually mentioning the article. Holt texts *"you're famous now, autograph my beer can."* Ivy sends heart-eye emoji. Lila calls twice and leaves a voicemail that says only, "breathe."

Crew stays behind the counter like an unofficial bodyguard, helping wrap books, carrying boxes, distracting tourists with football trivia. It's infuriating how natural he looks here—like the space was waiting for his height, his voice, his habit of humming when he counts change.

When the rush finally dies, I sag against the register. "You have no idea what kind of chaos you caused."

He shrugs. "I've been causing chaos professionally since college. I'm pretty good at cleanup, too."

"You think this is fixable?"

"Everything's fixable," he says. "Except maybe that reheated scone you burned earlier."

I throw a napkin at him. He catches it one-handed, of course.

He steps closer, voice lowering. "You know what I'm realizing?"

"What?"

"You're only really mad because you like me and the whole town knows before you got to deny it properly."

I open my mouth to argue. Nothing arrives. He grins like he's scored the winning play.

"Crew Wright," I warn.

"Bailey Hart," he answers, softer. "Relax. Let them talk. We'll write our own version."

The phrase slides under my ribs and lodges there.

By late afternoon, the gossip storm slows. Tourists drift out, locals retreat to dinner plans, and the shop smells like paper and forgiveness. Crew helps me close—stacking chairs, turning signs, pretending not to notice how my hands shake when they brush his.

At the door, he hesitates. "Dinner?"

I blink. "Now?"

"Now," he says. "Before the next crisis."

I should say no. I should send him away to preserve whatever's left of my self-control. But the way he looks at me—open, steady, patient—undoes all the reasons I built.

"Okay," I hear myself say. "But somewhere the Gazette can't find us."

He grins. "I know a place."

The place turns out to be the back deck of the Wright farmhouse, lit by string lights and a sunset so vivid it looks Photoshopped. Rowan's on grill duty with Dean, Lila and Ivy wave from the porch with a glass of wine, and the smell of cedar and smoke wraps around us like an embrace.

"This doesn't count as private," I murmur.

"It's family," Crew says. "They don't count as witnesses."

Dinner is loud, messy, and wonderful. Lila tells stories about her kids, Rowan teases Crew about his haircut, and I laugh until my cheeks ache. For a few golden minutes, I forget headlines and fear.

When everyone drifts inside for dessert, I stay out under the string lights. Crew joins me, two beers in hand.

"Peace offering," he says.

I take the bottle. Our fingers brush, causing a jolt to race up my arm.

"Still mad?"

"Less mad," I admit. "Mostly overwhelmed."

He leans on the railing beside me. "We can still take it slow. No one needs to dictate the speed at which we do anything."

I look at him, the way the light cuts across his face, how the edge of a smile lives there even when he's serious. "Crew, nothing about you is slow."

He laughs quietly. "Fair."

The silence after stretches long enough for the crickets to claim it. He murmurs, "I meant it, you know. About writing our own version."

I meet his gaze. "Then start the first line."

He reaches over and tucks a strand of hair behind my ear again. "Chapter fourteen," he says. "Where we stop pretending."

My breath catches.

The light flickers. The night holds its breath.

We don't kiss that night, but we do linger too long on the farmhouse porch, talking about nothing. Crew's hand brushes mine whenever he gestures, and every time, it feels like punctuation in a sentence we're still learning to write.

When he drives me home, the cab smells like pine, and the radio murmurs old songs we both know. The kind that pretend they're about heartbreak but really mean hope.

He stops at the lighthouse gate and kills the engine. The silence between us is tender, humming.

"Tomorrow?" he says.

"Tomorrow," I whisper.

He nods, starts to get out like he's going to open my door, then thinks better of it. His restraint feels louder than any kiss could.

When I climb the steps, I glance back once. He's still there, truck lights soft against the fog, watching until I vanish inside.

The following morning, gossip still buzzes around town, but softer now—like background static. People have other things to do: bake, fish, live. Maybe that's what forgiveness sounds like in a small town.

I shelve new arrivals, then scribble "Lighthouse Love" on a display chalkboard because leaning into the joke hurts less than hiding from it. Crew shows up halfway through the afternoon, carrying two coffees and a grin that could undo the weather.

"You renamed a display after us?" he asks.

"Branding," I say. "We're trending."

He laughs, then sets the coffees down and slides one toward me. "Guess we'd better give them something to talk about."

"Crew—"

He shakes his head. "Not that. Not yet." He glances around the shop, the shelves glowing in late light.

Before the dinner hour hits, Crew runs out for a bit, then reappears with two more coffees and a tool belt slung low like temptation disguised as competence. He looks like he belongs on a hardware calendar, and I should be arrested for noticing.

"What are we fixing?" he asks, already halfway to the back door that sticks when the humidity sulks.

"Door," I say. "And my reputation."

"Door first," he says, because he loves me with triage.

He kneels, tests the frame, and runs a thumb along the warped edge. "You know, if we shave a hair here and add a shim, it'll stop rubbing."

"I adore when you talk lumber to me," I say flatly. He grins without looking up, the corner that means I've been caught liking him.

We work shoulder to shoulder. He holds the door, and I hold the shim. His forearm brushes my upper arm, and my entire nervous system writes poetry I refuse to publish. The sound of the plane shaving the edge is clean, satisfying— curl after curl of wood peeling away like the door is sighing out its stubbornness.

"Try it," he says.

I tug the handle. The door swings as smooth as a promise.

I clap. He bows like a magician.

Payment is the unspoken permission to stay. He does,

leaning on the counter while I ring up a couple in matching rain boots who whisper that they're "Team Stay Gold" and wink like they were on the dock with us. I roll my eyes and take their money while Crew pretends he didn't hear and also looks smug.

At five, a squall scuffs the bay. Rain needles the windows sideways, and the shop turns amber and safe. Crew and I stand at the front just to watch the weather happen. My hand ends up on the glass. His ends up close enough that if I moved half an inch, we'd be threaded.

"Used to hate storms," I say, watching the surface pucker under wind. "Felt like the world was mad at me."

"And now?" he asks.

"I like how honest they are." I glance up at him. "How they arrive, make a mess, leave you clean."

He hums. "You sure you're not a poet?"

I snort. "I'm a bookseller with a diverse vocabulary."

"And you," he says, as if the sentence doesn't need anything else.

The squall passes. The light returns. The floorboards dry in patches that look like continents. I sweep the grit into little countries and push them into the dustpan like diplomacy.

I'm tired in the good way—hands used, brain sated, body vibrating with a quiet hum that isn't caffeine. Crew asks, "Dinner?" and I'm about to say no in the name of composure when Lila texts.

Lila: Dean says bring the quarterback. I made pasta. No press, only carbs.

CLOSING SHOP EARLY, I RIDE WITH CREW TO THE HOUSE on the canal where I always imagined someone rich and famous living. And now with Dean there, a billionaire in his own right, my vision came true. The thought leaves me wondering whether I can be right about things with Crew, too.

Dean and Lila's porch smells like basil and butter. A pitcher of something bright is on the rail. There are cushions Ivy bought in a fury because "the porch wasn't vibing." A child's chalk drawing on the step looks suspiciously like a lighthouse and a football holding hands. Lila probably staged it. I'll thank and mock her later.

Dinner is chaotic music. The table is too small and perfect anyway. Ivy flits and fusses and then sits and eats like a person deprived of joy, which she is not. Dean tells a story about a goat that was not his problem, then became his problem, and now lives behind their garage like a dignified roommate. Crew laughs, that low, real laugh he saves for here.

There's a moment—tiny and huge—when somebody tries to pass bread around me, and I reach for it at the same time as he does, and his hand overlaps mine. No one says a word. The contact is brief, practical, and unrehearsed. It feels like a wire spliced back together.

After dishes, the deck is string lights and breath. Lila puts on a playlist that would embarrass her best friend, Ashvi. Crew and I lean on the railing and watch the bay turn navy. The air cools, the wood warms, and I realize I'm not braced for impact. I'm leaning.

"Tell me something true," I say.

He thinks for longer than a joke needs. "I was going to quit."

"Football?"

He nods. "After the injury... after the surgery... I wasn't just afraid I couldn't play like before. I was afraid I didn't want to be that person anymore."

My throat goes tight. "And now?"

His gaze stays on the dark line where water meets sky. "Now I want a life that doesn't require me to outrun myself."

I don't say anything for a few breaths because I learned this summer the value of letting silence do its work. "You don't have to outrun anything here."

He nods, a small, grateful tilt. "That's the point."

There's a sweetness to the restraint we're practicing while with company I didn't know I had a taste for. It feels like we're choosing something on purpose, not falling and calling it fate.

He drives me back later, windows down, the truck smelling like pine and pasta. At the gate, he rests his forearms on the steering wheel and looks at me like the word *soon* is a physical thing he can hold between his teeth.

He says goodbye with a quick peck, nothing like we'd

shared earlier, but every bit the promise of more when I'm ready.

When I make it up the steps, the house feels like a held breath that finally lets go. I wash my face, tie my hair, crawl into bed with a book I've memorized, and fall asleep after the same paragraph I've loved for ten years.

The following days braid themselves into something I've never let myself have: ordinary joy. He shows up with breakfast sandwiches, and I pretend to critique them. I show up at the farm with jam and an opinion about fence posts that is not invited but is indulged. We fix three small things that needed fixing: the sticky window, the wobbly stool, and the way a section of romance had silently drifted into horror. The town's gossip turns into benevolent teasing. Mrs. Winthrop brings a knitted lighthouse cozy for no discernible reason. The high school librarian emails to ask if "Mr. Wright" will read for literacy night. I forward it to him and add: *Mr. Wright says yes.* He sends back a photo of the otter puppet saluting.

But it's not all soft edges. The world keeps trying to tug at the threads. An online sports blog runs a photo of us and speculates about "distractions." A Tennessee Stallions fan page debates whether my bookstore is good for team morale, as if books reduce yardage. Crew reads none of it. I read too much. We meet in the middle. I delete the app, and he listens when I say "this part scares me."

He doesn't tell me it will be fine. He says, "Tell me what I can do that helps," and then does it.

On a Thursday morning, I wake to a gray that feels like

a headache. The air is thick with the promise of rain and the certainty of something else. I go downstairs, make coffee, open my email, and freeze.

SUBJECT: Event Inquiry: A Page in Time

FROM: PR@StallionsHQ.com

My heart lurches as I click.

Hello Ms. Hart,

We'd love to coordinate a community appearance with Crew Wright at your bookstore—children's story hour with signed team posters, photo ops, and suggested press coverage.

Please confirm availability.

Best,

— Stallions PR Team

I read it twice. A third time. The words blur, sharpen, demand to be felt.

It's not bad, I think. It's not a takedown. It's a gesture. It's also a spotlight I didn't ask for, and a headline with my name baked in.

The lighthouse creaks as I hold my breath.

I forward the email to Crew with nothing but the subject line: *Press?*

He replies almost immediately.

Crew: Do you want this?

IT'S TWO SECONDS OF TYPING AND TEN YEARS OF learning to answer the right question.

> Me: I want the kids to have a day that feels like magic.

> Me: I don't want cameras in my kitchen.

> Crew: Then we say no to cameras. Yes to story hour. I'll call them.

THE SHAPE OF THE DAY UNCLENCHES. THE KNOT IN MY chest loosens by two notches. It doesn't disappear. I don't know if it ever will. But it loosens, and the breath that returns tastes like fresh air.

At three, we host an impromptu, unofficial literacy hour with no posters and no hashtags, just a semicircle of small humans and a quarterback with an otter on his hand. I sit on the rug beside them and watch him read like the words are a game he's playing with the room.

When the last kid leaves, one straggler lingers—a little boy with a chipped front tooth and a ferocious cowlick. He hands us a crumpled drawing of a lighthouse, a football, and a book with legs holding hands. In shaky block letters, he'd written **THANK YOU**.

Crew kneels to eye level and taps the page. "We'll hang this up where everyone can see it."

"Even the otter?" the kid whispers.

"Especially the otter."

The boy nods, solemnly satisfied, and runs for the door where his dad waits with a grateful grin. Crew watches them go, his mouth pressed into a line that is not quite a smile, not quite an ache. I know the feeling. It's what happens when the world gives you back a piece you didn't realize was missing.

We lock up early and sit on the floor with tea, backs against the counter. The shop clicks and settles around us.

He turns his head, studying me like I'm a map. "Tell me the thing you're still not saying."

I pick at a loose thread on my sweater. "That sometimes I feel like a footnote in the story of people who love bigger than I do."

"You don't love small."

"I specialize in quiet."

He considers. "Quiet isn't small. It's chosen."

The sentence lands in the exact place that still hurts and settles there like balm. I bump my knee against his and let my body say it for me.

Night crawls softly up the windows. We sit until the air cools enough to raise goose bumps on my arms. He notices, shrugs out of his hoodie, and drops it over my shoulders. The fabric smells like cedar and hard work and him. The hoodie is too big on purpose. I pull the sleeves over my hands, and he looks at me like I'm wearing victory.

"Tomorrow?" he says when he stands, like it hasn't become our liturgy.

"Tomorrow."

He goes. I stay. I sweep, wash the two mugs, and tuck the otter back into his basket like a coworker. Upstairs, I brush my teeth and laugh out loud at myself because I am happy and embarrassed to be happy in case the universe thinks it's bragging. I apologize to the stars for my audacity and then ask for more anyway.

At the window, I watch the beam turn and turn.

When sleep comes, it's easy. When morning comes, it's gentle. Unlike many from my past.

And when the next headline posts online—**STORY HOUR WITH STALLIONS QB?**—I do not flinch. Because the photo above the fold is the drawing with block letters, and the caption reads: *Thank you for the light.* Sure, the internet will spin it into whatever it wants. Coral Bell Cove will do what towns do: worry, argue, forgive, bake. But I will do what I have learned to do here: open the door, sweep the floor, let the beam spin, say *now* when I mean it and *soon* when I have to, and walk toward the person who keeps showing up with coffee, a wrench, and a willingness to let me set the terms.

By the end of that week, the door doesn't stick anymore. Neither does my heart.

And if the town wants to call it a chapter, fine. It is one. A long, slow, stubborn chapter where the plot isn't a twist but a choice made again and again under decent lighting.

I write the last line of the day on the chalkboard for no one and everyone:

Open for miracles at ten.

Then I lock up, climb the spiral, and fall asleep smiling, because the best thing about being known is that you're not alone in your own story. And the best thing about a lighthouse is that it never asks the sea to be less.

Tomorrow, he'll knock. Tomorrow, I'll say come in.

And tomorrow, as always, the light will turn.

Chapter Fifteen

CREW

*I*t's 6:03 a.m. when my phone vibrates off the nightstand.

The sound it makes when it hits the floor is how I feel most mornings lately—solid but slightly cracked. I'd been waiting to hear from Marcus for a few days after spending a couple of hours in Norfolk getting tests done on my shoulder. A necessary evil in the process of being the best I can be.

> Marcus: MRI cleared. You're good to start throwing again.

I STARE AT THE SCREEN, THEN OUT THE WINDOW WHERE the fields are still wrapped in fog. It should feel like good news. It does, a little. Mostly, it feels like a coin flipping in slow motion.

I toss back the covers, stretch until my shoulder protests, and mutter to the ceiling, "Guess we're back."

The ceiling, being a professional at ignoring my drama, offers no comment.

By eight, I'm down on the far end of Otter Creek Farm with Rowan. He's on the tractor. I'm supposed to be helping, but end up leaning against the fence, coffee in hand, pretending deep thought instead of actual work.

"Marcus said I'm cleared," I tell him.

He whistles low. "Hell of a thing. Thought you'd be happier."

"Yeah."

"Yeah?"

"It's complicated."

He cuts the engine, wipes his forehead, and gives me that brotherly look that means *don't make me drag it out of you.* "Complicated like you don't wanna go back?"

"Complicated like I don't know what going back means anymore."

Rowan squints. "Ah. Complicated like a woman."

I laugh. "You've been talking to Ivy."

"Maybe. She says your brain's about as steady as wet paint."

"She's not wrong."

He grins. "Then stop watching it dry and do something."

Doing something turns out to mean fixing the railing outside the bookstore. Again.

Bailey claims it's the sea air. I suspect it's fate's way of giving me excuses to hover.

She's already open when I get there, broom in hand, hair in a braid that makes concentration look better than any runway model ever could.

"You're early," she says.

"You say that like it's a crime."

"For you, it's suspicious."

"Fair."

I hold up the new bracket. "Figured we'd give this corner a fighting chance."

She eyes it. "What's the catch?"

"No catch. Just felt like fixing something that isn't me for once."

Her mouth twitches. "That's dark."

"Occupational hazard."

We work in easy silence. Or maybe not easy—more like aware. Every brush of her shoulder feels like a sentence we'll have to finish later.

When I stand to test the railing, she's right beside me, closer than she probably meant to be. The scent of coffee and cinnamon clings to her. My hand brushes her hip when I reach for the drill, and her breath catches, small but sharp.

I should step back. I don't.

"Crew..."

"Yeah?"

"Don't look at me like that."

"Like what?"

"Like you already know."

She's not wrong. I've known for years. I just didn't know what to do with it.

Later, while she's helping a tourist choose romance novels "that don't end in trauma," I wander the shop pretending to browse. My brain's doing a play-by-play commentary on how easy she makes it look—building peace out of paper and dust jackets.

When she laughs, I feel it in the spot my shoulder used to hurt. When she bites her lip to hide a smile, my pulse trips like it's late for practice.

I'm doomed, basically.

At lunch, I head to the pier where Lila sits cross-legged with her pen, scribbling in a notebook that looks more like therapy than journaling.

"You look serious," I say.

"Working on something." She hums to herself and tilts her head. "Also hiding from Dean. He thinks I'm napping."

"You're a menace."

"Runs in the family."

I sit beside her, legs dangling over the edge. "How's Bailey holding up?"

"She's pretending not to care that the entire town ships you harder than I ship my petri dishes."

"Noted."

Lila smirks. "She's good for you, you know. Even with her being one of my best friends."

"Pretty sure everyone thinks that."

"Because it's true."

"I'm trying not to screw it up."

"Then stop trying so hard." She runs a hand through her hair, twisting the ends just like she did when she was younger. "Just show up. That's all she's ever needed."

I look out over the water where the lighthouse gleams in the distance, its white tower cutting through the mist like it's showing me where to aim.

"Showing up's easy," I say quietly. "Staying might not be."

"Then make it be," Lila says. "You're Crew Wright. You turn impossible plays into touchdowns for fun."

"Yeah," I murmur. "But this time, I want more than a win."

By sunset, I find myself back at the lighthouse with takeout and no plan.

Bailey opens the door wearing paint-flecked jeans and a look that says she hasn't stopped thinking either.

"Hungry?" I ask.

"You bribed me with Thai food?"

"It's my love language."

"Your what?"

"Spicy noodles and poor emotional timing."

When she laughs and lets me in, the world rights itself just a little.

Dinner turns into talking. Talking turns into her sitting on the counter while I rinse dishes.

At one point, she reaches out to wipe sauce from my cheek with her thumb and doesn't move it fast enough.

Our eyes meet.

My hand lands on her thigh, light as a question.

The air between us isn't air anymore. It's possibility.

She swallows hard. "Is this still a bad idea?"

I whisper, "Probably."

Neither of us moves for a long, loaded heartbeat. Then she slides off the counter, her bare feet landing softly on the tile, and whispers, "Tomorrow."

It's the third time she's said it, and somehow it hurts worse every time.

That night, lying in bed, I can still feel the warmth of her skin under my hand.

Marcus's text about throwing again stares back from my phone, but all I can see is her standing in her doorway, light haloing her like she was made to be the thing I came home to.

And that's when I know I'm in trouble.

Because for the first time in my life, I want something I can't win by force.

Bailey Hart isn't a game. She's the whole damn season.

And I'm still learning how to play it right.

The following morning starts with trepidation and caffeine.

Mostly caffeine.

I'm halfway through my first mug when Rowan strolls in, kicks the kitchen chair like it owes him rent, and drops into it with a groan. "You look like a man with something on his mind," he says, stealing my toast.

"I have many somethings," I say. "All equally unhelpful."

He chews. "So... Bailey."

"Do we really have to do this before breakfast number two?"

"Yes."

I sigh. "She's—"

"Different?" he offers.

"Yeah. And not in the cliché way. Just... grounded. Real."

Rowan grins. "You mean she calls you out on your crap, and you like it?"

"Something like that."

He nudges my coffee mug closer. "Then you're screwed, brother. Because you only talk like this when it's not a fling." I know he's referring to the PR relationship I had with his current wife, Ivy, a couple of years back. We were friends and nothing more, but it took a while to convince my brother of that.

"I know."

"Does she?"

I glance out the window where the morning fog is still dragging its feet over the bay. "She knows enough. The rest... I think she's still deciding."

"Then don't make her decide alone."

Rowan stands, pats my shoulder, and leaves me with the kind of advice that sounds easy until you try living it.

By midmorning, I'm pacing outside *A Page in Time* like a guy auditioning for the role of "emotionally conflicted golden retriever."

Bailey's in the window, rearranging a stack of hardcover releases. She looks content in that quiet, dangerous way that makes you want to stay forever just to watch her exist.

I knock on the glass. She glances up, smiles, and gestures for me to come in.

"Good morning," she says.

"Define 'good'."

"You look like you wrestled a decision and lost."

"I did."

"Want to talk about it?"

"Not really."

She quirks a brow. "Then why are you here?"

"Because I don't know how to not be."

Her expression softens—barely—but it's enough to pull oxygen back into my lungs.

"Help me unpack these?" she asks, sliding a box cutter across the counter.

It's a small act of mercy, but I take it.

We fall into rhythm. She opens boxes, and I stack. She teases me for sorting romance alphabetically by *hotness of cover models*, and I tell her I'm a man of visual priorities. She tries to look unimpressed but bites back a smile that betrays her.

Somewhere between unpacking and shelving, I find myself watching her. The way she hums under her breath. The way she presses her lips together when concentrating. The way she steadies herself with one hand on the shelf, fingers tapping in rhythm like her body has its own metronome.

It's domestic and dangerous all at once.

"Stop staring," she murmurs without looking up.

"Didn't realize I was."

"You were."

"Can you blame me?"

She turns, mock glare in place, but her cheeks have that faint pink that tells me I'm winning the kind of game that doesn't have rules.

"You're trouble," she says.

"Maybe," I say, stepping closer. "But I'm the kind you like."

She opens her mouth—probably to argue—but Mrs. Winthrop barrels in just then with a basket of scones and a thousand opinions, and the moment shatters into harmless chatter.

That night, I'm back at the farm, watching game footage Marcus sent me while thinking about Bailey's laughter echoing in the aisles.

My phone buzzes.

Bailey: Thanks for helping today. Even if your "hot cover" system was questionable.

Me: Questionable? It was flawless.

Bailey: You sorted half the romance section by abs.

Me: You say that like it's a bad thing.

Bailey: It's a thing.

Me: You're smiling.

Bailey: No proof.

Me: Liar.

THREE DOTS APPEAR, VANISH, REAPPEAR.

Bailey: Good night, Crew.

Me: Good night, Bailey.

IT SHOULD BE SIMPLE. IT'S NOT.

I stare at the screen, thumb hovering, tempted to send something reckless like *I wish you were here*, but I don't.

Because if I say that, I'll mean it.

And meaning things around her feels like walking barefoot on glass—painful, grounding, addictive.

Two days later, Marcus flies in from Nashville after meeting with the Stallions GM for an in-person checkup. He's all business, clipboard and precision.

"You've got full rotation," he says, watching me throw. "Speed's coming back."

"Feels good."

"Still on board with the plan? Camp starts in three weeks."

Three weeks.

That used to sound like salvation. Now, it sounds like a countdown I didn't agree to.

"Yeah," I say automatically.

He eyes me. "You don't sound convinced."

"I am."

"You're lying."

I toss the football again, hard enough to sting my palm. "You're reading too much into it."

Marcus sighs. "Crew, you're cleared physically. But mentally? You need to decide what you want. Because the league eats indecision for breakfast."

He's right. He always is. But the image that flashes in my mind isn't the field—it's Bailey, standing on her porch in the glow of the lantern room, hair in the wind, eyes soft but fierce.

"I'll figure it out," I say.

"Do it soon," Marcus says, packing up. "Because if you're not all in, you're already out."

After he leaves, I head straight for the lighthouse. It's instinct now—like my compass is permanently set to her.

She's outside, perched on the steps with a mug in her hands and that sweater I like. The light behind her paints her in gold.

"Hey," she says.

"Hey."

"Rough day?"

"Something like that."

"Want to talk about it?"

"No," I admit. "Just... need to be near something that makes sense."

She pats the step beside her. "You're in luck. I make sense every other Wednesday."

I laugh, sit, and lean my elbows on my knees. The ocean hums across the way.

"Three weeks," I say quietly.

"For what?"

"Training camp."

"Oh."

"Yeah."

"Are you excited?"

"I was."

"Was?"

"Now I'm just... torn."

She studies me for a long moment. "You don't have to choose, you know."

"That's the problem. Feels like I do."

She doesn't offer an answer. Just reaches out, her hand resting lightly on mine. It's small, barely there—but the warmth of it travels straight through me like a live wire.

For once, I don't speak. I just sit there, hand in hers, watching the lighthouse beam sweep over the bay, thinking maybe this—this simple, quiet thing—is what I've been chasing all along.

By the time I leave, the stars are out, and the ache in my chest isn't from my shoulder anymore.

It's from knowing that whatever happens next, I'm already hers—and that might be the most dangerous play I've ever made.

The night swallows the road back to the farm, and I let it. Windows down, crickets stitching the dark together, the truck smelling like old leather and sawdust. I should be listening to rehab notes or a podcast about zone coverage, but all I hear is the way Bailey said *you don't have to choose* like it could be true if I let it.

The porch light is off. Mom's note waits on the counter—

meatloaf in the fridge, don't be a stranger, love you

—and I eat standing up, the way you do when your body's home and your head isn't. The house is roomy with everyone gone, echoes of old arguments and good birthdays tucked in corners. I take a shower, scrub until the day comes off, then stare at the ceiling fan as if it owes me answers.

Three weeks. Camp. Noise. The life I built from muscle and grit and Sunday night noise. It's still there—still mine, if I want it. But the image of stepping into a stadium now comes with a second overlay: a white tower against a navy sky, a woman on a porch, and a beam of light turning, as if it remembers me by heart.

I grab my keys again. I don't even try to pretend I'm not going back.

The lighthouse is a geometry of shadow and glow when

I pull up. The beam sweeps slowly, catching the edge of the railing, the brass at the door handle, and the curl of a fern in a pot Bailey swears she forgets to water, yet it thrives anyway. I knock once and immediately feel ridiculous. It's late. This is reckless.

The door opens fast, like she was already there. She's barefoot in an old T-shirt and soft shorts, hair twisted up, glasses sliding down her nose. Her mouth shapes my name like she's been practicing.

"Couldn't sleep," I say.

"Me either." She steps back. "Come in."

Inside, the shop is dim, the kind of quiet you whisper in out of respect. She flips a small lamp on behind the counter, and it throws a warm circle at our feet. The place smells like paper and citrus and her shampoo. It's criminal.

"I made tea," she says, like we've always had midnight tea. She pours and hands me a mug. Our fingers meet like they've planned it. "Did your shoulder hurt?"

"Only in the parts that aren't the shoulder." I set the mug down and rub a hand over the back of my neck. "Marcus says I'm good to throw. I keep imagining every version of what happens after."

"Which one makes your chest tighten?" she asks, honest as a scalpel.

"All of them." I huff out a breath, try a smile. "You ever wish for two bodies?"

She tips her head. "One for fear. One for joy."

"Yeah."

"I used to," she says. "Then I realized it was one body either way. Might as well let it hold both."

I sit with that. Too simple. Exactly right. The kettle clicks softly back to sleep as if it approves of the sentiment.

She moves around the counter and stands beside me instead of across from me, shoulder to shoulder. Not touching. Not *not* touching. We face the rows of spines like a small congregation at a safe church.

She listens, steady. "Tell me what you'd miss if you stayed."

"Hotel rooms at two a.m. where the minibar is the friend that wants to ruin you." I let out a laugh that isn't nice. "The way people love you when you're useful." A long breath. "The part where I don't have to ask what matters because the schedule decides."

Her silence is not passive; it's shelter. "And if you stayed here?" she asks.

"Salt air," I say, too fast. "My mom's porch. Rowan pretending he hates me. Fixing a door that actually stays fixed. Reading to kids who think the otter is real." I look at her. "You."

She doesn't flinch. She does look down, like the floor might take the heat out of the moment if we ask politely. "Those aren't small things."

"I know." I take a deep breath. "I'm trying to be the kind of man who doesn't make the big things sound small so they fit in his old life."

The clock ticks. The beam turns. I can feel the exact

place our bodies know we could step wrong and choose not to, and it makes the air taste like lightning.

"Come upstairs," she says suddenly, voice low. "I have"—her mouth tugs—"a loose window latch. Before the storm tomorrow."

I should grin. I don't. "Yeah," I say softly. "Let's fix it."

We climb the spiral, the narrow stairs forcing us closer than is safe. My hand rests to her left on the rail, hers to my right, and our knuckles pass each other every third step like a metronome. The lantern room is a planet of glow and shadow, the rug a faded map of somewhere we haven't gone yet. She leads me into the attached apartment and points at a window above the small kitchen sink. "There," she says, relief-shy from her own excuse.

I check the latch, the play in the hinge, and the gap where the frame bowed. "Shim will do," I murmur because it's easier to speak about lumber than all the pent-up desire rushing through me.

She stands beside me, holding the flashlight, her arm brushing mine every time she shifts the beam. "Do you ever worry," she says, and the light wobbles across my wrist, "that if you pick wrong, the other life will punish you?"

"All the time." I wedge the shim with careful pressure and feel the latch catch. "But I worry more that if I don't pick, both lives will."

We test the window together—open, close, clean slide, the click of the latch as satisfying as a solved chord. "Good," she says, pride lighting her face—my favorite ruinous thing. "Thank you."

"Payment accepted in tea and seven reckless seconds," I say, then immediately wish I had half the sense God gave a fence post.

She blinks. "Seven?"

"That's the number of kisses I can survive tonight," I say, not moving. "If you want to."

Silence. The rope hums. Somewhere below, a gull chooses violence against a trash can. She steps forward like the body knows before the brain does.

"Seven," she echoes, fingers finding the front of my shirt.

We don't rush. We inventory like this is a valuable thing that deserves care: the way her breath hitches; the way my hands hover at her waist and choose gentleness; the way we both laugh once, a small sound that breaks the fear in half. Then I bend, and she rises. Our mouths meet with the kind of gravity that's a choice.

One. Heat.

Two. The taste of mint and tea and her, my whole chest going unsteady.

Three. Her hand slides to the back of my neck, and I have to reset the world under my feet.

Four. My thumb traces her jaw, and her lips part, and I think I will live inside this exact second until I die.

Five. Her laugh in my mouth, the soft kind that means she's not bracing.

Six. The tiniest sound from me I've never made before. She answers with a sigh that's the map key to every yes.

Seven. We stop. Foreheads pressed. A breath shared like a stolen secret.

We don't move for a count of eight, nine, ten, because rules are real, and patience is a holy language, and I will learn it if it kills me. When we step back, our hands are still linked without either of us purposely doing it.

"Okay," she says, eyes bright and wrecked. "That was reckless."

"Measured," I whisper. "Science."

"I think I want to be reckless for longer. Reckless enough to think I'm enough to make you stay." She bites her plump lip, and the growing erection in my pants jerks at the movement.

"Sweetheart, you're more than enough reason to stay. Let me help you believe that."

My hand that gently touches her waist slinks up under the cotton of her shirt. The tips of my fingers glide along the soft skin of her waist, and her breath shudders with each gentle stroke.

"I love the feel of your skin," I moan as my hand reaches the underside of her bra. Bailey's breath hitches as I unhook the latches along her back, releasing the breasts I've been dying to get my hands on.

Her back arches as my lips find their way to the soft skin of her neck.

"Crew," she groans, her thighs rubbing against each other as she squirms against my touch. My fingers slip under the lace of her bra and gently caress her nipples. The sensation of her sensitive peaks hardening under my touch has my cock jerking within the confines of my jeans.

"Bailey."

"Hmm..." she replies as I press my lips to the corner of her mouth.

"Let me make you feel good. No rules. Just you and me. Will you let me?" I ask, my eyes snagging on the thick blankets she keeps folded in the corner of the lantern room.

"Yes," Bailey says with zero hesitation.

In a move I'll have to mentally play back later, I reach out and snag the end of one of the blankets and flick it on the hard, cold floor behind Bailey. She scooches back on instinct until she's seated in the same spot we met for tea all those days ago.

Sitting back on my heels, I let my eyes travel over her body, and I can't help but think about how long I've waited to have her like this.

"Take off your shirt," I demand, my voice gravelly to my own ears. Bailey's eyebrows lift, and her chest stops moving. But it takes only a second for her cheeks to redden before she tucks her chin toward her chest and slowly lifts the thin material over her head. The straps of her bra follow suit without me even having to ask.

God, she's gorgeous. Her nipples are a dusty pink against the paleness of her skin. I can still make out the subtle tan line from her bathing suits worn over the summer.

An animalistic jealousy gushes over me, thinking about other men taking in what's mine.

"Pants," I bark out as I fist the denim on my knees in an attempt to keep myself from reaching out.

Bailey dutifully follows and tosses her clothes on the remaining stack of blankets before lying back on her elbows, wearing only a pair of sensible cotton panties in the lightest shade of blue.

"Fuck, Bailey. You're beautiful."

She arches her brow as a slight breeze makes its way through the lantern room from the old windows. Her nipples stand at attention, begging me forward.

"Show me?" she asks, sitting forward. Bailey's hands go to her hips, and I immediately tell her to stop.

"Let me do that. You just lie back."

On all fours, I crawl my way over her body until our faces are aligned. I take in the slight quiver in her lips and the shimmer in her eyes. It's a look I know all too well. She's nervous and excited, the same look she got when she opened her bookstore.

I brush my lips across her jaw, moving from one side to the other as her fingers find their way under my shirt and trail across my hips.

Our lips meet, and my tongue begs her mouth for entrance. Her taste is something I'm starting to crave, and I fear it will never be enough.

Bailey's fingers inch toward the button of my pants, but I tear my mouth away from hers, halting her movements.

"No, sweetheart. Tonight is about you."

She looks up at me with glassy eyes, and I wish I had a way to capture her like this. "But what about you?" she asks, her fingers trailing along the dusting of hair on the center of my abdomen.

"Just let me make you feel good. You'll get your chance." With a smirk, I press a quick peck on her lips and make my way down to her chest, ignoring her rolling eyes and focusing on her swift intake of breath as my lips latch around one of her nipples.

As a soft moan escapes her lips, I quickly switch to her other nipple, making sure to give it the same amount of attention.

Beneath me, Bailey squirms, and I adjust my weight onto my good arm and use my other to hold her hip still.

Sparing a glance up at her face, I find Bailey watching me intently, her teeth snaring her plump bottom lip. Locking eyes with her, I reach down and slide my hand across the waistband of her panties before slipping it inside.

Immediately, my fingers are engulfed in her body's heat, and I've gotten nowhere close to her center.

"Am I going to find you wet, Bailey? Are you going to drench my fingers?" I ask, cinching closer and closer to the spot she yearns for.

"Crew." My name is a plea on her lips, and I find my resolve splintering away like leaves in a storm.

My fingers slip farther across her mound until I reach her sensitive folds, my thumb brushing against her clit. Bailey's entire body jerks at the contact.

"Fuck," I growl as I slip a finger inside her tight cunt, relishing in the obscene amount of heat. Pulling my hand free, I quickly steal a taste from my fingertips, my eyes nearly rolling back in my head at the flavor.

Gripping the edge of her panties, I rip them from Bailey's body, tossing them haphazardly across the room. I use my shoulder to spread her knees apart and lie in front of the most perfect pussy I've ever seen.

"Jesus, I can't wait to feast on you."

Bailey tries to cover up her sex, but I smack her hand away. "Don't."

"No one's ever," she whispers, and I feel both elation and anger. Joy at the fact that I'll be the first to have my tongue between her legs. Irritation at the fact that some dimwit didn't take the time to pleasure her.

"Well, it's my honor to be the first. I plan on being here a while. You just sit back and relax."

I focus on her pussy, using my tongue to lick slow, steady strokes as my thumb rubs circles around her clit. With the way her moans grow, I can tell she's already close.

I keep up the slow pace for a few minutes, then move my mouth toward her sensitive nub, using my lips and tongue to increase the pleasure. My fingers slip inside her channel, hooking at just the right spot, causing Bailey's legs to close around my head.

She could suffocate me at this moment, and I would die the happiest man. Unfortunately, the distraction does little to halt the fact that I'm about to come in my boxers—something I haven't done since I was in middle school, making out with Becky St. Claire behind the bleachers at a high school football game.

"Crew!" Bailey cries out, her hands fisting in my long hair as her walls tighten around my fingers.

"That's it, sweetheart. Come for me. Let me see you fall apart, baby."

"Oh my..." she moans as her back arches.

I slow my movements, crawling over her body to wrap her in my arms as she comes down from her high. It takes her a few minutes, but she turns to look at me as I brush my fingers through her hair, her body sated, her eyes dazed, a small grin growing.

"That was..."

"Perfect," I tell her, pressing my lips against hers. Thankfully, she doesn't pull away as she tastes herself on my lips.

Bailey's legs intertwine with mine, and I know she can feel the hardness pressed against her hip.

"Are you sure you don't want me to take care of that?"

"Maybe next time. Right now, I just want to lie with you in the moonlight."

Bailey cuddles closer, and as a shiver passes over her, I grab another blanket and drape it across our bodies. I won't let her stay up here long, but right now, the moment is too perfect to move.

"This is nice," she mumbles, her voice heavy with sleep.

This is exactly how it should be.

Words I say to myself, and one day, I'll bring myself to say them to her, too. For now, lying with her like this is more than I ever thought I deserved.

Chapter Sixteen

CREW

In the early morning light, I turn to go, hoping to fend off more small-town rumors. The universe, which has a timing I both resent and respect, chooses then to make my phone vibrate. I glance down. *David.*

Of course.

Bailey watches my face shift. "You can get it."

"It's nothing," I lie.

"It's not nothing," she says gently. "Take it."

I swipe. "Hey."

"You see PR's email?" David's voice is all brass tacks and calendar invites. "We'll loop local press into the story hour. Soft optics. Good for rehab narrative."

"No press," I say immediately.

"Crew—"

"No press," I repeat, quieter, in a voice I don't use with anyone else. "This is for kids. Not for cameras."

He exhales sharp. "You're leaving juice on the table."

"I'm leaving room for breathing." I look at Bailey. She isn't listening, not exactly. She's giving me privacy by staring very hard at the window we just fixed, lips pressed together like she's studying a text only she can see. "Set it up with the school only," I tell him. "Make it easy. If they say no, we don't do it."

Silence, the kind that means he's reorganizing his strategy. "Fine," he says at last, clipped. "But you're throwing for the official team doc and GM in Nashville on Monday. No more delays."

"I'll be there," I say, and my chest answers yes and no at the same time.

I hang up. She looks at me. "You didn't have to do that."

"I did," I say simply. "I can do noise. I won't do it to you."

Something shifts in her face—relief, thank you, a new kind of trust. She steps close, palms on my ribs, not pulling me in and somehow pulling me in. "You're dangerous when you're good," she says.

"Working on being consistently dangerous," I say, because if I don't joke, I'll say something like *I'd burn it down before I let it touch you*, and that's too much for a weeknight.

We walk back to the spiral, to the landing where we pretend good night is easy. She catches my hand on the rail, presses a kiss to the knuckles—light, devastating—and says, "Go home before our reckless seconds turn into days."

I go. Barely.

I wake at 5:12 a.m. to rain interrogating the roof. The storm arrived early, slanting in off the bay with opinions. The rehab band hangs off the chair's arm where I left it. I loop it around a porch post and start the routine Marcus wants. Rotations. Holds. Slow burn. I count breaths, not reps, because I am training a different muscle too—the one that chooses patience when my whole history begs for a sprint.

By eight, I'm soaked and happy and on my way to the shop with two coffees and a crooked grin. She opens at the exact second I knock, like a magnet and steel. We spend the morning making the kind of weather people could live inside: story hour at ten (the otter is a diva and demands grapes), a line of tiny raincoats, one dad who cries at the last page and pretends it's dust. Between the chaos, we exchange small looks that carry the weight of last night's seven seconds. I'm no good at hiding. She's getting worse at it, too.

At noon, a text from Marcus.

Marcus: Doc wants velocity video.
Tomorrow by 3.

I SHOOT HIM A THUMBS-UP AND A THIRTY-SECOND CLIP OF a clean throw into the net on the side lot. The shoulder sings on the follow-through, not pain, not warning—just the memory of how good it can be. I send it and picture the doc nodding in a room full of slow computers.

At two, the storm flexes. Wind shouldering the door. Windows rattling like a choir. Bailey looks up, and I'm already at the back entrance, checking the latch we fixed and verifying that the shim held.

"You okay?" I ask.

"I like thunderstorms," she says bravely. "But they can still scare me."

She then adds, "Stay until it passes?"

"You couldn't move me with a forklift."

We light candles even though the lights haven't flickered yet. We make cocoa. She puts on a record with crackles that sound like a campfire. We talk about nothing that matters and everything that does: the first book that broke us open, the first coach who yelled in a way that made us smaller, the places our parents got it right, and the things we forgive because it makes room for peace. My knee ends up against hers. She draws absent circles on my shin with her socked toe and doesn't seem to know she's doing it. I file the moment under *reasons I don't care if the stadium forgets my name*.

The power flickers twice and holds. The storm swears and moves north like it lost interest in us. We stand at the window and watch the bay calm down, the surface smoothing its dress like it's about to go somewhere fancy and lie about what it did all afternoon.

The door opens then without the bell—Rowan, dripping, grinning, carrying two boxes over his head. "Rescue drop," he declares. "Mom sent soup. I brought scones. Also news. The *Chronicle* wants a quote about 'the quarterback's community outreach of literacy excellence,' and I hate that sentence so much I came in person."

Bailey blinks. "You walked here in that?"

"Heroically," he says. "Give me a towel and deny me nothing."

We feed him, mock him, compose a fake quote that is 100 percent just adjectives, then delete it because our mothers raised us better. He leaves trailing puddles and goodwill.

When the door shuts, the shop moans. Bailey leans on the counter, tucking a loose strand of hair behind her ear. "I used to think storms were interruptions," she says softly. "This one feels like permission."

"Permission for what?"

"To stop bracing," she says. "To choose."

I don't touch her. I don't speak. I let her choose.

Her hands find my face, my jaw, my mouth, and the beam sweeps, and the record crackles, and if patience is a holy language, then we're fluent enough to invent our own dialect. We keep the number. We break it and reset it. We stop while we both still can and call it a win that feels cruel and exactly right.

Bailey's hands linger at my jaw for a second longer, like they didn't get the memo. Her thumb traces the corner of my mouth before it falls away, and I swear the record skips just from the shock of losing her touch.

The lighthouse beam sweeps across the front windows

again, pale and slow, and the whole shop exhales like it's been watching us.

"I should..." She clears her throat and straightens, palms smoothing down the front of her sweater. "Um. Check the windows one more time. Make sure we don't wake up to a saltwater aquarium in the reading nook."

Her voice shakes on the joke.

"Yeah," I say, even though I don't move. "Good plan."

We orbit each other for a minute, both pretending to care about anything that isn't the fact that we just stopped before we both did something we wouldn't be able to walk back from.

She goes to the big front windows, testing the latch with deft fingers. I go to the back door, check the deadbolt, and flip the sign even though we locked up twenty minutes ago.

The storm pelts the glass, wind howling down the alley like it's trying out for the ghost tour. Thunder rumbles low, close enough to vibrate the framed prints on the wall.

When I turn back, she's standing in the middle of the shop, arms wrapped around herself, staring at the ceiling like it might have answers hidden between the beams.

"You okay?" I ask quietly.

Her eyes flick to mine. "I keep thinking about the power going out," she says. "And how the emergency lights don't always kick back on. And then it's just me, alone with the ghosts and the romance section."

"You're not alone," I say, before I can swallow it back.

The words hang there. Bigger than I meant them to be.

Her mouth tips up on one side. "Right now, I'm not."

Something in my chest knocks hard against my ribs. "How bad is it supposed to get?" I ask, nodding toward the storm.

She blows out a breath. "Worse before it gets better. The weather alert said the bridge might close if the wind gusts stay this high. I was going to sleep upstairs." She nods toward the stairwell that leads to her little loft apartment over the shop. "Figured I'd beat the rush on the highway and avoid hydroplaning into the bay."

I picture her small space upstairs—books stacked three deep on every surface, that tiny kitchenette, the lumpy couch she swears is "perfectly fine." I picture her up there alone while the wind shakes the glass and the whole building hums.

I don't like it.

"You sure you're okay up there by yourself?" I ask, trying to sound casual and failing miserably.

Her gaze flicks to my mouth, then to my hands, then back up. "You offering to tuck me in, Wright?"

My brain shorts out for a second. "I—no. I mean, yes. Not like that. Unless you... I just meant—"

Her laugh is soft, tired, fond. "I know what you meant."

The record on the turntable reaches the end and clicks, the needle bumping lightly in the groove. She doesn't move to fix it, and neither do I. The silence feels louder as the storm rages outside.

"Stay," she says suddenly.

I blink. "Here?"

"No, at the gas station," she says dryly, then softens.

"Yes, here. The couch pulls out." She tilts her head toward the stairs again. "You shouldn't drive in this. And I... would feel better knowing I'm not the only one listening to the pipes rattle and wondering if the roof is going to peel off."

"Bailey—"

"Just stay," she says, voice quieter now, the joke falling away. "It doesn't have to mean anything we're not ready for it to mean."

I could make a stupid joke. I could say something about needing to check on the horses at the farm, throw up a shield of responsibility. That's what I've been doing for years—hiding behind duty, behind schedules, behind reasons.

But I remember her fingers on my jaw, the way she said permission to choose.

And how good it felt to let her.

"Okay," I say. "I'll stay."

Relief washes over her face so naked and bright that it hits me in the throat.

"Okay," she echoes, more to herself than to me. "I'll, um... make tea."

We climb the narrow staircase one in front of the other, her hand on the railing, my hand hovering just behind her in case she slips. The building creaks as the wind shoves against it, and my heart is pounding harder than it did in the fourth quarter of any playoff game I've ever played.

At the top of the stairs, she turns left into her loft. I've been up here a couple of times—once to carry up a box of used books some tourist donated, once when the sink backed up, and she called me instead of a plumber, like I know anything more than "turn it off and back on again."

It's exactly the way I remember: cozy, cluttered, more Bailey than any place on earth.

Mismatched mugs hang on hooks in the tiny kitchen. A string of fairy lights zigzags across the ceiling, casting a warm glow that softens the hard edges of the storm outside. There's a stack of books on the coffee table, another on the floor, and another serving as a plant stand.

She kicks off her shoes by the door, dropping her keys in a ceramic bowl shaped like an open book. "Make yourself at home," she says, moving toward the kitchenette. "Tea? Coffee? I also have hot chocolate if you want to embrace your inner child."

"Hot chocolate sounds good," I say, shrugging out of my jacket. My shirt clings to my back, dampened by the humidity and my nerves.

She pulls a tin of cocoa mix from the cabinet, moving around the little kitchen like she's done this a thousand times alone. I lean against the back of the couch, watching her putter, feeling weirdly dangerous and domesticated at the same time.

The kettle whistles after a minute, and she pours the water, stirring carefully. The scent of chocolate and vanilla fills the space, fuzzy and nostalgic.

She brings me a mug, fingers brushing mine as she hands it over. The contact is small. It still feels like a spark traveling the length of my arm.

"Thanks," I say, more gruffly than I mean to.

She curls onto the far end of the couch, tucking her legs under her, mug cradled between both hands. I take the other end, leaving a respectable gulf of cushion between us, like we didn't almost forget our own names downstairs ten minutes ago.

Rain batters the windows. The lighthouse beam sweeps across the glass, painting the room in pale arcs of light every thirty seconds. The storm is louder up here, somehow, closer.

"It's kind of nice," she says after a sip, eyes on the window. "Being forced to stop. The whole town will be tucked up in their houses, reading and baking and pretending they're not stalking the community Facebook page for drama."

I huff a laugh. "Yeah. Mrs. Delaney's probably already posted three blurry photos of the clouds with captions like 'Be safe, y'all' with seventeen exclamation points."

"Don't forget the weather app screenshots," Bailey adds, smiling into her mug. "With the arrows and circles drawn on like she's a meteorologist."

I watch her smile, the way it softens the tension around her eyes. God, I've missed this. Missed her. Not just the way she kisses or the way her hands tremble when she's nervous, but the way she turns everything into a story, even a storm.

"You okay?" she asks suddenly, turning that gaze on me. "You're awfully quiet for a guy who usually has an opinion about every play on the field."

I roll the mug between my palms. "Just... thinking."

"Dangerous," she teases, but her voice is gentle. "About what?"

You. Us. How I spent years pretending this didn't matter as much as it does.

"About earlier," I admit. "Downstairs. About how hard it was to stop."

Color rises in her cheeks, but she doesn't look away. "Hard for you, too?" she asks, and there's a hint of vulnerability in the question that makes my chest ache.

"Bailey," I say quietly. "You have no idea."

Her throat bobs as she swallows. "I do," she says. "Trust me, I do."

Silence falls again, heavier but not uncomfortable. The kind of quiet that has a pulse.

"I meant what I said," I tell her. "About wanting to go slow. Wanting to do this right."

"I know," she says. "And I meant what I said. About not bracing anymore."

Her fingers tighten on the mug. She sets it down carefully on the coffee table, then mirrors the motion with my cup, taking it from my hands and placing it beside hers.

Her knee brushes my thigh as she shifts closer. "Can I sit here?" she asks, even though she already is.

"Yeah," I say, my voice low. "You can sit wherever you want."

She moves into the space between us, thigh pressing fully against mine now. The warmth of her seeps through denim and muscle, straight into bone.

"I don't want to rush it," she says, eyes searching mine. "But I also don't want to pretend I don't want you."

My breath leaves in a rush. "Then don't."

Her hand finds my wrist, fingers sliding down to my palm like she's tracing all the times we almost held hands and didn't. She laces our fingers together, squeezing gently.

The storm rattles the windows. The lighthouse beam sweeps. Somewhere in town, a transformer pops, and the lights flicker once.

We don't move.

"I'm scared," she says suddenly, voice barely above a whisper.

I squeeze her hand. "Of what?"

She takes a shaky breath. "Of losing you again. Of... getting this wrong. Of giving you all my pages and finding out you only wanted the highlight reel."

I swallow hard. "Bailey," I say, my voice rough. "I've already seen the messy chapters. I was there for some of them, remember?"

Her laugh is watery. "You caused a couple."

"Yeah." The word tastes like regret and hope. "And I've spent a long time trying to figure out how to be worthy of a second read."

She stares at me for a long moment, like she's weighing something big and breakable in her hands.

Then she shifts closer, swinging a leg over my lap in one smooth, hesitant motion, settling down so she's straddling me.

My hands fly to her hips on instinct, fingers flexing against the denim. My brain short-circuits.

"Bailey," I rasp.

"I'm choosing," she says, eyes steady on mine. "I get to do that, remember?"

"Yeah," I manage. "You do."

She cups my face again, thumbs brushing my cheekbones. "Then let me."

Her mouth finds mine, slow and deliberate, and this time there's no tentative edge. No testing. Just the quiet, fierce certainty of a decision made and remade.

I kiss her back, pouring all the words I don't trust myself to say into the press of my lips, the angle of my jaw, the way my hands tighten on her waist like she's the only solid thing in a world that keeps shifting.

Her fingers slide into my hair, tugging gently, and a sound escapes my chest I wouldn't recognize on a replay. She swallows it with a soft, desperate noise of her own.

The storm rages outside. Up here, the world narrows to the couch, the heat of her thighs bracketing my hips, and the taste of chocolate and peppermint on her tongue.

She breaks the kiss first, breathing hard, forehead resting against mine. "Crew," she whispers. "I want—"

She doesn't finish, but I know. I know because it's the same want that's been sitting in my chest like a live wire every time I've looked at her for years.

My pulse pounds in my ears. "If we go there," I say hoarsely, "I'm not going to be able to... pretend this is casual. That it's just a storm thing."

"I don't want casual," she says immediately. "If I wanted casual, I'd be at the bar making bad decisions with tourists who mispronounce 'Coral Bell Cove.'"

"Fair." My smile is thin, shaky. "You deserve better than my version of bad decisions anyway."

Her hands slide down my neck to my shoulders, fingers splaying over my chest like she's memorizing the shape of me. "I deserve someone who shows up," she says. "Who doesn't run the second things get messy. Who lets me be messy."

"I'm right here," I say.

"Are you?" she whispers.

The question lodges under my ribs.

I think about all the times I pulled back. The times I let fear and loyalty to other people dictate the way I treated her. The way I treated myself.

I take a breath deep enough to hurt. "Yeah," I say. "I am. I'm scared as hell, but I'm here. And I'm not going anywhere unless you tell me to."

Something fractures in her expression—something brittle and old. Her eyes shine.

"Okay," she says, voice thick. "Then stay."

Chapter Seventeen

CREW

Bailey's mouth finds mine again, softer this time, like a promise instead of a challenge. I kiss her back, my hands sliding up her spine, feeling each notch and curve through the fabric, mapping her like a route home.

She shifts in my lap, and I suck in a sharp breath. Her smile turns a little wicked, a little shy. "Still sure you want to take it slow, Wright?"

I let out a strangled laugh. "Define 'slow'."

She leans in, lips brushing my ear. "We've been slow for years."

The truth of that rolls through me, heavy and undeniable.

I turn my head, nuzzling into the curve of her neck, breathing her in. Vanilla and paper and something uniquely Bailey.

"Okay," I murmur against her skin. "Then maybe tonight we can... speed up a little."

Her breath stutters. "Good," she whispers. "Because if I have to stare at your mouth for one more second and not taste you, I might actually combust."

"I'm a professional," I say, voice rough. "I can handle a little heat."

She snorts, then dissolves into a gasp as I trail slow, reverent kisses along the line of her jaw.

Her hands fist in the back of my shirt. She rocks against me, and every nerve ending I have lights up.

I pull back just enough to look at her. "Bailey, tell me what you want."

Her eyes hold mine, steady and sure, even as her cheeks flush. "I want you," she says. "All of you. No half-measures. No pretending we're not already in this up to our eyeballs."

My throat goes tight. "Okay."

I stand, hands firm on her hips, lifting her with me like she weighs nothing. She lets out a surprised laugh and wraps her legs around my waist, arms looping around my shoulders.

"You could've just asked me to move," she says, breathless.

"Where's the fun in that?" I murmur, pressing a quick kiss to her cheek.

She laughs again, the sound bright and disbelieving, like she can't quite believe this is happening. Like I can't either.

The fairy lights cast soft, warm halos on the walls as I carry her the few steps toward the bedroom alcove. It's more of a nook than a room—a double bed pushed against the far wall, a quilt in muted blues and greens, a stack of books on the nightstand threatening to avalanche.

I pause at the threshold, heartbeat loud in my ears. "Last chance to kick me back to the couch," I say, voice low. "Tell me to stop, and I'll sleep out there, no questions asked."

She cups my face again, thumb brushing the faint line of a scar at my chin from a tackle gone wrong years ago. "I'm not going to change my mind in the next five steps," she says softly. "If I do, I'll tell you. I promise."

"Okay," I whisper. "Okay."

"Tell me if you want me to stop," I add as I reach forward and unsnap the button on her pants. The zipper quickly followed, its clicking noise meshing with our heavy breaths.

I watch the goose bumps grow on her arms as I kneel and slip her legs free of the pants. I smirk at her sudden gasp as I lean forward, grabbing the globes of her ass in each of my large palms, and press my lips against her thighs.

My hands trail higher as I stand, taking in every inch of her soft skin, as they grip the hem of her shirt and lift it over her head.

"Your turn," Bailey mumbles as she reaches for the hook of her bra.

I waste no time ripping my shirt over my head and sliding my pants down my legs, shucking them somewhere in the room.

"You're like...perfect. It's really not fair."

"You know what else isn't fair?" I ask as she slips out of

her panties. I reach my arm around her waist and tug her naked body against mine. "Having you here like this and having to practice some sort of self-control."

"Maybe you could lose it, just for a little bit," she whispers as her small hand wraps around my cock.

By the time we hit the mattress, the storm has become a dull roar in the background, like the ocean is trying to climb the cliffs and eavesdrop.

Bailey lies beneath me, hair fanned out on the pillow like spilled ink, eyes wide and dark and so damn open it makes my chest ache.

"Hey," I murmur, brushing a thumb over her cheekbone.

"Hey," she echoes, a tiny smile curving her lips. "You okay?"

"Pretty sure I'm better than okay," I say. "But, you know, jury's still out until the fourth quarter."

She snorts. "Are you really making sports metaphors right now?"

"It's how I cope with nerves," I confess.

"You're nervous?" Her brows lift in soft surprise.

"I'm about to sleep with the girl I've been in love with since she spilled coffee all over my playbook in high school," I say bluntly. "Yeah, I'm nervous."

Something in her gaze softens, melts. "You were in love with me?" she whispers.

"Past tense?" I counter.

Her breath catches. "Crew..."

"I was an idiot," I go on because if I stop now, I might

not start again. "I had no idea what to do with it. I didn't want to screw up your life, or mine, or my brother's, or—"

She presses a finger gently to my lips. "Hey," she murmurs. "We can unpack the tragedy of our teenage communication skills later, okay? Right now, I just... I want to be here. With you. All the way here."

My chest feels too small for my heart. I turn my head, kissing her fingertip. "All right," I say, the word a promise.

Her hands slide up my arms, over my shoulders, grounding me. "Stay with me," she whispers. "In your head. Don't go replay old tapes while you're touching me."

"I won't," I say. "I'm right here."

Bailey wiggles closer and presses her mouth against mine again, only this time she slips her tongue between my lips. She groans as I shift my hips against her stomach. My hands grip her ass, my fingers digging into the flesh, as she continues to explore my mouth. I rock against her twice, then use more strength than I could ever muster to pull myself back.

She makes her way down my body until her face aligns with my cock. Her tongue reaches out tentatively and licks the head of my dick. My hands fist the quilt on her bed as it takes all my willpower not to grip her hair and fuck her mouth.

Bailey must sense my need as she uses one hand to grip the base of my cock and uses her lips and tongue to make wet paths along the shaft. She watches me as her lips open toward my tip. My cock is barely going to fit, but I don't give a damn. I want to claim her mouth.

"Open your mouth wider, sweetheart."

She not only widens her mouth just a bit, but her pale thighs part just enough for her to slip her free hand between her legs.

"Ah, fuck. That's it. Touch yourself. Make yourself feel good."

Her whimpers of pleasure synchronize with my moans as my dick reaches the back of her throat. From the corner of my eye, I watch her hand move in quick circles as she rubs her clit.

When my balls tighten up, that little vixen uses her free hand to cup them, squeezing just enough to sting.

"Coming!" I growled before I could release myself into her mouth. But Bailey surprises me as she swallows every ounce that lands in her mouth. There's a small dribble that she swipes with her tongue, sighing as she does.

Bailey sits back on her heels, her clit-rubbing hand now resting gently on her thigh. Her lips are red and well used, and she smiles, pleased with herself.

Sitting up, I grip her ass, lifting her into the air and against me. God, she's so fucking small. Her legs immediately wrap around my waist. The heat of her exposed pussy enfolds around my cock. Even though it'd been thoroughly used, it jerks to life.

I ignore my erection for a moment, kissing Bailey instead. I'm growing addicted to her mouth. I'm hooked on her tongue and the way it dances against mine. It's simply the way she fits against me. I'm absolutely certain that when I slide my cock into her tight channel, I'm going to be addicted to her pussy.

"Take what you want. Ride my cock."

Twice, the tip of my cock almost slides inside her tight sheath, and I know we'd regret it in the morning if I let us keep going without protection.

"Condom?" I ask through gritted teeth, though I can't help imagining what it would be like to feel her without anything between us. But neither of us is ready for that level of commitment yet.

"What?" Bailey questions as if entranced by her own pleasure.

"Condom? Do we need one?"

"I... um..." She licks her lips, lids heavy with lust.

"Let me take care of this, sweetheart."

She groans as I lift her off my lap and set her on the bed next to me. I look around the room to find my pants and quickly make my way to the material, grabbing my wallet where I'd stashed a couple of condoms for emergencies. Glancing at the expiration, I sigh, realizing it's a week away, then tear the foil with my teeth. My cock is overly sensitive as I slide the latex down my erection. As much as I want to watch Bailey bounce up and down on my dick, I'm not sure I can withstand it at the moment. I'm likely to blow my second round too soon as it is.

"Lie back, beautiful," I tell her as I move to the bed and lie on my side. Everything before had been hot and heavy, but I want to remember this moment with her.

I reach out to stroke Bailey's hair, tucking the wild wisps

away from her face. She's relaxed, and her eyes blink slowly as she turns her face toward me.

"Crew?"

"Hmm?"

"I'd really like you to fuck me now."

Smirking, I move between her legs, keeping my cock just a few inches from her sex. My hands are on either side of her head as I hold my body above hers.

"Are you sure?" I ask her, rocking my hips forward, sliding my erection against her pussy.

"One-hundred thousand percent."

"How does my girl want it?" I ask as I shift my weight onto my good arm. My eager hand craves the feel of the heat pulsating between her legs. She writhes under my touch.

"I just want to feel you," she groans, and her legs try to pull me tight against her body. "I need to feel you."

Removing my hand from her cunt, I grab my pulsating cock and guide it toward her entrance, slapping the top of her mound covered in trimmed dark brown hair before gliding downward through the folds. Even with the condom, I can feel her heat radiating around my tip.

Aligning the head at her entrance, I slowly guide my erection deeper inside her pussy. The walls tense around me like a fist, and it takes everything in me to keep from plunging to the hilt to feel her clutch me completely.

Sweat begins to bead along my hairline as I pause, waiting for her tightness to adjust to my cock's size. Bailey's eyes pinch closed, and for a second, I worry I've hurt her. I begin to pull back, but then I feel her hand on my ass, her fingers clutching the muscle.

"Don't stop. Please."

"Are you sure?" I ask through clenched teeth.

She practically growls without saying a word, her eyes popping open in rage.

I rock into her as deep as she can take me. I'm only able to fit a little more than half of my shaft inside her before her body stops me. She's so petite that I'm afraid of hurting her by going any farther.

Pulling back out fully, I then slide my cock inside her sheath again, blessedly aware of how her walls grip me. Grabbing the back of her right leg, I hitch her knee closer to her chest, plunging into her again.

"Yes," she purrs, her back arching at the same time.

Beneath my hand, her leg starts to quiver after a few more thrusts.

"Tell me what you want," I say, my breath exhaling in quick pants.

"Faster. Touch my clit," she wheezes as her other leg wraps around my waist, digging her heel into my ass.

Reaching up, I grasp the pillow positioned against the headboard and shove it under her hips. With the lift of her ass, my cock slips deeper into her pussy.

"Yes! Oh my God!"

Leaning forward as I continue to thrust my aching erection in and out of her sex, I brush my lips against her mouth. "Crew. Not God. And you'll call out my name when I make you come." I slip my hand between our bodies, my fingers skimming her tight bundle of nerves as I rest my forehead against hers. "Fuck, I'm close."

"Me too," she whimpers, her hips rocking in time against my hand as she climbs toward her release.

I feel her walls quaking as my dick rubs that special spot inside her sex. When she comes screaming my name, Bailey's nails clench my back, digging into my skin as she holds on while riding out her orgasm. The moment her tight walls squeeze my cock like a clenched fist, I pour myself into the condom.

My body jerks from the exertion, and I try my best to move off Bailey, but she surprises me when she wraps her arms around my neck and holds me close while dropping her legs on either side of my hips.

The room is quiet except for our ragged breathing and the soft percussion of rain against the windows.

The lamp light flickers from her nightstand and blurs at the edges of my vision. My pulse is finally beginning to come down from "overtime" levels. Bailey is sprawled half on top of me, her cheek pressed against my chest, one leg thrown over mine like she's staking a claim.

My hand moves lazily up and down her spine, tracing the little bumps I learned by heart tonight.

She hums, the sound low and content, vibrating against my ribs. "That," she murmurs, "was... not casual."

I huff out a laugh that feels suspiciously like a choked sob. "No," I agree. "That was pretty much the opposite of casual."

She tilts her head back to look at me, hair mussed, lips a

little swollen, eyes soft and still somehow sharp enough to see straight through me.

"You okay in there?" she asks, tapping lightly over my heart.

"I think my brain is still trying to reboot," I admit. "It might be stuck on the loading screen where you—"

She slaps a hand over my mouth, laughing. "Do not narrate it," she says, cheeks flushing. "We both know what happened. My nervous system is still processing it in 4K."

I grin against her palm, then kiss the heel of her hand. "Fine," I say. "I'll keep the play-by-play internal."

"Thank you," she says primly, settling back down with a sigh. "Although, for the record, if this were a game, I'd say we both put some impressive numbers on the board."

"Are we really turning this into a stats review?" I ask, amused.

"Sorry," she says. "I cope with vulnerability by making jokes. It's very mature of me."

I tighten my arm around her, anchoring us both. "It's my favorite thing about you," I say quietly. "Well. One of them."

She goes still. "You have a list?"

"Of favorite things?" I chuckle. "Yeah, Bailey. I'm not exactly subtle."

"List them," she says.

"Now?"

"Yes, now. You can't just casually mention you have a list and then not share. That's illegal."

"Pretty sure it's not," I start, then trail off when she

gives me the look. The one that used to undo me in high school and apparently still does. "Fine," I say, dragging my hand slowly up and down her back in thought. "Your laugh. The way you snort when something actually gets you."

She groans. "Oh my God, start with something flattering."

"It is flattering," I protest. "It means you're not faking it."

She pokes my side. "Next."

"The way you talk about books like they're people," I say, more serious now. "Like they have feelings you're worried about hurting."

Her expression softens. "That's just... basic empathy."

"Maybe," I say. "But I like it. I like that you get defensive on behalf of fictional characters."

She makes a thoughtful noise. "Okay, I'll allow that one."

"I like that you can't stand when people dog-ear pages, but you'll write in your own books like you're having a conversation with them," I say. "And how you always pretend you don't care about the tourists' opinions, but you light up when they come back from vacation and tell you your recs made their trip."

She buries her face in my chest. "Stop, I'm actually going to cry."

"I like that you care enough to cry," I say, dropping a kiss on the top of her head. "That you didn't harden up just because life gave you reasons to."

Her shoulders shake slightly under my hand. "Crew," she whispers.

"And I like that you invited me to stay tonight," I add. "That you chose me."

She lifts her head again, tears bright in her eyes, but there's a stubborn tilt to her chin. "I'll probably need reminders that I'm allowed to keep choosing you," she warns. "Years of training myself not to... it doesn't undo overnight."

"I have nothing but time," I say. "I can run the drills with you as long as it takes."

She laughs wetly. "Of course, you turned it back into sports."

"It's my thing," I say. "You're stuck with a guy whose whole personality is metaphors about fourth quarters and overtime."

She studies me for a long moment, then reaches up and brushes her fingers along my jaw. "There are worse fates," she says softly. "I've read about all of them."

I thread our fingers together over my chest. The simple weight of her hand in mine feels more intimate in some ways than anything we did a few minutes ago.

Outside, a particularly strong gust hits the building, making the windows rattle and the bed frame creak.

Bailey tenses instinctively. I tighten my hold on her.

"Hey," I murmur. "I've got you."

"I know," she says after a beat, relaxing again by degrees. "My logical brain knows the shop has survived storms way worse than this. My anxiety brain, however, is convinced we're about to be airlifted into Oz."

"If we wake up in Oz," I say, "you're in charge of directions. I'll just follow you around and pretend I know what's going on."

"Good," she says. "Because I'm not giving you control of the yellow brick road after you tried to shortcut the scenic route tonight."

I raise a brow. "Shortcut?"

She smirks. "You were ready to sprint for the end zone, Wright. Don't pretend otherwise."

"I was ready to respond to the play you were calling," I correct, tapping her nose lightly. "You moved first."

She flushes, but there's pride in it. "Yeah," she says. "I did."

The quiet that settles after that feels different. Not heavy, exactly. Full.

"What happens now?" I ask before I can talk myself out of it.

Her brows knit. "You mean, like, immediately? Because immediately, I'm thinking we should probably drink some water and maybe stretch, because I am not twenty-two anymore and my hamstrings are—"

"Not what I meant," I cut in, laughing. "I mean... with us. Tomorrow. The next day. When the storm's over, and the town goes back to gossiping about bake sales and who's repainting their porch."

"Oh." She drops her gaze to our joined hands, thumb

rubbing slow circles over my knuckles. "I don't know," she admits. "I know what I want, though."

My heart climbs into my throat. "What do you want?"

She lifts her eyes again, and there's no hesitation there now. "I want you," she says simply. "In my life. For real. Not just as the guy I almost dated once upon a time. Not just as the brother of my friend. Not just as the football star who blew back into town with a bum knee and a hero complex."

"Hey," I protest. "My knee is very sensitive about that description."

She smiles, then sobers. "I want you as my partner," she says. "My person. The one I call when the roof leaks or the car won't start or a book breaks my heart. The one whose hand I reach for first when something good happens, or something terrible."

The room tilts for a second. "Bailey," I manage. "You're going to give me a heart attack before I even get to play another season."

Her face falls a fraction. "Too much?"

"No," I say quickly. "Not even close. I just... I didn't want to push you into something you weren't ready for."

"I've been ready for a long time," she murmurs. "I've just been scared. And tired. And busy convincing myself that wanting you was the same thing as asking for drama."

"And now?" I ask.

"Now I'm tired of being tired," she says, eyes fierce. "I'm tired of putting myself last. I'm tired of deciding for other people whether or not I'm worth the trouble. If you think I am, then... I want to try. Really try."

I swallow hard. "Okay," I say, the word rough. "Then we try."

She searches my face. "You're sure? This isn't just storm brain talking?"

"Look at me," I say.

She does.

"You think one night is enough to flip some switch I haven't been able to shut off for years?" I ask quietly. "I don't suddenly love you because we slept together, Bailey. I already did. This just... finally matches the reality to the feeling."

Her inhale is sharp, shaky. "You love me," she repeats, like she's testing the words for cracks.

"I do," I say. "I'm not expecting you to chuck confetti and say it back right now. You can take your time. But I need you to know I'm not in this halfway."

She stares at me, eyes swimming, chest rising and falling quickly. For a second, I think I've gone too far.

Then she whispers, "I love you, too."

It lands like a hit and a healing all at once.

I close my eyes for a second, letting it wash over me. When I open them again, she's still there, still watching me like she's not sure if she's just broken something or fixed it.

"Okay," I say, a little breathless. "That was faster than I expected."

She laughs, tears spilling over now. "I've been—" Her voice cracks. She tries again. "I've been saying it in my head for months, Crew. Years, probably, if we're being honest. I just didn't trust my mouth not to... ruin everything."

I pull her up, cradle her face in both hands, and kiss her, slow and deep and as gentle as I can make it.

When we break apart, we're both breathing hard again, but this time the urgency feels less like hunger and more like relief.

"We're a mess," I murmur.

"Speak for yourself," she says, wiping her cheeks with the back of her hand and sniffing. "I am a very put-together independent business owner who just happens to be naked in a storm with her ex-almost-boyfriend who is now apparently her actual boyfriend."

"Is that what I am?" I ask, a stupid grin tugging at my mouth.

She pretends to think about it. "Hmm," she says. "Yeah. I think so."

"Good to know," I say. "I'll have new business cards printed."

She snorts. "Crew Wright: Professional Boyfriend. Rates negotiable."

"For you?" I murmur. "I work for bookstore credit."

Her eyes go soft again. "Dangerous offer," she whispers. "I could keep you forever that way."

"That's kind of the point," I say.

She burrows back against my chest, sighing. "Is it weird that I'm relieved we had The Talk after we had sex?" she asks, voice muffled. "Is that backward?"

"I don't think there's a right order," I say. "We've been doing everything out of order since we were sixteen."

"True," she says. "Might as well keep the theme going."

We lie there for a while, just breathing, the rhythm of her rising and falling chest syncing with my own.

Eventually, she mumbles, "If we fall asleep, you're not allowed to freak out in the morning and pretend this didn't happen."

"I won't," I say immediately.

"I'm serious," she says, poking my ribs lightly. "I've seen the movies. I've read the books. Guy panics, girl pretends she doesn't care, twelve chapters of avoidable angst."

"Are you really using romance tropes as a cautionary tale?" I ask, amused.

"Yes," she says. "This is my area of expertise."

"Okay, expert," I say. "What's the correct trope for tomorrow morning?"

She considers. "Soft morning after with shared toothbrush jokes, coffee, and maybe some slightly awkward but honest conversation," she decides. "Followed by a gentle re-entry into the world where we resist the urge to overshare with the entire town for at least forty-eight hours."

"So no posting a selfie with the caption 'Stormed his castle, 10/10 would recommend'?" I ask.

"Oh my God," she groans, laughing. "Absolutely not. If we're turning this into a public-relations rollout, it has to be a slow-burn reveal. Think strategically timed holding-hands moment at the farmers' market."

"I don't know if I can wait that long to hold your hand in public," I say.

She squeezes my fingers. "You don't have to wait in private," she whispers.

I tighten my grip. "Good. Because I'm not letting go anytime soon."

Another gust of wind rattles the window. The lights flicker, then stabilize.

Bailey yawns, her body relaxing more fully against mine. "If the power goes out," she mumbles, already half asleep, "you have to tell me a story."

"What kind of story?" I ask softly.

"One where we get a happy ending," she says, words slurring.

I press my lips to her hair. "Deal. Though I think we just wrote the first chapter."

She hums, a little pleased sound, and then her breathing evens out, slow and steady.

I lie there in the flickering light, listening to the storm rage and the woman I love sleep on my chest, and for the first time in a long time, I don't feel like I'm waiting for something to go wrong.

I feel like I'm exactly where I'm supposed to be.

The storm finally starts to ebb sometime in the deep hours, the rain easing from a furious drumline to a steady, sleepy patter. My eyes grow heavy, but I force myself to stay awake a little longer, just to memorize this.

Bailey. The way her hand twitches in her sleep, fingers still locked with mine. The quiet little puff of air every third breath. The warmth of her thigh over my hip like a seat belt.

Tomorrow, there will be questions. Siblings. Teammates. Small-town speculation. Logistics about my rehab schedule and her shop hours, about how we fit our lives together in ways that don't look like they do in the books on her shelves.

But tonight, there's just this.

Grabbing my phone, I do something I've been avoiding for the last few days—I write an email.

COACH—

Cleared throwing well. I'll be in on Monday. I also want to talk about role and pace. I'm not the kid I was. I can give you everything I have. It just might not look like what it used to. If that's a problem, tell me now so I don't sell you something I can't stand behind.

I READ IT TWICE, THREE TIMES, THEN HIT SEND BEFORE I let fear dress it in different words. I stare at the screen until the sent confirmation stops pulsing. Then I text Bailey.

Me: Sent Coach my thoughts.

SHE REPLIES WITH A PHOTO OF THE OTTER IN A triumphant pose.

Bailey: Proud of my quarterback.

I SAVE IT LIKE A TEENAGE IDIOT AND REFUSE TO BE ashamed.

I sleep hard. When dawn threads the blinds, I feel taller, like a bone set correctly overnight.

The next day is player logistics and adults using acronyms in emails. Before I take their requested video, I stop by the shop. Bailey presses a kiss to my cheek for luck and slips a note in my pocket I don't read until I'm back at the farm.

You don't have to become smaller to fit the life you want. I'll make more room. -B.

I throw the ball into the net and rush around trees as if they're offensive linemen, sending the video to the coaches, feeling like nothing more than a pawn.

My phone buzzes.

Coach: Let's talk Monday. Proud of you, kid.

I SMILE AND DON'T APOLOGIZE FOR HOW BIG IT IS.

When I head back to the lighthouse for the afternoon shift I pretended wasn't mine, the bay looks wide enough to hold both lives. Maybe it is. Maybe I'm the one who wasn't.

I park, jog up the path, and stop dead at the sight waiting at the gate: a news van at the curb. A guy with a camera on his shoulder. A woman with a mic adjusting her hair in the side mirror. My chest drops and then hardens. The email, the boundaries, the polite no—we did all of it. They came anyway.

Before the old panic can rehearse the old dance, Bailey steps out onto the porch, stance small but immovable, chin up. She sees me. Doesn't wave. Doesn't mouth a warning. Just looks at me like I already know how to walk through this with her.

I do.

I walk up the steps and take her hand like we always meant to do it in front of everybody. The reporter turns, smile bright and sharp. "Crew, Bailey—can we grab you for just a minute about the story hour?"

"No," I say, calm. "But you can email the team. They'll send a statement."

She tries again, a different angle. "Is this official? Are you two—"

"It's a bookstore," Bailey says, voice even. "And it's a school event. Please don't film the kids."

The camera guy drops the lens a fraction, human under the job. The reporter falters, then recalibrates. "We'd love a feel-good—"

"Then run something else, maybe the bookstore's fundraiser." I nod at the camera. "That'll do more good than our faces."

We wait. It's less a standoff than two people testing whether the other side recognizes the difference between a story and a life. The mic lowers an inch. The camera goes to standby. The reporter nods, one professional to another. "We'll email," she says. "Good luck with your return."

"Thanks," I say, meaning it.

They leave without footage. I can't make that happen most days in my world. Today we did. It feels like a new muscle firing.

On the porch, Bailey exhales so slow it's almost invisible. I squeeze her hand once and don't let go. "Reckless?" I ask, with a grin I can't stop from breaking the tension.

She shakes her head, laughing with her whole body. "You're unbelievable."

"Consistent," I say.

She steps in and puts her forehead to mine in a move that now lives rent-free under my sternum. "Tomorrow," she whispers our now inside joke, and we both know tomorrow is closer than it's ever been.

"Tomorrow," I answer, and for the first time in a long time, both halves of my life nod at the same time.

Chapter Eighteen

BAILEY

It's raining again.

Of course it is. Coral Bell Cove has two moods—*sunny gossip* and *melodramatic rainfall.* Today, it's both.

By noon, the storm moves off, leaving everything slick and shining—the kind of quiet after that feels like the world holding its breath. The clouds hang low and heavy over Coral Bell Cove, and the air smells like salt and rain and second chances.

Crew arrives in his typical fashion, this time with an entourage of teen boys following his every footstep. Thankfully, they scatter away when I flip the CLOSED sign on the bookstore and place my arms around Crew's waist, tilting my lips toward his in a kiss that I know will spread like wildfire through the neighborhood.

We walk down to the dock because the house feels too small for everything sitting between us. The boards are damp under my bare feet. The water laps soft and steady against the pilings, patient like it knows something we don't.

"Remember that fundraiser senior year?" I ask, toes curling over the edge of the dock.

Crew glances over, mouth twitching. "Which one?"

"The one where someone thought selling date bids was a good idea."

He groans. "Oh God. Don't remind me."

I laugh, full and bright, because for the first time in a long time, it doesn't hurt to remember. "You went for six hundred dollars."

"Because Jenny Decosta bid half of it to mess with Sawyer," he says.

"And then Tanner stole the card and—"

"—and read your note to the entire gym."

The laughter fades, leaving something quieter, heavier. The space between us fills with all the words we never said.

"You didn't defend me," I say finally. It comes out soft but steady.

He drags a hand through his hair, that same boyish gesture I've seen a hundred times. "I didn't know how."

"That's not an excuse."

"I know," he says, eyes on the horizon. "I was seventeen and stupid and terrified of looking like I cared more than I should've."

"And now?"

He meets my gaze then, something raw and real flickering there. "Now I'm older and still stupid. But I don't care who knows I care about you."

I swallow hard. The wind picks up, tugging at my hair, and when he reaches out to tuck a strand behind my ear, his thumb grazes my cheek. That small, familiar touch undoes me.

I lean in, just enough for him to close the distance.

The kiss is slow and certain, soft at first—an apology, a confession, a beginning. The taste of salt air and rain clings to his lips. His hand slides to the back of my neck, steady and warm, and my fingers bunch in the collar of his shirt, holding him there because I can't remember what it felt like not to.

The world narrows to breath and heartbeat and the quiet ache of finally.

When I pull back, I press my forehead to his. "You always did have terrible timing," I whisper, smiling even as my heart stumbles.

He laughs against my mouth. "Pretty sure this is the best timing I've ever had."

And for once, I believe him.

We head back to the bookstore, hands barely brushing against each other. The electricity sizzles and is ready to scorch us without a moment's notice.

We slip through the back door, directly into the kitchen, and before I can set my keys on the counter, Crew grabs my hand and tugs me against him. His lips immediately find the sensitive spot between my neck and shoulder.

"Crew," I moan as my body rocks back against the growing stiffness in his pants.

His hands come around my body, one wrapping around my waist while the other slips under my shirt, grasping one of my heavy breasts.

My keys drop to the floor, and I couldn't care less where they land.

"I need to have you, baby. I'm dying for you."

"Take what's yours."

A growl echoes in the small room, and in a flash, I find myself twisted around and his mouth crashing against mine.

Clothes come off with greedy hands until they're strewn across the room. Pants dangling from a cabinet pull, a shirt hanging halfway out of the sink. Utter chaos.

Crew backs up until he crashes into a chair. Instead of brushing it aside, he sits down, taking me with him. My legs straddle either side of his hips, positioning his cock right at my entrance. With barely the chance to take a breath, one of Crew's hands grips my hip while the other wraps around his shaft to guide himself inside my pussy.

"Oh..." I moan as my body adjusts to his size.

Crew's hand that was around his dick moves to caress my breast, urging me to move.

"That's it, sweetheart, take what you want. Make yourself feel good."

Just his voice does enough to make my body frantic for more. More friction. More kisses. More everything.

Barely able to touch the floor with more than the tips of

my toes, I rock against Crew, loving the way his hips move against my clit with each thrust.

Crew's hand fists in my hair, tilting my head back so his lips can assault my neck before he wraps his other arm completely around my waist, holding me still as he pistons his cock in and out of my sex.

My legs quake beneath me, so I know my orgasm is close.

"Crew."

"I know. I'm close, too. Let me feel you fall apart."

Somehow, his thrusts increase in speed until we're both plummeting over the edge toward our release.

"Fuck," Crew barks as he holds our sweaty bodies together. "You've ruined me, Bailey. Nothing compares to this."

Too exhausted to reply, I can't help but think to myself that he's absolutely right. Nothing will ever compare to being like this with Crew. I can only hope that my heart won't break if he decides to leave.

Chapter Nineteen

CREW

Sunlight crawls through the old lighthouse window, spilling across the bed in slow gold stripes. The air smells like salt and cinnamon and her. I don't move for a while. Bailey's head is on my shoulder, her hair a mess against my chest, her breathing steady. Every time she breathes, it feels like the world quiets a little.

This shouldn't feel like peace. I've spent my entire life in motion—stadiums, airports, cameras, noise. Peace was always the thing after a win, the silence that came too late. But this—her weight against me, the creak of the beams, the gulls outside losing their minds over breakfast—is something else.

She shifts, murmurs something half dreaming, and her leg slides over mine. My brain short-circuits. I stare at the ceiling, counting heartbeats. If I move, I'll wake her. If I don't, I might combust.

So I lie there and try to memorize it instead. The

freckles on her shoulder. The small scar near her elbow. The way her fingers twitch like she's always chasing something, even in sleep.

When her eyes finally blink open, she looks at me like she's surprised I'm still there.

"Morning," she whispers.

"Morning."

"You're staring."

"Trying to figure out how I'm supposed to leave this bed ever again."

Her soft laugh wrecks me. "You start by moving your legs."

"Not happening." I tighten my arm around her waist. "You're a hazard."

"Crew Wright, accused of being lazy in bed. Film at eleven."

I grin. "That'd be the first accurate headline they've written about me."

Her smile falters just slightly, and the reality rushes back in—the gossip, the cameras, the noise waiting beyond the bay. I reach up and brush my thumb across her cheek. "Hey. No one gets to ruin this. Not even them."

She nods, but her eyes say she's already building the walls again.

We end up in the kitchen anyway because the cat threatens mutiny if breakfast is late. She moves around the narrow space like she's dancing, barefoot and half awake, wearing my T-shirt that hangs low enough to make me forget what coffee is for.

"You're staring again," she says without looking up.

"Occupational hazard."

"You were a quarterback."

"Exactly. Reading the field."

She shakes her head and hides a smile behind her mug. "You're impossible."

"And you like it."

"Unfortunately."

I steal a piece of toast, and she smacks my hand. It feels normal, dangerously normal. And that's what scares me most—how easily I could stay.

Around midmorning, her phone dings. I know the sound of bad news before she even reads it.

"*The Gazette*," she says. "They want an interview. The lighthouse program."

"Or the quarterback sleeping in your bed."

"Probably both."

My jaw locks. I cross the room, take the phone gently from her hand, then set it face down on the counter. "You don't owe them anything."

"I owe the kids visibility for the reading fund."

"They'll twist it, B."

"I know."

Her shoulders sag, and I hate that I can't fix it. Football taught me to bulldoze problems. This isn't that. This is a woman trying to protect her quiet, and me being the noise she invited in.

"Let me handle it," I say.

She glances up. "And what—charm them into silence?"

"If that's what it takes."

"You can't fight every battle for me, Crew."

"Maybe not," I say, voice low. "But I can stand next to you while you fight."

Something flickers in her eyes—relief or love or both—and then she's moving, pressing her forehead against my chest. "You make it really hard to stay mad at you."

"That's the idea."

The rest of the day plays out like a movie that refuses to end. We fix the wobbly back bookshelf together. I hold the boards while she drills, pretending not to stare at the way her ponytail keeps slipping loose. We eat lunch on the porch steps, sharing one sandwich because she forgot to buy bread again. We argue about what counts as "classic literature." She claims *Pride and Prejudice* is superior. I counter with *Friday Night Lights*, and she throws a pickle at me.

The shop opens after lunch, and I stay because leaving feels wrong. I restock shelves, read to the kids, and let the town ladies corner me with questions about my "return to fame."

Bailey watches from behind the counter, pretending to check receipts, her eyes soft but uncertain. I know that look. It's the same one I used to give the scoreboard when time was running out.

When the last customer leaves, the quiet between us feels alive.

"Stop looking at me like that," she says.

"Like what?"

"Like you're about to say something reckless."

"I was," I admit. "But I'm saving it."

"For when?"

"For when you're ready to believe I mean it."

Her breath catches. "You're terrible at small talk."

"I'm really good at bad timing."

The predicted hurricane swells far off the coast, bringing with it a storm that rolls in just before closing. She locks the front door, and thunder hums through the floorboards. I'm standing too close, but she doesn't move away. The air shifts, dense and electric.

"You should probably head home before the road floods," she says.

"I'm already home."

She shakes her head, half smiling. "You're infuriating."

"Persistent," I correct, stepping closer. "Difference of semantics."

"Crew—"

"Bailey." I reach out, trace a line down her arm, and stop at her wrist. Her pulse jumps beneath my fingers. "Tell me to go."

She doesn't.

The lightning flashes once, and then we're kissing—slow, unhurried, inevitable. The kind of kiss that erases names and seasons and every bad decision that came before it.

When she pulls back, breathless, she whispers, "I don't want to complicate things for you."

"You simplify it," I say. "You. Me. That's it."

Her laugh is a broken sound. "You make it sound so easy."

"It could be."

She looks up at me, rain glinting on the glass behind her. "Then don't make me regret it."

I don't answer her with words.

I answer her with my hands—gentle at first, like I'm asking permission even though we're already past that point. My palms slide along her arms, memorizing the way she fits against me, the way her breath stutters when I pull her closer. There's nothing rushed about it. No urgency except the kind that's been building for far too long.

She presses her forehead to my chest, and for a second we just breathe together, the storm roaring outside, the lighthouse holding steady around us like it's done for a hundred years. When I tilt her chin up again, her eyes are dark, searching. Trusting.

"Tell me to stop," I murmur.

She shakes her head, fingers curling into the front of my shirt instead. "Don't."

That's all it takes.

We move together, not toward anything specific, just toward each other—backing into the room, hands exploring, mouths finding familiar places that suddenly feel new again. Every touch feels deliberate, like we're making a promise without saying it out loud. Her laugh dissolves into a soft sound against my neck, and I feel it everywhere, right down to my bones.

I guide her down, slow enough to let the moment

stretch, to let it mean something. She watches me the whole time, like she's afraid if she looks away, it'll vanish. I don't rush. I don't need to. The anticipation is its own kind of heat.

When I finally lower myself beside her, she reaches for me immediately, anchoring me there. As if I might disappear if she doesn't. I kiss her again—deeper this time, fuller—and everything else fades out. The storm. The future. The careful lines we've both been walking.

For a while, there's only this. Warmth and closeness and the quiet certainty of being exactly where we're supposed to be.

Later, the lighthouse smells like coffee and rain again. She's lying beside me, tracing idle shapes on my chest. I'm pretending not to count how many heartbeats until I have to tell her.

"I got a call," I finally say.

"From?"

"Nashville. Training camp wants me to check in next week."

Her hand stills.

"I don't even know if I'm ready," I say. "But I have to find out."

She nods, staring at the ceiling. "Of course."

"I'll come back."

"I know." Her voice is steady, but her eyes aren't. "You always do."

I reach for her hand, link our fingers. "I don't want this to feel like goodbye."

"Then don't make it one."

DAWN COMES TOO SOON. I PACK MY BAG WHILE SHE makes coffee, both of us pretending it's just another morning. She stands on the porch in my sweatshirt, hair in a braid, trying to look unshakable.

"I'll call," I promise.

"Drive safe," she says.

"Bailey."

She meets my eyes. There's so much in them—fear, pride, everything I've ever wanted.

"Come back to me," she says.

"I will."

I kiss her once more, taste salt and coffee and the kind of goodbye that doesn't end. Then I climb into the truck, start the engine, and watch her fade in the rearview mirror until she's just a shadow against the rising sun.

The road stretches ahead, slick and empty. My chest aches like a bruise I can't tape over. Somewhere behind me, the lighthouse beam cuts through the fog—steady, stubborn, waiting.

Chapter Twenty

CREW

The road to Nashville is a long breath you forget you were holding. Cornfields give way to billboards that promise you a new you if you just buy this, wear that, smile here. I keep the radio low—white-noise country about trucks that never break and women who always forgive—and let the miles stack like reps.

David calls somewhere past the state line. "Hotel's booked. Suit steamed. Lines in your inbox."

"I'm not reading lines."

"Then you'll wing it. You're charming when you're cornered."

"Not anymore."

Silence sharpens. "Don't get precious on me, Crew. We need this. Sponsors need to see you're pliable."

I stare at the dotted white line and consider a hundred answers that would end this quicker and messier. "Sponsors need to see I'm a person."

"You're a product," he snaps before he can make it sound like love. He swallows and tries again. "You're a person when we win. We do this right, everybody eats."

"Bailey isn't everybody."

"She's... a bookstore," he says, like the word can be filed under quaint. "She'll be fine."

"She's the point," I say, and hang up because growth is not letting a conversation finish carving you down to the old shape.

The next call is Laramie, my agent. "You going?"

"I am."

"Good. Eyes open. No closed-door signatures. Record with your memory. Don't give them a monologue. Make them interrupt themselves. They'll tell you everything they're afraid of if you let the silence stand."

"What do I do with the fear?"

"Whose? Theirs or yours?"

"Mine."

She chuckles. "Put it in your pocket and bring it home. I'll label it and file it with the rest."

"Copy."

"Crew?"

"Yeah."

"Proud of you for walking in and not out."

The words land where I keep the fourteen-year-old who thought respect only came after the hit. "Trying not to be benched by my own life."

"Attaboy."

I lose her to a dead zone, and for a few blessed miles, it's just me and the hum of decisions I haven't made yet.

Nashville looks like itself—glass and steel and murals and men with microphones. The facility looks like a spaceship wearing a varsity jacket. I park in the staff lot because old habits don't surrender easily, clip my visitor badge to my hoodie like I still belong, and walk in through the door where the custodians smoke on their break. They nod; I nod back. Tribe recognizes tribe.

The lobby smells like new rubber and old money. Screens loop footage of me and not-me: touchdowns, sidelines, a slow-motion smile someone once told me to save for fourth quarters and commercials. A receptionist with lashes for days gestures me toward Conference B. "They're ready for you."

They always are when there's something to take.

I pass the weight room—empty this time of day—and feel my body tilt toward it like muscle memory is magnetized. I pass the film room and catch my reflection in the dark screen: a man who learned to read defenses and is learning to read himself. I pass the hall of framed jerseys and stop at mine, the one from the season the city decided winning was everything. I touch the glass. It's colder than it looks.

"Crew." Harris's voice is the same it's always been—pleasant over a blade. He's at the end of the corridor, hands in his pockets like a reasonable man. David's next to him, smile pinned tight.

"Harris. David."

We shake hands because being a professional is a habit too.

"Appreciate you coming in," Harris says, pivoting into the conference room. It's gray and glass and very impressed with itself. A carafe of water sweats on a credenza. Three folders sit at my seat like decisions have already been made for me.

"We'll keep this quick," he says. "We know you've got... coastal engagements."

Land mines called books and porch lights. "Quick works," I say, and don't sit.

David clears his throat. "Sponsor slate is excited about your 'journey.' We just want to capture a little texture. Let folks see you're still *their* guy."

"I'm not," I say, and watch the sentence land like a fumble in a quiet stadium. "I'm Bailey's guy. This town's guy. My own, for once."

Harris's smile doesn't move. "We can hold both things."

"You tried," I say, nodding at the folders. "Which one's the 'I surrender my spine' packet, and which one's the 'I pretend to be contrite about fabricated clauses' packet?"

David goes pale. Harris's eyebrow does a trick it does when he's impressed and furious. "You've been talking to your agent."

"Like she's my friend," I say. "Because she is."

"Agents investigate," Harris says. "They don't advise."

"They do both when the people being investigated make it easy."

Harris steeples his fingers. "Let's start over. You're here

because we want to support your next chapter—mentor track, analyst deals, civic leadership. You get paid, we look smart, and the town gets its little lighthouse on a brochure with our logo somewhere tidy. Everyone wins."

The way he says *little lighthouse* makes something old and volatile light match after match along my spine. "No logos," I say.

"Don't be dramatic."

"She's not a backdrop."

"She?" he says lightly. "We're discussing property."

"Language tells on you."

"Language is what kept you employed," he says, smiling. "Also, talent. We haven't forgotten how much you gave us."

Gave. Past tense like a verdict. I steady myself on the back of the chair and decide not to throw it through a window. "I'm not taking the shoot. I'm not reading your lines. If you want to talk about my future like I'm in the room for it, we can. If you want me on a leash for the sake of optics, call a different dog."

David flinches. Harris folds his hands. "Poetry aside, we have obligations."

"So do I," I say. "To a place that keeps saving me in small ways. To a version of myself that's not always apologizing for existing."

Harris opens a folder and slides a document two inches forward. "This is called *mutual benefit,* Crew. Read the numbers before you light yourself on fire for a bookstore."

Harris's smile thins. "We control narrative when narrative threatens value. You've always known that. We tried to keep you on the field."

"By using her as leverage."

He tuts. "The world is leverage."

"Yet," I say softly, "the people who keep it turning are the ones who put their hands out and *pull,* not *push.*"

He watches me for a beat. "How long did it take you to rehearse that one?"

"Three months," I say. "Every night I watched her lock the door and leave the porch light on anyway."

David clears his throat, voice hoarse. "Just do the spot, Crew. We'll make the clause go away. We'll say it was… over-enthusiasm from legal. We'll drip a donation at Christmas. We'll—"

"—name a bench," I say, mouth bitter. "No."

Harris leans back. "Then here's *our* no: we suspend you. Administrative leave pending review. You don't talk about internal matters. You don't step in front of a microphone without a handler. If you do, we call it breach, and we call your sponsors, and we call your agent, and we call the station that thinks it wants you in a suit, and we remind them that live television prefers predictable men."

My heart does the thing it does left of panic and right of peace. "Predictable men don't come home."

"Some do," he says. "The smart ones."

"I'm not smart like that anymore."

"Be careful," David says quietly, and I hear the version of him that used to throw me passes and tell me to keep my chin tucked. "They're not bluffing."

"I'm not either."

Silence stretches like a new muscle. Harris breaks it. "You've got tonight to think. Tomorrow we announce one of two things: your future with us, or your departure. Make me proud and let me give you a hug for the cameras."

"Or?" I ask.

"Or I shake your hand like a man and release you with cause," he says, and the word cause sits on the table like a snake. "That's the path where you crawl under fences for the rest of your life."

I think about fences. About the way a little boy looks at you when you sign his library card and ask him what he loves to read. About the way Bailey moves through her own shop like the world is meant to be tended. About goats that need corralling and shelves that need leveling and a lantern that needs rope and patience. About the way my own breath sounds when I'm not performing it.

"I've done enough crawling," I say. "If you're going to call it cause, at least tell the truth about the cause. A man who stopped being your favorite story because he learned to read his own."

Harris's mouth twitches—approval he doesn't want. "Seven a.m.," he says, standing. "My office. Wear something fans can get behind."

"Jeans and stubbornness?" I ask.

"Those will do."

We don't shake hands. David follows me to the door and grabs my elbow before I'm out of polite distance. "You okay?"

"I will be."

"This is bigger than you, Crew."

I nod. "That's why I'm small on purpose."

He flinches like I hit him with a word.

The hotel room is beige and humming when I shut the door behind me. I don't turn on the lights. Nashville glows through the blackout curtains like the city is trying to apologize for being itself. I sit on the edge of the bed, pull the paper bag out of my duffel, and open Bailey's note.

You're allowed to want the quiet kind of win.
P.S. The cat is pretending to be impartial but he
slept on your pillow for three minutes and then
judged me for noticing.

I laugh. I cry. Both are small, and both are mine.

My phone buzzes.

Laramie: So?

Me: They want me pliable. I'm not. 7am. He'll try to hug me for a camera or gut me for a quote.

Laramie: Good. Don't sign. Don't smile. I'll be in the lot. Bring your spine.

Me: It's packed.

Laramie: Proud of you. Also, sleep.

I DROP THE PHONE, LIE DOWN ON THE BEDSPREAD THAT smells like bleach and a thousand men wondering who they are when they're not being clapped for. I close my eyes and try to hear the lighthouse beam even from here—the slow, stubborn sweep of home sounding out the dark.

Sleep comes in two-minute plays. Every time I wake, the room is the same, and I'm a little less afraid.

At 5:26, I give up pretending. I shower, dress in the jeans and stubbornness, and leave the tie on the dresser like a relic of a version of me I don't love anymore. The sun is bleeding into the edge of the city when I hit the sidewalk. I can almost taste salt that isn't here.

At 5:58, I step into the lobby.

At 5:59, I see them—Harris by the elevator, crisp as a threat; David beside him with a face that looks like it has said too many almost-apologies; a glass door that leads to a day that will try to make me invisible.

At 6:00, I square my shoulders and walk like gravity remembers who's in charge, and for once, it isn't the room.

And then—because the universe loves drama and I'm trying not to—my phone buzzes in my back pocket. I ignore it. It buzzes again. And again. The receptionist glances up. Harris's eyes sharpen. David checks his watch like time could be trained.

On instinct, I pull the phone out. One text. Unknown

number. A photo of the lantern room window shot from the bay at night, our silhouettes faint where brick meets glass.

Unknown: Beautiful view. would hate for anything to block it. 8 a.m. broadcast— don't be late.

I LOOK UP, AND HARRIS SMILES LIKE HE DIDN'T JUST TRY to set the sky on fire with a match he can't hold.

"Shall we?" he says.

I put the phone face down on the counter and tell my pulse to stop sprinting. If they want me afraid, they can watch me breathe instead.

"After you," I say, and walk toward the elevator like a man who finally learned you can be terrified and still refuse to run.

Chapter Twenty-One

BAILEY

The shop smells like paper and rain, the kind of scent that usually calms me, but today it feels like a weight pressing into my ribs. The storm outside finally broke overnight, and the lighthouse hums with it—low, constant, like a pulse I can't match.

I've already wiped down the counter twice, restacked the front display, and alphabetized the new shipment of romances that came in this morning. Normally, I'd lose myself in it—spines lined like soldiers, covers gleaming under the soft light—but every time I touch one, I think of his hands instead.

He texted last night before bed:

Crew: Made it to Nashville. Don't let Dean near the power tools.

. . .

I READ IT FIVE TIMES. TYPED A DOZEN REPLIES. SENT ONE.

AND THEN—NOTHING.

Now it's almost noon, and my phone is a quiet, accusing thing beside the register. I've checked it so many times that the screen's greasy with thumbprints. Still no unread messages. No call.

He said it was just a quick meeting. Forty-eight hours, tops. But Crew Wright isn't the kind of man who goes quiet. When he's upset, you hear it—in his voice, in his body, in the way he exhales before he says something honest.

I stare at the display of bookmarks near the register. Lila made them for the fall festival last month—pressed flowers sealed under resin, each one a little world frozen in place. I pick one up, trace the stem of a daisy, and pretend I don't feel like that's what I'm doing too. Waiting for time to melt.

The bell over the door jingles, and Ivy steps in carrying two coffees and a smile that's too bright to be real. "You look like you're trying to murder that bookmark," she says, handing me a cup.

"I'm not," I lie.

"Uh-huh." She leans against the counter, hip cocked, hair escaping her braid. "You heard from him?"

I shake my head. "Not since last night."

Her voice softens. "He's probably buried in meetings. You know how those guys love to hear themselves talk."

"Yeah," I say, wrapping my hands around the cup. The warmth seeps into my fingers but doesn't reach anything that matters. "Just... it's not like him."

Ivy's eyes search mine. "You're doing that thing where you tell yourself it's fine while your insides are setting fires."

"I'm not—" I start, then stop, because she's right. I'm exactly that.

She nudges me gently. "You want to come by the studio later? I'm dropping off that set list for the charity event. We're pretending to be organized."

"I can't. The new shipment's still in boxes, and the book drive paperwork's due tonight."

"Bailey..."

I give her the look that says *please don't make me talk about this right now*. She reads it, sighs, and lets me have my silence. "Okay. But call if you need to vent or... break something."

"I'm not breaking anything," I say, voice too steady.

She grins. "Then I'll do it for you."

When she leaves, the quiet rushes back in like a tide. The lighthouse creaks, the breeze drags another breath across the windows, and I wonder when home started feeling like a question.

By three, the sky's cleared to a pale gray that smells like salt and second chances. I close up early and walk down Main Street, hoping movement will trick my body into thinking I'm fine.

Coral Bell Cove moves at its own rhythm—kids chasing each other past the bakery, Mr. Daniels setting out pumpkins in front of the hardware store, the chatter of tourists who think they've found something untouched. Every person I pass smiles, waves, asks about the book drive. Normal things. Simple things.

But every sound feels half a second too slow, every color dimmer than it should be. Like the world forgot to plug itself in when Crew left.

I stop at the café window, watching Ivy inside talking to a group of women. Her laugh carries even through the glass, soft and unguarded. She looks up, catches my reflection, and lifts a brow that says *come in.*

I shake my head. Not today.

My stomach twists. It's not jealousy, exactly. It's envy of ease—the way she's learned how to live loud again after being dragged through the tabloids, the way she can trust that love stays.

I walk on, past the docks, where the water laps lazy against the boats. Crew's truck isn't there, of course, but I still look for it. Habit's cruel that way.

The air tastes like brine and metal. Somewhere, a gull screams like it knows things don't end quietly.

When I get back to the lighthouse, dusk is already

bleeding into the edges of the sky. I flip the porch light on before I even unlock the door. He always teases me for that —calls it my "welcome mat for ghosts."

Inside, the shop glows soft, golden. Cozy. It should feel safe. Instead, it feels like pretending.

I sink onto the stool behind the counter, phone in my lap. I tell myself not to check it again. Then I do.

Nothing.

I open our thread anyway, scrolling through old messages. His last picture—the one he sent from the truck —still makes me smile. The way he holds the camera too low, jaw shadowed, the world behind him a blur of motion. *Made it to Nashville.*

He looks tired in it. I didn't notice before.

My chest tightens, and I drop the phone onto the counter like distance might shrink if I stop holding it so hard.

The storm outside has moved on, but the wind still pushes against the windows. The lantern beam sweeps across the room, throwing soft light over the books, the plants, the cup he left half-drunk on the windowsill two days ago.

I trace a finger over the rim, then close my eyes.

"Don't let them make you smaller," I whisper, the words tasting like prayer.

The floor creaks. For a heartbeat, I think it's him— stupid, hopeful instinct. It's just the building settling. Or maybe it's me.

The following morning, I wake early, the air heavy and still. The ocean's calm again, that eerie hush after a storm. I make coffee, feed the cat, and watch the first light hit the water through the kitchen window.

He should've texted by now.

I tell myself maybe his phone died. Maybe he overslept. Maybe the meeting ran late. But each maybe sounds thinner than the last.

By eight, I've checked the news, the team page, his fan accounts—nothing unusual. Just recycled interviews, old highlight clips. The digital version of pretending everything's fine.

When I unlock the shop, Rowan's already outside with a box of donated books balanced on his hip. "Morning, sunshine," he says. "You look like you fought a ghost and lost."

"Coffee hasn't worked yet," I say, opening the door.

He follows me in, setting the box on the counter. "You good?"

"Fine."

He gives me a look that says he's not buying it. "You sure? I can threaten someone on your behalf. I'm versatile."

"I'll keep that in mind."

He grins. "You always do."

When he leaves, I stand behind the counter, hands pressed flat to the wood. The grain feels like a heartbeat under my palms. I wonder if that's how Crew felt—trying to steady something that won't stop moving.

By noon, the bookstore fills with the quiet chatter of regulars. Mrs. Landry drops off her weekly cookie bribe. A kid from the high school asks for something "that doesn't suck" for his lit class. I find him *The Outsiders* and tell him it's about staying gold. He shrugs but smiles.

Normal. I can do normal.

Until I can't.

Because when the shop finally empties and I'm alone again, the quiet presses in harder than before. My phone buzzes once—my heart stutters—but it's just a weather alert.

And that's when the fear shifts into something else. Not panic. Not yet. Just that low, humming certainty that something isn't right.

I pick up my phone again and type. *Just checking in. How'd the meeting go?*

I delete it. Type again. *Miss your face. Also, your favorite kid broke the display shelf.* Delete that, too.

Finally, I send a single word. *Home?*

The message hangs in the air, blue bubble glowing like a promise I don't believe.

The dots appear for half a second—then vanish.

I stare at the screen until it goes black.

Outside, the lantern beam sweeps over the water, slow and steady, the same as always. But it feels like it's searching this time.

Searching for him.

And maybe for me, too.

The next day starts with fog.

The kind that blurs the horizon until sky and water forget which one is supposed to be blue.

I open the shop anyway. Habit wins over sense.

The bell jingles, the cat yawns, and the smell of ground beans from the café next door slides under the door like an invitation to act normal.

I make it until ten. Ten whole minutes before checking my phone again.

Nothing.

There's a hollow space where his name should be.

Every hour that passes stretches it thinner, like silence can actually tear.

By eleven, I give up pretending and take the box of donation forms down to the café. Mrs. Lopez will want the paperwork for the town fundraiser anyway, and I can't keep pacing the aisles of the shop without going insane.

The bell above the café door rings when I step in, warm air kissing my face. The smell hits—sugar, espresso, cinnamon—and for a second I almost remember what peace feels like. The place hums with low chatter, spoons against mugs, a guitar humming from the radio.

"Bailey!" Mrs. Lopez waves from behind the counter, hair pinned up, lipstick smudged from smiling too much. "You working or hiding?"

"Maybe both," I say, sliding the box onto the counter. "Book drive totals. Coral Bell Elementary hit their goal."

"That's my readers!" she beams, already flipping open

the folder. "You staying for coffee? You look like you need it."

I manage a half smile. "Do I?"

"Like a woman holding back the tide with a paper cup," she says, and doesn't wait for an answer before calling to the back, "Jessica, two lattes!"

I sit at the counter, twisting the paper napkin in my hands.

The TV in the corner plays muted news—sports recap, scrolling headlines, some anchor mouthing excitement that doesn't reach her eyes. It's background noise, like usual.

Mrs. Lopez slides a mug toward me. "How's your fella? He's still in Nashville, right? That quarterback?"

The napkin tears in half in my fingers. "Yeah. Just meetings."

She nods, satisfied, then moves on to the next customer, leaving me with steam and caffeine and a silence that feels anything but quiet.

I sip, burn my tongue, and glance up, just as the screen cuts to a press conference.

I don't register the words at first. Just the image. A long table, team banners, microphones lined up like a firing squad. Harris at the center, smiling. David on the far right, pretending he belongs. And Crew—

Crew looks like someone I almost recognize.

He's in a tailored suit, hair pushed back too neat, eyes shadowed. His smile is the kind that hurts to look at—half a muscle too tight.

The anchor's voice rises, clear over the café hum: "...and

the Tennessee Stallions are proud to welcome back quarterback Crew Wright, officially returning for next season after successful rehabilitation and a renewed partnership with our sponsors..."

My heart stops.

The words fall wrong.

Renewed partnership.

That's the phrase he swore he'd never let them use again.

I set my coffee down, too hard. Liquid splashes the counter.

"...Mr. Wright, how does it feel to be back?" a reporter asks from offscreen.

Crew leans toward the mic, and for a second, his lips part like he's about to speak the truth. But then something shifts—his eyes flick sideways toward Harris, a warning or a reminder—and what comes out is measured, flat, someone else's voice wearing his mouth.

"I'm grateful," he says. "The team has always believed in me. I'm looking forward to moving past distractions and focusing on what matters."

Distractions.

That's what he calls me now?

The air leaves my lungs like it's been punched out.

Someone in the café laughs at another table, a sound too bright for this moment. Mrs. Lopez hums to the radio. The world doesn't notice I've gone still.

I stare at the screen, at the way his hand tightens on the

table, fingers flexing once like he's trying to hold on to something invisible.

Harris smiles wider, leans closer, says something low I can't hear. Crew nods.

The camera pans, and for a flicker—just a single heartbeat—Crew's eyes meet the lens. And I swear he's looking for me.

That tiny, desperate thing that passes through his expression—it's gone before I can name it. But it's there. The real him, buried under PR polish and contract chains.

The screen shifts to an ad. Bright colors. Laughter. The world keeps moving.

I'm still frozen.

Mrs. Lopez looks over. "You okay, honey?"

I nod, but the word doesn't reach my throat. "Yeah. Just... spilled my coffee."

"Want a towel?"

"I'm fine," I manage, already grabbing my bag. "Sorry—bookstore needs me."

She calls something after me, but I don't hear it.

Outside, the air cuts cold against my cheeks. I walk without direction, phone clutched in my hand like a lifeline that isn't one. The waves slap against the dock in slow, deliberate rhythms. Somewhere, the gulls scream again.

I stop at the edge of the pier, wind tugging my hair, the lighthouse small but steady in the distance.

He looked at the camera. He *looked at it like it was me.*

Something inside me steadies—not the fear, not the hurt, but something sharper. Resolve, maybe.

If he can't say what's happening out loud, then I'll find out myself.

The water shivers with light as the lantern sweeps across it, one steady pulse after another.

I whisper to the horizon, to him, to whoever's listening,

"I'm coming to get you back."

And for the first time since he left, I let the storm break.

Chapter Twenty-Two

CREW

The handlers move like they've done this a thousand times—one hand on my back, one hand gesturing down the corridor, murmuring things I don't bother to hear. The hallway smells of hairspray, coffee, and nerves. Every surface gleams. I can see my reflection in the polished floor: a suit that doesn't feel like mine, a face that looks older than the man who left Coral Bell Cove yesterday.

A reporter in the front row raises his hand. "Crew, there's been a lot of speculation about your time away. What would you say to fans who worry about your focus?"

My cue card answer waits in the folder before me. I don't look at it. "I'd tell them focus never left. It just... learned different targets."

Laughter ripples. Harris's smile tightens.

Another reporter. "You've had a lot of media attention

around personal relationships. Can you comment on how that's impacted your career?"

Harris leans toward his mic. "We'd like to keep today about football—"

"No," I say quietly, and the word cuts through the room like feedback. "It's fair."

I look at the cameras. "Distractions happen when people forget you're human. I haven't."

The room stills. Harris's knee presses into mine under the table—his silent *shut up*.

I give them the smile they want. "I'm grateful to the team, the sponsors, the fans." My voice sounds even, calm. "I'm looking forward to the season."

Flashbulbs strobe. Questions pile. I answer each one the way a trained man does—measured, polite, every syllable a leash. Inside, my pulse drums against my ribs, steady, furious.

The last question comes from a woman in the back. "You've spoken about mentorship and second chances. Is there anyone you'd like to thank personally?"

Bailey's name sits on my tongue like a live wire.

I swallow it. "Too many to list," I say instead.

Applause again. Harris stands. The event dissolves into handshakes and photo ops. I shake them because that's the choreography. Cameras flash. Someone claps me on the shoulder. I let them.

The lights dim. The crowd disperses. The door to backstage closes, and the air finally tastes like oxygen again.

David exhales beside me. "That went well."

I turn to him slowly. "Did it?"

"Better than it could have. You stayed on message. Sponsors are already happy."

"Glad to make the puppeteers proud."

He flinches. "Crew—"

Harris walks in, phone to his ear, voice smooth. "Yes, it was perfect. Yes, he was perfect. We'll send the reel to marketing in—" He hangs up and smiles at me. "You handled yourself beautifully."

"I lied for you," I say.

He shrugs. "You lied for yourself. For your career."

"No," I correct, voice quiet. "For your comfort."

The room temperature drops by a degree. David shifts uneasily.

Harris pockets his phone. "You think you can burn this machine down and still walk away clean? You're welcome to try. But remember—public sympathy is a fickle thing."

"I don't need sympathy."

He steps closer. "Then what do you need?"

"Truth," I say, and smile because the truth scares him more than rage.

His jaw flexes. "You're not stupid, Crew. You want to go back to your little lighthouse, fine. But this—" He gestures toward the empty stage. "This is what feeds the town that feeds you."

"Bailey feeds herself."

Harris laughs. "You really believe that shop can compete with a franchise check? You think love keeps the lights on?"

"Yeah," I say softly. "Actually, it does."

David clears his throat. "Let's all take a breath—"

But I'm done breathing their air. "I'm finished."

Harris tilts his head. "With what?"

"All of it. You, the sponsors, the act." I pull the microphone badge from my lapel and set it on the table between us. "You can keep the script. I'm taking my voice."

He watches me for a beat, calculating. "You walk out now, you'll never play again."

I think of Bailey, then wordlessly I turn, walking down the hall toward the exit. My footsteps echo—steady, deliberate. Behind me, Harris says something low to David. David doesn't answer.

Outside, night has settled over Nashville. The parking lot gleams wet from a drizzle that didn't earn the name rain. My truck waits where I left it. I open the door, slide behind the wheel, and sit in the dark for a long time.

The city buzzes around me—sirens, laughter, a billboard flashing my own face with the caption *Back and Better*.

I start the engine. The sound fills the cab, warm and rough, the only honest thing I've heard all day.

As I pull onto the highway, my phone lights up with missed calls, messages, notifications I don't read. The skyline shrinks in the mirror.

Bailey's lighthouse glows in my mind like it's calling ships home.

The fury finally breaks, quiet and clean, leaving only purpose behind.

The next time they try to speak for me, they'll have to find me first.

The city fades like a bruise under the rain.

One last flash of blue neon glows on the wet asphalt before the skyline disappears behind me completely, and I finally—finally—breathe.

Not the shallow, camera-ready kind. The real kind.

My knuckles ache where I've been gripping the steering wheel too tight. My pulse has slowed, but that restless hum under my ribs hasn't. It's not anger anymore. It's something sharper. Purpose, maybe. Or the kind of calm that only comes after you've already decided what to lose.

The GPS voice tells me to stay on the interstate for 200 miles. I kill the sound and drive in silence.

Headlights slice through the dark. Every mile marker feels like another layer of noise falling away. Nashville, the press conference, Harris's smug face—all of it shrinks in the rearview until it's just me and the hum of tires on wet pavement.

The rain is steady now, a soft percussion against the windshield. It reminds me of nights on the farm, lying awake in the loft listening to storms roll across the fields. I used to count seconds between thunderclaps, pretending that meant control.

Tonight, I don't need to count. I just drive.

Bailey's name sits somewhere behind my sternum, steady and certain. I picture her behind the counter of *A Page in Time*, sleeves pushed to her elbows, pencil tucked behind her ear. Probably pretending not to notice when her glasses slide down her nose. She never lets me push them back up for her, says she doesn't need rescuing. She's right.

But God, I miss the way she lets me try.

The highway stretches out, endless and wet, and my reflection in the window looks like a man I almost recognize. Not the quarterback. Not the brand. Just the guy who once handed a girl a tattered copy of *The Outsiders* and told her to keep it because she loved it more than he ever could.

Stay gold, she wrote inside the cover. Her handwriting is looping, stubborn, and beautiful.

I still have that book. It's on the passenger seat now, beside my phone, buzzing with messages I don't answer.

By the time the "Welcome to Virginia" sign flashes by, dawn's threatening the horizon. The air smells like salt and earth—like home.

I stop at a diner just past the state line, order black coffee, and sit in the corner booth watching the rain taper off. No one recognizes me here. Just another tired guy in a hoodie, staring out the window like he's waiting for something to shift.

The server fills my cup again without asking. "Long night?"

"Long life," I say, and she laughs softly, patting my shoulder before walking away.

I think about Bailey's face when she used to laugh like that—unrestrained, head tilted back, eyes crinkled. The kind of laugh that hit you in the chest and made everything make sense.

I wonder if she laughed after the press conference. Or if she just turned off the TV and let the silence do what I didn't have the guts to.

That thought twists something inside me, sharp and deep.

I throw down some bills, grab my keys, and head back to the truck. The air's cold now, clean. It cuts straight through the haze.

The drive to Coral Bell Cove is muscle memory. The roads narrow, the pine trees crowd close, and the world gets quieter. Every curve feels like peeling back time.

When I hit the first stretch of coastline, I roll down the window. The smell of brine and sea grass fills the cab. I breathe it in like it's medicine.

The sign at the edge of town still reads: **Welcome to Coral Bell Cove—Population 4,817**

Someone's painted a tiny seashell above the "C." Bailey, probably. She always said details mattered.

Main Street's asleep when I roll through. The bakery is dark except for the faint glow of the ovens. The lamppost by the dock flickers like it's thinking about quitting. Everything is the same, and everything is different.

Otter Creek Farm sits quiet on the hill, the barns still and silver in the early light. I pass it, heading straight for the water.

The lighthouse appears through the fog like it always does—solid, defiant, impossible to ignore. The bookstore's porch light glows, soft and golden, a beacon for the lost and the stupid. I pull over, kill the engine, and sit for a long time.

Every muscle in my body wants to run to her door, but fear keeps me still. Not the big, life-and-death kind. The smaller, crueler one—the fear of watching her eyes shutter when she sees me.

I close my hands around the steering wheel until the leather creaks.

She deserves better than half-apologies. She deserves the truth.

When I finally get out, the night air hits like salt on an open wound. The wind off the bay carries the faintest trace of her—vanilla, old paper, and something uniquely Bailey.

The porch steps creak under my boots. The CLOSED sign sways in the window. The place smells like rain and ink and second chances.

I knock once. Twice.

No answer.

I should leave. Let her sleep. Let her choose when to see me. But before I can turn away, I hear the soft tread of bare feet. The lock clicks. The door opens, and there she is.

Bailey.

Her hair is in a tangle, her eyes rimmed red, but she's never looked more like home. She's wearing my old Stallions hoodie—gray, frayed at the cuffs, the one she used to sleep in when she thought I didn't notice.

Her breath catches when she sees me. "Crew."

"Yeah." My voice scrapes out low, rough. "It's me."

She blinks, like her brain's fighting to catch up. "You— how did you—"

"Drove," I say simply.

Her gaze flicks over me, taking in the suit jacket, the

exhaustion, the rain still dripping from my hair. "You're supposed to be—"

"Somewhere I didn't want to be," I finish for her.

A thousand words live in the silence between us. The rain, the headlines, the lies, the press conference.

She finally breathes, the sound small and shaky. "I saw you on TV."

"I figured."

"You looked..." Her voice falters. "Trapped."

"I was."

Her throat works. "And now?"

"Free."

The word lands heavy. True.

Her eyes search mine, like she's trying to see if I mean it. "You left all of it?"

"All of it," I say. "The sponsors. The contracts. Harris."

Her laugh breaks, part disbelief, part heartbreak. "You really are insane."

"Maybe." I take a step closer, close enough to see the faint freckles across her nose. "But I'm done letting someone else own my story."

Her lips tremble. "And what story's that?"

"The one that ends here," I say quietly. "With you."

Her breath stutters. The sound of the ocean fills the space between us.

She doesn't move when I reach up and brush a strand of hair from her cheek. Her skin is warm, soft. Her eyes close on a shiver.

For a heartbeat, everything in me tilts toward her—every nerve, every memory, every word I didn't say.

Then she opens her eyes. "You shouldn't be here."

"I should," I whisper. "I needed to be."

The way she looks at me—torn between anger and relief—undoes me completely.

"You can't just show up after all that and expect—"

"I don't expect anything," I cut in. "Just a chance to explain."

She swallows. "Then explain."

"I said things I didn't mean because they told me to. I let them control the story because I thought it was the only way to keep everything together. But the truth is—everything I was holding on to wasn't worth what I almost lost."

Her eyes glisten. "And what was that?"

"You."

She lets out a broken sound, half laugh, half sob. "You always did know how to ruin a girl's defenses."

"I'm not trying to ruin anything," I say softly. "I'm trying to rebuild."

For a long moment, she just stands there, breathing me in like she's deciding whether to believe me.

Finally, she steps back, her voice barely above a whisper. "Come in before you freeze."

The air between us shifts, softer now, something like surrender.

I step inside.

The door closes behind me with a quiet click, sealing us in. The room smells like books and salt and her shampoo. A candle burns low on the counter, wax pooling in the shape of a heart that's been melted and remade.

Bailey crosses her arms, watching me like she's still deciding whether this is real. "So what now?"

"I figure that out here," I say. "With you. If you'll let me."

Her lips curve—not quite a smile, not quite forgiveness. "We'll see."

And for the first time since I walked off that stage, the world feels right again.

Chapter Twenty-Three

BAILEY

The latch catches with a soft metallic sigh, and just like that, he's inside my world again. The heater hums. A single lamp throws a pool of light across the counter, catching the gold in his hair and the salt on his shoulders. He looks too big for the space—broad, tired, still carrying the noise of stadiums even while standing on my worn rug.

I fold my arms because I need somewhere to keep my hands. "You're dripping on the floor."

He glances down. Water darkens the boards around his boots. "Add it to the list of things I need to fix."

"You don't get to start with the floor," I say, sharper than I mean to. "There are other things broken first."

He nods once. "Yeah. I know."

Silence stretches. The air smells like rain and paper and the cinnamon candle that's been burning since before midnight. He takes a step closer, then stops as if the room itself has drawn a boundary.

"You look tired," he says softly.

"I've been running a business," I answer. "And watching press conferences I didn't want to see."

His jaw tightens. "I didn't want you to see that."

"Then you shouldn't have said what you did."

"I had to."

"You didn't." My voice trembles on the edge of breaking, so I turn toward the counter, pretending to tidy a stack of receipts. "You always think the only way through something is to let it hurt you first."

He exhales slowly, the sound rough. "And you always think walking away makes it stop hurting."

That hits too close. I press my palms flat against the counter until the sting in my hands steadies me. When I finally turn around, he's closer—close enough that I can see the small scar above his eyebrow, the one he got senior year when he tried to impress the class by catching a pass he never should've attempted. Some things never change.

"Why did you come back?" I ask.

"Because everything else started to feel like lying," he says simply.

There's a softness in his voice that wasn't there before, an ache that pulls at something deep inside me. I want to stay angry. I want to remind him how many nights I sat here waiting for a text that never came. But instead, I whisper, "You left me to defend your silence."

"I know." His eyes find mine, steady, apologetic. "I'm done being silent."

He moves toward the stove, rubbing his hands together like he's trying to warm them. "Do you still have that kettle that wheezes like a dying seagull?"

I blink. "You remember that?"

"I remember everything." His smile is small, cautious. "You'd set it on before you started reading, and it'd scream right at the best part."

A reluctant laugh slips out of me, light and startled. "It still does that."

He reaches for it automatically, then stops. "Can I?"

I nod. Watching him fill the kettle and set it on the burner feels intimate in a way that almost hurts. His movements are slower now, deliberate, like he's trying not to break anything—including me.

When the kettle finally starts its familiar whine, he leans back against the counter beside me. We stand shoulder to shoulder, not touching, staring at nothing. The quiet between us hums louder than the stove.

"I don't know how to do this," I admit.

"Me neither," he says. "But I know I want to."

He turns then, fingers brushing a strand of hair from my face. It's the lightest touch, but it sets my pulse sprinting. I should step away, but I don't.

"Bailey," he murmurs, voice hoarse. "I meant what I said. I left all of it. I'm not choosing between the game and you anymore."

"You can't just erase that world."

"I'm not erasing it. I'm walking away from the part that stopped feeling like mine."

The kettle shrieks, startling us both. I turn off the burner, grateful for the excuse to move, to breathe. I pour two mugs, hands trembling only a little, and slide one toward him.

He takes it but doesn't drink. "This feels like déjà vu."

"Because we've done this before," I say quietly. "You show up, you promise, and then—"

"This time, I stay." The words are quiet but unshakable. "I'm done running plays written by someone else."

Something in his tone makes me believe him, even as every defense I've built insists I shouldn't. I stare into my cup. Steam curls up and blurs my vision until I'm not sure if it's fog or tears.

"I don't know if I can trust you again," I whisper.

"Then let me earn it."

I look up. His eyes are the color of stormwater— dangerous and steady. He doesn't reach for me again, doesn't push. He just waits.

Outside, dawn starts to bleed through the windows, gray turning to gold. The light catches the dust motes in the air, making them shimmer like tiny possibilities.

I take a slow breath. "You're still dripping on the floor."

He smiles, small and genuine this time. "Guess I should mop."

And somehow, absurdly, I laugh. The sound breaks the last of the tension, leaving room for air. He laughs too, low and quiet, and for a second, it feels like the world has finally exhaled.

I set my cup down and look at him—really look. "You're not forgiven," I say.

"I didn't ask to be," he answers. "Just asked to stay long enough to try."

And when he says it, something in me unclenches. I nod once. It's not yes, not yet—but it's not no, either.

Outside, the gulls start their morning racket. The kettle clicks as it cools. The first true light of day spills through the windows, painting his profile in gold.

And just like that, I realize the storm might finally be over.

Chapter Twenty-Four

CREW

The next day, the Read-In tastes like victory and vanilla. Kids left sticky fingerprints on the camera lens, Mrs. Winthrop cried into a scone, the inspector autographed a copy of *Goodnight Moon* like a reluctant celebrity, and the 8 a.m. "clean story" they tried to roll out died sputtering in the comments under a tidal wave of otters and heart emoji. Laramie texted me a screenshot of a national sports feed: **STALLIONS QB LEADS LITERACY BLITZ; LEAGUE STATEMENT: "WE SUPPORT COMMUNITY."**

I spend the first hour fixing the back gate I promised Bailey I'd repair, which is a metaphor I don't have the energy to unpack. The hinge is stubborn. So am I. When it finally gives, the satisfying pop is almost obscene.

Bailey leans in the doorway with a glass of lemonade that would shame the sun. "Look at you," she teases. "Handyman heartthrob."

"I'll have you know I'm multitalented." I lift the drill like a trophy. "Gate whisperer, scone consumer, amateur ring-light assassin."

She bites her smile and passes me the glass. Our fingers brush. That familiar voltage runs my spine like a fast route. The porch is empty. The town has jobs and casseroles to deliver. For the first time in days, the lighthouse feels like it's just ours.

"Close the door," I say.

Her brows flick up. "Bossy."

"Focused."

She steps back, toe nudging the door shut. The latch clicks—the one I replaced, the one that doesn't rattle now when the wind has opinions. I set the drill down and take two steps, erasing the distance.

We've been living in borrowed moments—stolen kisses between hearings and press calls, a hand on her back while she reads, a forehead press that says more than any speech —because chaos has been loud and we've been louder. Now the quiet stands up and stretches and asks if we remember how to use it.

"Hi," she says against my mouth.

"Hi," I answer into hers.

It feels different after saying it on camera, after the pier, after the warehouse. Not heavier—truer. She curls a fist in the front of my shirt and pulls me with the confidence of a woman who made a town bend and a corporation blink.

We don't race. We drift, bumper boats/carousel horses/something with bells and a slow smile. Her back finds the wall. My hands find the curve of her waist. The room finds a warmer temperature than the thermostat suggests. She tastes like lemon and stubborn. I kiss the laugh from the corner of her mouth and the worry from the line between her brows. She slides her palms under my shirt and relearns a map she's already memorized.

"Door's locked," she murmurs, breath tickling my throat. "Right?"

"Double," I promise, and press a kiss to the hinge of her jaw because it makes her shiver. "Triple if you ask nicely."

"You think I ask nicely?" She hooks her fingers in my belt loops and walks me backward, slow as a hymn, toward the stairs. "I make lists."

"Bossy," I repeat, and let her win.

We climb, kissing like we have time now—like the world isn't waiting downstairs with consequences and calendars. The lantern room windows make small, square paintings of the bay, lightning stitching silver through the water. The floorboards creak like they're rooting for us. In the bedroom, the cat does us the favor of leaving, tail high, like he refuses to participate in our poor choices.

Her sweater comes off; my breath does, too.

I don't rush. I want her aware of every second of it—my hands sliding up her sides, my thumbs tracing the familiar lines I've missed more than I let myself admit. I kiss her shoulder, the hollow of her collarbone, the inside of her wrist where her pulse is writing my name. She laughs when I drop a kiss just below her ear; I laugh when she noses along my jaw and finds the place that makes my knees consider surrender.

We're careful with my shoulder and reckless with everything else.

"Crew," she whispers when I slow down on purpose, mouth hovering at her sternum, hand warm and steady at her hip. There's a plea in it. There's power, too. She's not shy with me anymore—not hiding in any of the places she used to keep quiet.

She drags me up by my shirt and kisses me like gratitude and challenge at once, like she's daring me to keep control. I answer by backing her toward the bed, letting her feel the promise of what I'm not giving yet. Her fingers clutch at me, impatient now, and the sound she makes when I break the kiss to trail my mouth lower is worth every second of restraint.

We fall together, air knocked out in the best way. It's heat and hush and the sheet tangled in my calf. It's the kind of closeness that makes words useless and makes breath do the talking. When she arches, I cover her mouth with mine to catch the sound; when I groan, she bites my lip like I'm a secret and she's bad at keeping them.

We hover right up against the line we promised to imply and stay there—delicious, relentless. My hand slides under and up; hers answers, nails grazing down my back. The room smells like salt and us. The world narrows to a pulse we sync without trying, a rhythm that feels inevitable.

Clothes end up in random piles across the room. My cock eases into her slick center like it's found its way home.

My heart lurches in overwhelming feelings with every thrust. And when we both fall over the edge, I can't imagine being anywhere else.

After, we don't spring apart. We melt. My forehead rests against hers. Her fingers draw lazy circles at my nape. I count the beats in my chest and realize they're not sprinting—they're steady. That terrifies me in a way that feels like joy.

"You're dangerous," I tell her, voice rough.

"Occupational hazard," she says, smug and wrecked.

"We're keeping the door locked," I decide.

"Until lunch," she agrees, and then remembers she owns a business. "Or until Ivy breaks in with muffins."

"She would."

We lie there, the ceiling fan whispering encouragement, and talk about nothing—lists for the week, the inspector's surprisingly poetic signature, the way Rowan's goat ate a cease notice like performance art. We don't talk about Nashville yet. But the conversation moves toward it like a tide.

She traces the tape peeking from under my shirt. "You have the call with the GM tomorrow."

"I do."

"And you know what you'll say?"

"I do," I say, because I promised her slow and honest, and I intend to be both. "I'm not taking the mentor role because it's cleaner for the press. I'll take it if it's right for me."

"And if it's not?"

"I walk," I say, and feel the weight and light of it together. "I stay here more. I work the farm. I try my hand at commentating games; maybe broadcasting. I coach the high school kids if Coach Allen will let me. I read to otters with a British accent and let the internet roast me. I fix every hinge in this place twice."

She smiles without looking at me, which means it's the kind that belongs to herself. "I won't let you give up something you love out of fear."

"And I won't keep something that only loves me when I'm useful."

We go quiet. The wind fingers the lighthouse skin and makes the glass hum. The water hisses against the rocks like a whisper you tell yourself when you're brave.

"I want you here," she says, voice so soft I might be the only one who ever gets to hear it. "But not if here means small."

"Here is not small," I say, and kiss her knuckles for emphasis. "Here is precise. That's harder."

She turns her head and meets my mouth with hers like we're signing something sacred. Then she sighs and rolls out of bed, sheet wrapped around her to preserve a shred of dignity we burned an hour ago. "We should open."

"We did," I murmur, not moving.

"Crew."

"Fine." I sit up, wince fresh, grin anyway. "I'll make the porch respectable while you pretend to alphabetize and actually read."

"Accurate," she says, and kisses me once more, quick, like a tip.

Downstairs, the day resumes its small-town shape. Lila organizes a volunteer list with the quiet ferocity of a general. Ivy prints REOPENED signs that feature the otter puppet in a hard hat. Rowan replaces two loose shingles on the back addition while Dean times him and yells splits. Mrs. Winthrop returns with actual legal counsel ("He's very handsome," she confides, "and knows what a variance is."). The inspector drops by "just to say we're on the schedule," and leaves with a lemon bar because kindness is our favorite weapon.

The GM calls earlier than expected. I take it on the side steps, looking at the water because it keeps my jaw from doing things my temper will regret.

"We want you," he says. "But the room changed. You know that."

"I do," I say. "So let's change with it."

Pause. Papers shuffle. Someone murmurs offscreen. "You're proposing...?"

"I come in as QB2 when needed," I say. "Half season. I mentor Jax, not as a prop, but because he's good and deserves someone who actually cares. I get Tuesday-Thursdays flexible so I can be in Coral Bell Cove when we have major town events—yes, I said town events—and you stop putting my personal life in your PR decks."

He laughs like he respects me against his will. "That's a lot of leverage for a guy with a shoulder the papers say is 'hot garbage.'"

"Then don't take it," I say calmly. "But it's the only way you get me and the town in the same season without wrecking both."

"We can commit to a window," he hedges. "Maybe not that wide."

"Then commit to honesty," I counter. "If I'm a brand to you, say it to my face. If I'm a man, treat me like one. If you want the comeback story, you get the parts that happen off the field, too."

He sighs. "You were easier when you just threw."

"I was worse," I say.

"We'll talk at the facility in three days," he decides. "Bring your proposal. Bring your conditions."

"I'll bring scones," I say, and hang up.

Bailey steps out with two paperbacks and Holly Golightly sunglasses, which she wears only when she's feeling chaotic. "How'd it go?"

"They want me," I say. "I want me, too. We're negotiating."

She hands me a book. *The Art of Slow Miracles.* "Homework."

"Fair." I tap the other paperback. "That one for me, too?"

"No," she says sweetly. "That one's to prop the door."

Afternoon softens into the kind of light that makes everything look like a photograph you keep on your fridge with a dumb magnet. Kids come in for popsicle-bright picture books.

At five, a delivery I didn't order arrives: a new sign for the shop, hand-carved, gilt edges, elegant script. A note:

From anonymous donors who think your door should shine as stubbornly as your light.

Bailey runs her fingers over the letters like braille. "We can accept this," she decides, "because sometimes strings are just ribbon."

"Sometimes," I agree, and don't tell her I know exactly which billionaire and which pop star paid for it, because the point is that they did it quietly.

Dusk finds us on the dock with takeout in boxes and bare feet on wood still warm from the sun. The water has turned the color of a good bruise. The lighthouse beam ticks its metronome. The town is a murmur behind us.

"We're winding down," Bailey says, like a promise she's testing out loud.

"Soon," I say. "Not tonight."

She tips her head onto my shoulder. "One more storm?"

"Probably," I say. "One more negotiation, one more hearing, one more man who thinks he can narrate us better than we can."

"And then?"

"And then ordinary," I say, like it's the fanciest thing I've ever ordered. "Porch dinners. Friday night games, even if I'm on the sideline. You pretending you don't need help with inventory, and me pretending I don't love being asked.

Goat invasions. Ivy's songs. Lila's lists. The cat hating me with dignity. Us, tired in good ways."

She's quiet long enough to make me nervous. Then she says, "Make me a list."

"Of?"

"Ordinary."

So I do, whispering it into the bay like a vow. "You in that cardigan with the elbow patch you refuse to fix. Me fixing it just to make you mad. Waking up to your hair trying to fight the pillowcase and losing. You reading to me on storm nights. Me reading to you when your voice is tired. Soup on the stove that ruins the wooden spoon. Your grandfather asleep in his chair and snoring like a tractor, and we love him more for it. A porch swing that doesn't squeak because I got it right the second time. The lantern room staying dry because we did the roof and because I learned how to say 'we' without choking. A kid from town showing up with a football and a question and me saying yes. You handing me a paperback and saying, 'This one will hurt, but in a useful way.'"

Her hand finds mine and squeezes once, then twice. Morse we invented for ourselves. *Yes. Yes.*

We eat. We laugh. We behave indecently for a minute when the moon climbs, and the pier is empty, and the wind covers our sighs. It's heat and implication and the sweet feeling of her tucked against me, breath in my neck, my palm spread over her stomach like a promise. I tuck her under my arm and stare at the black ribbon of the horizon and think of the boy I was who thought legacy was a stadium, and the man I am, who knows it's a porch light and a stubborn bookstore and a woman who kept a note that once made her small and turned it into a lighthouse.

"Tomorrow," she whispers.

"Tomorrow," I echo, and for the first time in a long time, it sounds like a place instead of a delay.

On the walk back, my phone pings with a calendar alert I forgot I set months ago: **Nashville – Report to camp.** I stop under the streetlamp and stare at it. Bailey watches me watch it.

"You can say no," she says.

"I can say *not like that*," I answer, and swipe away the alert. "I can say *I'll come, but I will not leave.*"

She links our fingers. "That's a very Coral Bell Cove kind of sentence."

"It's a very you sentence," I say.

Back at the lighthouse, the porch light burns steadily. We climb the steps, and before we go in, she stops and pulls me by my shirt into a kiss that feels like punctuation. Not a period—an em dash. A continuation.

"Lock the door," she murmurs against my mouth.

"Deadbolted," I promise.

We let the night have the town. We keep the lighthouse for ourselves. And somewhere between the second laugh and the third kiss, winding down stops sounding like an ending and starts sounding like the right kind of beginning.

Chapter Twenty-Five

BAILEY

I wake to the smell of coffee drifting up from downstairs, to the sound of seagulls and a hammer tapping rhythmically somewhere along the boardwalk. The town feels alive again, lighter, as if Coral Bell Cove had collectively exhaled. Every porch flag is flying, every window chalked with hearts and book quotes. Even the air seems grateful.

Crew's side of the bed is empty except for the imprint of his body and the cat curled on his pillow like a smug crown. I stretch, my muscles humming in that way that isn't sore so much as satisfied, and smile into the sheet. The last few days have been chaos, and somehow we survived them with more than we started with.

Downstairs, Crew is barefoot, hair damp from a shower, standing at the stove in a T-shirt that says **READ LIKE A CHAMPION TODAY**. He's flipping pancakes with unnecessary flourish, singing off-key to whatever old country song is bleeding from the radio. There's batter on his cheek and a grin that could power the entire lighthouse.

"Morning, boss," he says when he sees me.

"You're in my kitchen," I remind him, tying my robe tighter.

He slides a plate toward me. "Breakfast diplomacy."

The pancakes are uneven and perfect. He leans a hip against the counter and watches me eat, eyes soft. "You realize yesterday we broke the internet."

"I realize the internet is easily broken," I say. "We just gave it something wholesome to panic about."

He laughs, pours more coffee, and the sound wraps around me like sunlight through the windows.

When the courier knocks an hour later, the moment shifts. The envelope he hands me is thick, official, stamped with the emblem of the Virginia Coastal Heritage Foundation. My name is typed neatly beneath **A Page in Time Preservation Grant Application.**

My fingers tremble. "It's early."

Crew wipes his hands on a towel and joins me. "Open it."

I do. The words blur at first, then sharpen. *Congratulations.* Approved. Full award amount. Restoration of the lantern room authorized under the Virginia Historic Revival Initiative.

I blink, laugh, maybe cry. Crew picks me up off the floor like I weigh less than relief and spins me until the cat yowls from the counter.

"You did it," he says into my hair.

"We did," I correct. But then I see the fine print—*matching funds required within thirty days.*

My stomach dips. "There's a catch."

"There's always a catch," he says, setting me down gently. "How much?"

I tell him. He whistles low. It's not impossible, but it's large enough to sting.

He squeezes my shoulders. "We'll figure it out."

By noon, half the town knows. Coral Bell's grapevine moves faster than Wi-Fi. Mrs. Winthrop brings champagne and scones "for tax purposes." Ivy prints *RESTORE THE LIGHT* posters in pastel blues. Lila starts a spreadsheet titled **MATCHING MIRACLE FUND.** Crew builds a donation box out of reclaimed wood and hand-paints *HOPE BUYS HINGES* across the top.

We set it by the register. Within an hour, it's half full of bills, coins, and one IOU written in crayon from a kid named Henry who promises "to sell seashells if necessary."

The shop hums all day. I'm signing receipts when Crew ducks behind the counter and whispers, "Close your eyes."

"I'm working."

"Close them."

I do. Something cool and metallic brushes my wrist—a tiny silver charm shaped like a book, strung on a thin chain.

He fastens it. "For luck."

When I open my eyes, he's smiling, shy and smug at once. "Thought you could use some backup magic."

I touch the charm. "You're ridiculous."

"Effective," he says. "That's what matters."

Late afternoon drips gold through the windows. Crew climbs a ladder to hang the new *A Page in Time* sign, and I stand below pretending not to stare at the way his T-shirt rides up when he stretches.

"Straight?" he calls.

"Steadier than you," I call back.

He laughs so hard he nearly drops a screw. "You sure about that?"

"Positive."

The banter fills the empty spaces that fear once occupied. For a few hours, there's only paint, laughter, and the rhythmic hush of the tide.

When he comes down, streaked with sawdust, he kisses me like he's rewarding teamwork. "Perfect alignment," he murmurs.

"You mean the sign?"

"Sure," he says, eyes glinting. "That, too."

At sunset, his phone rings. The Nashville number flashes across the screen. I see it before he does, and something inside me twists.

He answers, tone polite, neutral. "Hey, Laramie. ... Yeah, I've been thinking about it."

I busy myself with the register, pretending not to listen, though every word lands like a pebble on my ribs. *Commentator role. National network. Travel schedule.*

When he hangs up, I'm reorganizing books that were already alphabetical.

"Big opportunity," he says carefully.

"It sounds like it," I say, not looking up.

"It's not what I planned," he adds. "But it could mean stability. Flexibility, even. Half the season here, half there."

I finally meet his eyes. "And which half has a lighthouse?"

He winces, stepping closer. "Hey. I'm just... thinking."

"I know." I force a smile. "Think loud so I can keep up."

He cups my cheek, thumb tracing the edge of my jaw. "You're part of every version of the plan, Bailey."

"Promises are cheap," I whisper.

"Then let me prove it expensive."

We cook dinner together—seafood pasta that smells like the ocean itself. He chops garlic with exaggerated skill; I pretend not to flinch when he drops half of it on the floor. We drink wine from mismatched mugs, dance barefoot in the kitchen to old records that skip every third line.

When the song slows, he spins me once and catches me against him. The laughter fades but the closeness doesn't.

"I missed this," he says.

"Dancing?"

"Being still with you."

He brushes his lips against my temple, then lower, until the question in the air answers itself.

The rest unfolds like music we already know. The world narrows to his hands, my heartbeat, the slide of breath between us. He tastes like wine and something untranslatable. We move to the rhythm of a tide we've been denying since spring. It's tender, heated, reverent; the kind of intimacy that feels like a secret you both already told.

Afterward, the lighthouse beam sweeps through the

window, slicing silver across the ceiling. He traces it along my skin like he's memorizing coordinates.

"This feels like forever," he murmurs.

"It feels like right now," I correct, because I've learned not to measure time in promises.

He smiles against my shoulder. "Then let's stay here a while."

Later, when sleep should be winning, I lie awake listening to the wind. The cat sprawls between us like Switzerland. Crew's breathing evens out. I reach for my phone to set an alarm for the inspection tomorrow.

There's a new message.

> Laramie: Don't celebrate yet. We found something in the grant files. Call me first thing.

THE WORDS BLUR, THEN SHARPEN. MY CHEST GOES COLD.

I stare at the ceiling, the lighthouse beam slicing light and shadow across the room, and feel that old dread crawl back in—the one that whispers peace never lasts here.

Outside, the sea keeps breathing. Inside, I stop.

Chapter Twenty-Six

CREW

The glow from the lighthouse cuts across the room in measured rhythm, steady as a pulse. Every sweep paints her skin in light and shadow. Bailey's asleep, tangled in the sheet, the cat perched like a tiny sentinel at her feet. It's peaceful—the kind of peace that makes a man superstitious.

My phone screen still burns against the nightstand.

> Laramie: Don't celebrate yet. We found something in the grant files. Call me first thing.

LARAMIE DOESN'T USE WORDS SHE DOESN'T HAVE TO. *Don't celebrate yet* means *the ground's about to move.*

I lie there, staring at the ceiling, running through possibilities. Fraud. A clerical error. Someone claiming the lighthouse belongs to the town, not her. Or worse—someone trying to tie her name to mine again, twist it into another narrative.

I roll onto my side and watch her breathe. The way her lips part slightly with every exhale, the curl of her fingers against the pillow. She trusts the quiet. She trusts me.

I promised her ordinary.

But ordinary keeps coming with asterisks.

The sun rises early, and so does the restlessness. I slip out of bed, careful not to wake her, and head downstairs. The floorboards creak, but the sound feels familiar now— like the house acknowledging me.

Coffee first. Thinking later.

By the time Bailey pads down in one of my T-shirts, hair messy, eyes half-closed, the pot's half-empty, and my nerves are worse.

"You're awake early," she mumbles, grabbing a mug.

"Couldn't sleep."

She blinks at me over the rim. "I saw the text. I'm sorry."

I nod.

Her shoulders tighten. "You think it's bad?"

"I think Laramie doesn't spook easy."

Bailey sets her cup down. "She said to call her first thing. It's barely six."

"Then we're first."

She presses the speaker icon before I can protest. The phone rings once. Twice.

Laramie answers, voice too sharp for morning. "Wright."

"We're both here," Bailey says.

I add, "What did you find?"

"The grant came from the foundation, yes—but the matching-fund clause? That was added later. A supplemental file uploaded by a secondary reviewer."

Bailey frowns. "Meaning?"

"Meaning someone piggybacked the legitimate approval with a condition that doesn't exist. Someone inside the process inserted a fake clause designed to make you default."

I grip the counter. "To disqualify her?"

"Exactly," Laramie says. "And if you default, the lighthouse goes to the backup preservation entity—Sanford Coastal Media."

I swallow. "David."

"Or the people above him," Laramie says. "Follow the letterhead, and you'll see a holding company three layers deep. I'm sending you the documents now."

My phone buzzes with the email. It's all there—stamps, signatures, falsified dates. Someone's been playing chess while we've been playing checkers.

Bailey's voice shakes. "Can we fix it?"

"Yes," Laramie says. "But quietly. Public filings could take months. If you push too hard, they'll counter with injunctions. Let me work some angles first."

Bailey nods, even though the agent can't see her. "Do what you need to. Just... tell me if it's going to cost us more than the lighthouse."

Laramie's silence says enough.

After the call, Bailey leans against the counter, staring at the charm on her wrist. The one I gave her.

"You okay?" I ask.

She laughs, short and tired. "Define 'okay'."

"Breathing."

"Barely."

I take the mug from her hand, set it aside, and pull her against me. "We've beaten worse."

She presses her face into my chest. "You make it sound like a game."

"No," I whisper. "Like a promise."

For a long time, we just stand there, the coffee cooling between us.

By midmorning, the shop is open, but Bailey isn't behind the counter. She's upstairs with the files spread across the floor, tracing timelines, matching fonts, cataloging inconsistencies.

Lila drops off pastries and war-grade caffeine, then takes one look at Bailey's expression and says, "Whoever did this should start running."

I man the register. I'm not built for stillness, but today, I hold it because she needs it. Customers come in whispering encouragement, dropping cash into the donation box, and promising to write letters to the foundation.

By noon, the cat is judging us from the railing, and Bailey is muttering code sections under her breath.

I crouch beside her. "Eat something."

She points at the stack of papers. "Not until I figure out

who typed this fake clause. There's a watermark that doesn't match the rest of the file."

"You're terrifying."

"Flattering won't distract me. I watch a lot of *True Crime*."

I lean closer. "It might."

Her lips twitch. "You're insufferable."

"But effective," I say, stealing a bite of her pastry. "You taught me that."

She shakes her head but finally sits back, exhaustion replacing adrenaline.

We take a walk at sunset because Lila insisted on "airing the conspiracy brain." The town feels different now—proud, protective, a little dangerous in its unity. Every porch we pass waves, every window glows. Coral Bell doesn't just root for you; it circles the wagons.

Bailey's quiet beside me, hands buried in her jacket pockets. I reach over, threading my fingers through hers.

"You're somewhere else," I say.

"I'm in three places at once," she admits. "Past me is terrified. Present me is furious. Future me is trying to remember how to sleep. My grandfather is probably rolling over in his grave."

"Let me help with that sleeping one."

She glances up, a spark returning to her eyes. "You offering to read me a bedtime story?"

"Only the spicy chapters," I say.

She laughs, full-bodied this time, and it sounds like hope.

The late rain that rolls in after midnight is lazy, with more wind than rain. Bailey lights candles in the kitchen, the flames flickering against the old brick. We make tea because pretending to be civilized is easier than acknowledging how close the fear sits beneath the surface.

She's wearing one of my hoodies, sleeves swallowing her hands. The hem hits just above her thighs, and I'm halfway to forgetting every rational thought I've ever had.

She catches my stare. "What?"

"Nothing."

"You're staring."

"Just cataloging," I say. "For posterity."

"Posterity, huh?" She steps closer, eyes teasing but soft. "You always this poetic when you're about to do something stupid?"

"Only with you."

I set my mug down, reach for her, and the world narrows again.

This time, there's no rush, no interruption, no crisis banging on the door. Just us. Her breath, my heartbeat, the thunder rolling miles away like an approving drum.

I kiss her slowly with reverence. She answers like she's been waiting all day to remember what it feels like to be wanted without conditions.

Within my large hands, I gather her wrists and pin them above her head and against the arm of the sofa while my mouth assaults her neck.

"I love your skin."

"Crew," she whimpers, squirming against me. My hips cushion her legs, pinning her in place.

"What do you need, sweetheart?"

"I... I need your hands and mouth... everywhere."

"Take off the hoodie," I command, ripping the athletic pants from her legs as my gaze is glued to her glistening center. I place my hands on her thighs, holding her legs apart as she sits up to remove her top.

Her breasts bounce as they're freed from her lacy bra. She tosses the delicate material onto the floor next to her pants and hoodie.

My eyes dart up from her pussy to her breasts, triggering a growl from deep within my chest.

"Fuck. Baby, I'm so hungry for you. I... I can't promise I'll be gentle with you."

Lifting her hand, she softly runs her fingers through my brown hair. I do very little to fight back the animalistic purr that sounds from my throat.

"Shit, I don't deserve you," I confess as I bend forward and latch onto a nipple while one of my hands slips between her legs.

Rapidly, my body goes up in flames as I pay special attention to her most sensitive areas. I grow needier with each passing second. My name is an unrecognizable groan from Bailey's lips.

My mouth climbs up her legs toward her cunt as she quakes against my lips.

"Now, be a good girl, and let me make you come."

Our kisses grow frenzied, and our hands wildly stroke bare skin. It's both too much and not enough.

I slip a hand between her legs, running my finger back and forth along her wet slit. It's already coated in her arousal, but grows wetter with each pass.

Her breaths become pants as I continue swirling around her clit until she's quivering. Against my lips, she cries out, her orgasm crashing over her like a tidal wave.

"God, you're gorgeous when you come," I say as I pull my hand free, still yearning for more.

As she settles back down, I move until my face is between her legs. I lap at the wetness, murmuring to myself how much I enjoy indulging in her.

While Bailey's lost in her own pleasure, I pull back and slip a condom onto my cock. The large erection points toward Bailey like a stiff mast as I lean over her. I press my lips against hers, rock my hips back, and then surge into her.

"Oh!" she cries out as my cockhead runs across the spot most women aren't sure actually exists.

Raising one of her bent legs, I glide my cock over the sensitive spot again.

"Crew," she whispers, clawing at his back.

"Fuck, Bailey, I can feel you tightening around me. You're so fucking snug. I'm not going to last much longer." I nearly growl as she shifts a hand between her legs. "That's it. Touch yourself. Make yourself come."

As I sit up on my knees to give her more room to work

her fingers, I plunge in and out of her tight sheath. Beads of sweat run down the sides of my face and chest.

"Shit, sweet girl. I can feel you," I pant as she rocks her hips against mine. "Take what you need."

Suddenly, flashes of pleasure rocked across my spine. Bailey's back arches not long after from such a powerful release.

"Yes." My moan only drags out her orgasm further.

After a few more pumps, I grunt with my own orgasm, joining her in a well-sated heap on the couch.

The rest is a blur of warmth and skin and quiet gasps swallowed by the dark. It's not about escape; it's about arrival. About choosing the storm and finding peace in the middle of it.

When it's over, we stay tangled together on the couch, her head on my chest, both of us breathing hard but easy.

"You think we'll ever get a week without a plot twist?" she murmurs.

"I'd be bored," I say.

She pinches my side. "Liar."

"Maybe a little," I admit. "But I like the view."

She hums. "You mean me or the lighthouse?"

"Both," I say, kissing her forehead.

Hours later, the rainy weather's moved offshore. The clock blinks 2:17 a.m. when my phone buzzes again—Laramie.

I glance at Bailey, asleep again, curled against me, peace finally finding her. I slip out from under her carefully, heart pounding.

The screen lights the room in blue as I type back.

Her reply comes through seconds later.

The thunder outside is long gone, but the echo it leaves in my chest feels like the start of something worse.

I step out onto the porch barefoot, the boards still holding a trace of the day's warmth. The beam from the lantern room sweeps over the bay, one long blink every thirty seconds. I've started timing my thoughts by it—one for calm, one for panic.

When the phone buzzes again, I answer.

"Laramie."

"Sorry for the hour," she says. Her voice carries the grit of too much coffee and too few hours of sleep. "You asked for the name."

"I did."

"It's not David," she says. "He's involved, but someone higher ordered the insertion. The signature's falsified but traced from digital correspondence originating inside the team's legal department."

My stomach drops. "You're saying—"

"Your general manager," she finishes quietly. "Harris."

I squeeze the porch railing until the old paint bites my palm. "He wouldn't."

"He would if he thought forcing you into the public sphere would save the franchise's image. The clause was designed to fail, Crew. They expected Bailey to default, and then they'd ride the sympathy wave into a sponsorship deal. One tidy loop."

The world tilts. The man who coached me from college recruit to franchise quarterback, the one who visited me after the surgery with a Bible verse about second chances— he turned us into strategy.

Laramie continues, "We can build a case. I just need you to stay quiet for forty-eight hours. Let me gather the proof."

Quiet. The one thing I've never been good at.

"Copy that," I say. My voice sounds like it belongs to someone else. "Thanks."

"Crew."

"Yeah?"

"She's safer than you think," she says. "That lighthouse has teeth."

Then the line goes dead.

I sit on the porch steps until the sky starts graying at the edges. The cat squeezes through the door and curls beside my foot, purring like it knows better than to ask. The sea smells clean, almost sweet after the storm.

Inside, Bailey stirs. "You're brooding," she mumbles, voice still thick with sleep.

"Always," I say.

She wraps the blanket around her shoulders and joins me. "Bad news?"

"Complicated news."

"That's your polite word for betrayal."

I give a humorless laugh. "You're getting too good at reading me."

She bumps my shoulder. "Occupational hazard."

I tell her everything—Harris, the clause, the plan to use us. By the time I finish, her coffee's gone cold and her jaw's set in that way that makes smart men run.

"So he wanted to save the team by destroying your life," she says.

"Pretty much."

"And he thought I'd crumble under paperwork."

"People always underestimate librarians," I say.

"Booksellers," she corrects automatically. Then she sighs. "What do we do?"

"Wait forty-eight hours."

She snorts. "You don't wait well."

"Neither do you."

We sit there while the sun climbs out of the water. For a second, everything feels suspended—like the calm right before kickoff. I used to live for that tension. Now it just feels expensive.

By midmorning, the town knows something's wrong again, though not the details. Coral Bell's gossip chain runs on instinct, not information. Mrs. Winthrop shows up with muffins "for stress," Lila with legal pads, and Ivy with a playlist titled **Burn It Down but Gently**.

Bailey handles them like the pro she is—gracious, grounded, funny even. Watching her, I realize she's changed. She doesn't shrink from chaos anymore. She orchestrates it into rhythm. The girl who once left town because someone humiliated her now runs a community that would riot for her.

I want to tell her that, but I know she'd brush it off, so I just fix another hinge in silence.

At noon, I call Marcus because I need to hear from someone who still believes in clean hits and honest work.

"You sound like a man balancing on the fifty-yard line," he says.

"Feels that way," I admit. "Harris forged grant documents."

"Jesus."

"Yeah. We've got proof coming. But Laramie wants quiet."

"You going to give it to her?"

"I'm trying."

He chuckles. "You always did confuse patience with weakness."

"Maybe I'm learning."

"Maybe you're finally listening," he says, and hangs up before I can argue.

Afternoon brings a strange peace. The lighthouse inspection required by the grant passes without a single note. The inspector shakes Bailey's hand and calls the place "a marvel of responsible preservation." She nearly cries, and I nearly tackle him in gratitude.

We celebrate with sandwiches on the porch. The wind's warm, the bay glittering. For five whole minutes, we pretend this is what normal looks like.

Then her phone buzzes. A text from an unknown number.

Unknown: Nice inspection yesterday.
Shame about what's coming.

SHE SHOWS ME THE SCREEN. MY STOMACH KNOTS.

"Laramie?" I ask.

"She'd call you, not text me."

I grab the phone, take a screenshot, and forward it.

> Me: You seeing this?

NOT FIVE MINUTES LATER, I GET A RESPONSE.

> Laramie: Already have a PI tracing.
> Stay put.

BAILEY BITES HER LIP. "YOU THINK IT'S JUST HARRIS?"

"Could be anyone connected to him."

She shakes her head. "They won't stop, will they?"

"Not until we stop them."

Her eyes find mine—steady, unflinching. "Then let's finish it."

We decide to go public, but on our terms. A live town-hall stream from the porch, just like the Read-In, except this time the story's not children's books, it's the truth. Ivy sets up cameras, Dean drafts the statement, and Rowan offers goats for background ambience ("optics," he says).

While they plan, Bailey disappears upstairs. I find her in the lantern room, staring at the water.

"You sure about this?" I ask.

She nods. "I'm tired of waiting for permission to exist."

I step behind her and wrap my arms around her waist. "Then we'll tell it loud."

She leans back against me. "You're not scared?"

"I'm terrified," I say. "But you taught me fear doesn't mean retreat."

We stand there until the sun drops low, our reflections merging in the glass.

The broadcast goes live on my social media page at dusk. The town gathers again—kids on blankets, adults on folding chairs, half the coast watching online. Bailey sits beside me, her hand steady in mine.

"Good evening," she begins, voice clear despite the wind. "You've heard a lot of stories about us. Some true, some... creative. Tonight, we'd like to tell you our own."

I talk about second chances, about the difference between fixing a shoulder and fixing a life. She talks about building something worth fighting for, how light only matters when you share it.

The comments flood in—hearts, encouragement, the occasional troll drowned by kindness. For once, it feels like we control the narrative.

Then, mid-sentence, the screen behind us flickers. Static. A logo.

The feed cuts to a prerecorded segment—Harris at a podium, press cameras flashing. His voice is smooth as ever. "Due to ongoing investigations, we've placed Crew Wright on administrative leave. We wish him the best as he focuses on personal matters."

Gasps ripple through the crowd. Bailey squeezes my hand. I stare at the screen, every muscle locking.

Laramie's number flashes on my phone. I answer without looking away from Harris's smug face.

"Crew," she says, breathless. "It's moving faster than expected. He leaked his own statement early. We're intercepting the files now. Do not—repeat, do not respond publicly."

Too late. Bailey's already speaking into the mic. "You don't get to narrate this one, Coach."

The crowd roars approval, but I know what's coming next—legal threats, media vultures, endless noise. The beam from the lighthouse sweeps over the porch, catches Harris's face frozen on the paused feed, and throws his shadow long against the wall behind us.

I look at Bailey, steady in the chaos, and realize we've crossed the point of no return, but if it means giving everything up for her, then it's worth its weight in gold.

Chapter Twenty-Seven

BAILEY

I don't hear the truck pull up. I feel it. The way the floorboards hum beneath my feet, the way the gulls scatter like gossip, the way the air changes shape around him before he even opens the door.

Crew Wright walks into a room like gravity remembers who's in charge.

He's covered in morning—damp hair, a day-old stubble, shoulders carrying the weight of decisions that haven't even been made yet. He's still the man who can silence a room with a look, but now there's something else, too. A quietness that didn't exist before. A calm he didn't have when he arrived in Coral Bell Cove months ago, limping through my door with a tote full of kids' books and a heart he swore was temporary.

He sets his keys on the counter, glances at me, and exhales. "You saw the message?"

"Yeah." The image—the grainy shot of us through the

lantern room glass—still burns behind my eyelids. *Would hate for anything to block it.* It wasn't just a threat. It was a reminder that fame never forgets your forwarding address.

I cross my arms, forcing myself to meet his gaze. "You handled it?"

"Mostly." His jaw flexes, and I can tell *mostly* means *barely contained violence, disguised as strategy.* "Laramie's got the files. The kid came through. We're safe—for now."

For now. The two words I hate most in the English language.

I grab a rag and start wiping down the counter even though it's already spotless. "So that's it? They'll just... stop?"

He shakes his head. "They'll circle until they realize the story isn't theirs anymore."

"And when will that be?"

"When we decide it is."

His voice has that low certainty again, the kind that makes my chest hurt because it sounds like home and danger at once.

He walks closer, slow enough for me to back away if I want to. I don't. His hand finds the edge of the counter, fingers brushing mine just enough to make the air tilt.

"Bailey," he says quietly, "I'm sorry."

"For what?"

"For every time I thought silence was safer than showing up."

I drop the rag. "And now?"

"Now I'm done hiding."

He means it. I can feel it in the space between us, in the way he's looking at me like I'm both reason and result. But I also know him—his need to fix what he didn't break, his instinct to shoulder every burden in reach.

I touch his arm, just above the scar that cuts across his tricep. "You can't fight everything, Crew."

He tilts his head. "Who said I'm fighting?"

Before I can answer, he leans in and kisses me.

It's not desperate. It's not gentle either. It's something truer—like the quiet after thunder. His lips taste like salt and black coffee and the kind of apology that doesn't need words.

When he finally pulls back, I whisper, "That's cheating."

He grins, brushing his thumb along my jaw. "Effective."

"Infuriating."

"Still effective."

I roll my eyes, but my smile gives me away.

By noon, the shop is full. The donation box has been replaced with a carved wooden one that Rowan made, shaped like a tiny lighthouse. A little plaque reads *Light belongs to everyone.*

Kids are sprawled on the rug again, reading, drawing, dreaming. I sit among them, sorting through new titles, and for the first time in weeks, my heartbeat matches the rhythm of the room.

Crew crouches beside me, passing books like a glorified assistant. He's wearing a worn baseball cap, the bill shadowing his eyes, and every time he looks up, something inside me unravels a little.

"You know," he says, voice low, "this might be my favorite version of rehab."

"Folding cardboard and corralling toddlers?"

"Beats media training."

One of the kids—Henry, the one who wrote the IOU for seashell money—looks up. "Are you two married?"

Crew chokes on air. I nearly drop *The Velveteen Rabbit*.

"No," I manage.

Henry frowns. "You should be. You talk like my grandparents."

Crew recovers first. "Old and loud?"

"Gross but in love. Yuck," Henry says cheerfully and goes back to coloring.

Crew leans closer, his shoulder brushing mine. "Can't argue with the wisdom of children."

"Don't start."

"Wouldn't dream of it."

He's lying. I can hear it in his smile.

That night, we walk the beach. The sky's bruised purple, the waves gentle, the air thick with that pre-storm electricity Coral Bell seems to thrive on.

I kick at the foam curling over my toes. "You ever think we're just living inside some cosmic joke?"

"All the time."

"Maybe we should start laughing."

He slides his arm around my shoulders. "Or maybe we change the punchline."

We walk in silence for a while, our steps falling into

sync. When we reach the dock, he stops, hands in his pockets.

"Bailey, what do you want?"

I look up. "Right now?"

"In general."

I take a breath. The truth tastes simple. "I want to stop surviving my own story."

He studies me, jaw tightening. "Then write a new one."

"With you?"

"If you'll have me."

The words hang there, fragile and certain. The beam from the lighthouse sweeps over us, a single flash of silver on water, and I realize something that breaks me open— every time that light passes, it's not looking for danger. It's looking to guide someone home.

I reach for his hand. "Then don't stop showing up."

He pulls me against him, forehead resting against mine. "Not even if you tell me to."

"Good," I whisper. "Because I won't."

We end up back at the lighthouse, the air humming with something too big for language. He kisses me before the door closes, and the world goes quiet. His hands slide under my shirt, mine in his hair, our breaths uneven but certain. It's not the desperate kind of need anymore—it's the belonging kind.

Later, tangled in sheets and moonlight, he whispers, "You know the thing about storms?"

"What?"

"They always leave the sky cleaner."

I smile against his chest. "Poetic."

"Effective."

I laugh, half asleep. "Still infuriating."

He kisses the top of my head. "Good night, Lighthouse."

And for the first time in years, I don't dream of leaving.

THE COURTHOUSE SMELLS LIKE DUST, INK, AND NERVES. It's not the grand kind of courtroom you see on TV—just paneled walls, humming lights, a ceiling fan that's seen too many summers. Still, it feels like history is being decided here, and a part of me wishes I'd worn armor instead of a navy dress that wrinkles if you breathe wrong. Given the potential public nature of the parties involved, I was surprised at how quickly our case was heard.

Crew sits beside me, hand warm over mine. He's in a dark suit that fits him too well for comfort—not just the fabric, but the way it settles on a man who's spent his life in uniforms and jerseys. Laramie's lawyer team representing us stands in front, posture sharp enough to cut the tension in half.

Harris sits on the opposite side of the aisle, his tie knotted so tight it looks like it's choking him. When our eyes meet, his expression flickers—not guilt, not fear, just calculation. The kind of look that measures outcomes instead of people.

The judge enters. Everyone stands. The room exhales.

Our lawyer speaks first, voice steady. She lays out the

chain of emails, the falsified clause, the screenshots, and the intern's witness statement, who risked everything to tell the truth. Every syllable is a nail driven into the lie that tried to bury us.

When she finishes, the judge leans back, tapping a pen against his file. "Mr. Harris, do you have counsel?"

Harris clears his throat. "Yes, Your Honor. But I believe there's been a misunderstanding."

Crew leans closer and whispers, "He's about to redefine that word."

The judge's gaze doesn't waver. "Mr. Harris, the court doesn't appreciate creative definitions."

There's a murmur through the gallery—reporters, locals, friends who turned up because Coral Bell shows up when it matters. Ivy's in the back row, wearing sunglasses indoors like she's ready for a press conference. Lila's scribbling furious notes like this is a group project she refuses to fail.

Harris tries to spin a narrative about "administrative miscommunication," but the judge cuts him off with the efficiency of a man who's heard every version of *it wasn't me*. "The court finds that the matching-fund clause was inserted fraudulently and that all subsequent threats of default are null. The grant stands. Ms. Bailey Hart retains full ownership of the property."

The gavel hits. The sound is small, but the relief is seismic.

Crew squeezes my hand once, hard, like he's checking if this is real.

We persevered, and I get to keep the lighthouse and the grant.

Outside, the air tastes like sunlight and exhaustion. Cameras flash. Reporters shout questions about *the comeback*, about *redemption arcs*, about *the football star who found love in a lighthouse.* Crew shields me with his arm and a smile that isn't for them—it's for me.

"Do we say anything?" I whisper.

He leans down. "Not to them."

Then he looks straight into a camera lens and says, "Sometimes light just finds you."

It's the kind of line that'll end up in headlines, sure, but it's also true, and I love him for meaning it.

Back at the lighthouse, the town has already turned victory into a festival. Someone strung bunting across Main Street. Mrs. Winthrop baked an entire fleet of pies. The donation jar now reads *For Future Storms.*

Crew and I sneak through the back to avoid getting kidnapped by gratitude. He collapses onto the couch like he's been holding the planet up single-handed.

"You know," he says, "I thought winning would feel louder."

"It's the quiet kind of win," I tell him. "The kind you have to sit still to hear."

He looks at me, eyes soft. "I'm not great at still."

"You're learning."

He grins. "Effective."

I throw a cushion at him, and he catches it one-handed, the way muscle memory always will. Then he leans forward, elbows on his knees. "I'm done with them, Bailey."

"The Stallions?"

He nods. "They offered to 'revisit terms.' Said I could go back to mentoring next week if I sign their apology script. I told them I'm writing my own."

I blink. "You're walking away."

"I'm walking toward something better."

"And that is?"

He reaches out and touches the charm on my wrist. "This. You. Kids who come here to read. A place where I'm not a headline. And I'm actually excited about the part-time broadcasting job."

I swallow hard. "You're sure?"

"I'm done choosing the roar over the quiet."

Tears prick my eyes before I can stop them. "You'll miss it."

"I'll miss throwing passes," he admits. "But maybe it's time I learn to catch."

That night, Coral Bell throws an impromptu bonfire on the beach. Music, laughter, too many marshmallows. Crew's brothers show up with beer and bad jokes. Ivy sings, barefoot in the sand, her voice carrying across the waves. The song isn't about us exactly, but the chorus feels like it is: *you can't cage a tide, but you can build a shore worth coming home to.*

Crew pulls me into the circle of light. "Dance with me."

"There's no music."

"There's always music," he says, and hums against my temple until I find the rhythm, too.

We sway, the fire painting us in gold. People cheer when he dips me dramatically, then groan when he kisses me because apparently, small towns like their romance PG. He kisses me anyway.

When the fire burns down to embers, we stay long after everyone drifts away. The lighthouse blinks steady in the distance. He pulls me into his lap, wraps his arms around me, and the world goes very, very quiet.

"What happens now?" I whisper.

He thinks for a long time. "We build something that doesn't need fixing."

"Like what?"

"Like this," he says, and tilts my chin until I'm looking at him. "Like us. Like mornings that don't start with a fight we didn't pick."

I laugh softly. "That sounds suspiciously domestic."

"Terrifying, isn't it?"

"Completely."

He kisses me again, slow and deep, and for once, there's no noise in my head, no countdown to disaster. Just salt, wind, his hands steady on my skin, and the faint hum of a town that finally gets to rest.

Weeks pass in the kind of blur that feels like living instead of surviving. The repairs are finished. The grant funds arrive. The lighthouse reopens officially on a Friday that smells like salt and lemon cake.

Kids line up to climb the stairs, parents take photos, and the town declares it an official holiday. Crew gives a short speech, charming and irreverent, the kind that makes everyone laugh and then cry a little. When it's my turn, I manage exactly five words before emotion takes my voice.

"Thank you for coming home."

Crew squeezes my hand and whispers, "You nailed it."

Later, when the crowd thins, we climb to the lantern room alone. The sun's setting, the beam ready to start its work again. He wraps his arms around me from behind.

"Looks different from up here," he murmurs.

"How so?"

"Less like something we saved. More like something saving us."

I rest my hands over his. "You know what's funny?"

"What?"

"I used to think light was just... light. Now I think it's a promise."

He presses a kiss to the back of my neck. "Then let's keep it."

We stand there until the first sweep of the beam cuts through the dusk, steady and sure, reaching for anyone still out there looking for a way back.

EPILOGUE – BAILEY

The first cool snap of fall tastes like apple pie and sea salt, and Coral Bell Cove dresses for it—jack-o'-lanterns on every stoop, mums the color of sunsets, scarves that exist mostly for attitude. The lighthouse gleams like it knows it's pretty. New flashing, fresh paint, that quiet creak a building makes when it's satisfied.

I turn the OPEN sign at A Page in Time and step onto the porch with two mugs. Crew's at the rail fixing a stubborn shutter hook with the reverence of a man who worships at the altar of *things-that-click*. He wears a faded Stallions hoodie because irony is a love language, and a ball cap that's survived more weather than the rest of us.

"Report," I say, handing him coffee.

"Hook defeated. Porch secure. Cat judging." He nods at the windowsill, where the cat blinks like we're late for his nap.

The town hums behind us: Rowan's goats arguing with a

bale of hay on the back of his truck, Ivy rehearsing a chorus over by the gazebo, Lila directing volunteers with a clipboard and the subtle authority of a benevolent pirate. The Fall Read-In blossoms at noon—blankets, cider, story time under strings of lights we'll pretend we hung straight.

"Happy anniversary," Crew says casually.

I blink. "Of what?"

He bumps my shoulder. "Of the first day you let me behind the counter without a background check."

"That was a lapse in judgment."

"Best lapse you've ever had," he says, sipping. "Top three, at least."

He spends his mornings coaching quarterbacks at the high school, his afternoons here or at Otter Creek Farms, his evenings being the kind of neighbor who moves porch furniture before storms. It's the time of year when he'll jet across the country for broadcasting gigs on the weekends. I follow along because I'm always up for a new adventure like the ones I read about.

He said no to the word *brand* and yes to a life that smells like coffee and grass. Harris took an *early retirement* that was neither early nor voluntary. The league apologized in beige and donated to the foundation in a shade of contrition I accepted because money for historic buildings doesn't have a conscience.

"Come on," Crew says, eyes bright. "Lantern room."

"We have, like, twelve minutes until children descend."

"Twelve is so many." He laces his fingers with mine and tows me up the spiral, the familiar, loved climb. The glass is newly polished for the evening tours; the brass gleams; the beam naps until dusk.

He stops where the light makes a perfect square on the floorboards. "Right here."

I squint at him. "Are we... having a feelings meeting?"

"Possibly." He pats his hoodie pocket. "But with props."

"Dear God."

He takes out a paperback. *The Outsiders.* My copy—the one with the soft, wrecked spine, the one that hid a note once, the one that changed the weather of my life.

My throat goes tight. "Crew—"

"It's not the old note," he says quickly, all dimples and nerves. "That one did its job. This is an update."

He opens to the middle. A new card peeks out—cream, edges deckled like it belongs in a better century. His handwriting, reckless and neat all at once:

Stay, Gold—C.

Heat rushes to my cheeks. "That's not how the quote goes."

"I took liberties. I'm a local now."

He goes to one knee. Not dramatic; not performative. Just a man kneeling in a lighthouse because that's where his light is.

The ring is simple—thin gold, a single solitaire larger than I'd ever seen. When it hits the glass glow, it throws a small, stubborn flare.

"Bailey Hart," he says, voice low and steady, "be the

chapter after every cliffhanger with me. Marry me. Let's keep the light, together."

There are a hundred ways I could make a joke right now, a thousand ways to buy myself a second with humor. But we've done enough stalling. The cat isn't here to judge; the beam's off; the day holds its breath.

"Yes," I say, and it's easy. "Obviously."

He laughs—relief and joy in one sound—and slides the ring onto my finger. He stands and kisses me, slow and sure, and the room drops away until all that's left is breath and the taste of apple and the feeling of choosing the same future at the same time.

Below, the doorbell jingles and a little voice shouts, "Is story time now?" We break apart, foreheads touching, grinning like teenagers with good secrets.

"Later, we tell everyone?" he whispers.

"After story hour, if it hasn't already started spreading," I confirm, because priorities.

We take the stairs hand-in-hand, and when we step onto the porch, the town looks brighter—as if it was waiting to exhale with us. Crew squeezes my fingers once, then peels off to help Rowan rig the microphone while I set out the picture books. Mrs. Winthrop appears at my elbow as if conjured, eyes suspiciously glossy when she spots the ring.

"About time," she murmurs, pressing a tissue into my palm and a lemon bar into my other.

Ivy starts the set with a soft verse that sounds like a blessing. Lila cues me with a nod. The kids swarm the rug, knees banged, smiles wide, the future noisy and unafraid.

I open *The Day the Crayons Came Home* and sit. Crew drops to the floor across from me, long legs folding into kid-shape without complaint, a quarterback among crayons. He winks when Green complains about dinosaur duty; he growls dramatically for Beige; he leans in when I read the last lines about belonging and coming back.

The beam will wake at dusk, and when it does, it will sweep the bay like always, catching windows and waves and the corner of a brass ring that promises the steadiness we built the long way. Tomorrow, I'll order more copies of my favorite books, and he'll fix another hinge that we both will pretend squeaks. We'll fight about who takes out the recycling and who gets the hot water. We'll count donations for a new railing and argue over paint chips named after the weather. We'll keep showing up.

"Again!" Henry shouts when I close the book.

"Twice is the legal limit," Crew tells him solemnly. "It's in the bylaws."

The crowd groans. I sigh theatrically, flip back to page one, and start again—because that's what you do when something good ends. You begin it, and then you begin it again.

Crew catches my eye over a sea of knees and crayons. He taps his chest once. *Home.*

I nod—one beat, then two. *Home.*

THE END

STAY IN TOUCH

Newsletter: http://bit.ly/2WokAjS
Author Page: www.facebook.com/authorreneeharless
Reader Group: http://bit.ly/31AGa3B
Instagram: www.instagram.com/renee_harless
Bookbub: www.bookbub.com/authors/renee-harless
Goodreads: http://bit.ly/2TDagOn
Amazon: http://bit.ly/2WsHhPq
Website: www.reneeharless.com

ACKNOWLEDGMENTS

To my family—thank you for being my constant and my calm. Your love, patience, and unwavering support carried me through long nights, early mornings, and the moments when the words felt just out of reach. You ground me, believe in me, and remind me every day why these stories matter.

To my incredible editor, Jenny—this book is better because of you. Your insight, encouragement, and thoughtful guidance strengthened every layer of this story. Thank you for pushing me to dig deeper, trust my voice, and grow as a writer. I'm endlessly grateful for your belief in both me and these characters.

To my proofreader, Crystal—thank you for your sharp eye and meticulous care. Your attention to detail ensured every page was polished and ready, and I appreciate your dedication more than words can say.

To my earliest readers, Patricia and Lisa—thank you for

being there from the very beginning. For loving these characters, for your honest feedback, and for cheering me on when I needed it most. Your enthusiasm fueled my own, and this journey wouldn't be the same without you.

And to you, dear reader—thank you for choosing this story. For turning the pages, feeling the emotions, and welcoming these characters into your world. Your support makes every word worth it, and I'm so grateful you're here.

ABOUT THE AUTHOR

Renee Harless is a USA TODAY bestselling author with an affinity for wine and a passion for telling a good story.

Renee Harless, her husband, and children live in Blue Ridge Mountains of Virginia. She studied Communication, specifically Public Relations, at Radford University.

Growing up, Renee always found a way to pursue her creativity. It began by watching endless runs of White Christmas - yes even in the summer – and learning every word and dance from the movie. She could still sing "Sister Sister" if requested. In high school she joined the show choir and a community theatre group. After marrying the man of her dreams and moving from her hometown, she sought out a different artistic outlet – writing.

To say that Renee is a romance addict would be an understatement. When she isn't chasing her kids around the house, working her day job, or writing, she jumps head first into a romance novel.

www.ingramcontent.com/pod-product-compliance
Lightning Source LLC
Chambersburg PA
CBHW020336010826
48970CB00012B/1148